About the Author

John Rowe was a professional soldier for fifteen years. Educated at Sydney Grammar School and at Duntroon Military College, he was on active service in four wars: the Malayan Emergency, Kashmir, Borneo and Vietnam, where he was promoted to major and served with the US 173rd Airborne Brigade and the Australian Task Force.

Since leaving the Army he has published six novels and a *Time-Life* history on Australian soldiers in the Vietnam War. He is currently working on a new series of novels, a trilogy with an Australian military background.

For details of his other books, visit his website at
www.johnrowebooks.com

Other Books by John Rowe

McCabe PM (1972)
The Chocolate Crucifix (1973)
The Warlords (1978)
The Aswan Solution (1980)
Long Live the King (1984)
Vietnam, the Australian Experience (1987)

Count Your Dead

A Novel of Vietnam

John Rowe

SYDNEY UNIVERSITY PRESS

First published in Australia by Angus and Robertson Publishers, 1968

This revised paperback edition published 2013 by Sydney University Press

ISBN 978-1-74332-358-8

A revised ebook edition is available from John Rowe Books. www.JohnRoweBooks.com

Email: JohnRoweBooks@gmail.com

To Marianne

Glossary

arty – artillery
ARVN – Army of the Republic of Vietnam (allies of the US)
azimuth – bearing, or direction of march
bonzes – Buddhist monks
CBU – Cluster Bomb Unit
Charlie – Viet Cong forces (enemies of the US)
C-and-C ship – command-and-control helicopter
Dustoff – medical evacuation helicopter
FAC – Forward Air Controller
frag orders – fragmentary orders
gassho – ritual gesture made by pressing the palms of the hands together
JUSPAO – Joint United States Public Affairs Office
L of C – Line of Communications
LZ – landing zone
MACV – Military Advisory Command Vietnam
number twelve – lousy
ralliers – surrendered Viet Cong
R & R – rest and recreation leave
ROTC – Reserve Officers' Training Corps
slicks – troop-carrying helicopters
the Two – Intelligence Officer
USAID –US Agency for International Development
VC – Viet Cong

1

The emergency came at three o'clock in the morning. Still groggy with sleep and the effects of the half bottle of bourbon he'd drunk through the poker game that had finished only two hours before, Morgan tried to force himself to concentrate as the excited non-com explained the early reveille.

"Battalion commander wants all company commanders to report for briefing in thirty minutes, Captain Morgan."

"Why? What the hell's going on?" He sat up on his stretcher, pushed aside the nylon poncho liner he used as a sheet, and blinked through his mosquito net at the white disc of light hurting his eyes.

"And turn that goddam flashlight someplace else."

"Yes, sir. Sorry, sir. All I know is it's an Operation Eaglehawk emergency. Company to be ready to move in an hour."

Morgan swung his legs over the side of the stretcher onto the packed earth floor of his hexagonal tent, feeling with his toes for his rubber-thong shower shoes. His hand groped into the circle of light on top of the empty ammunition crate which served as a bedside table for his cigarettes and lighter.

"As soon as you've passed the word to saddle up to the rest of the company, organise me some coffee ... and tell the top sergeant to come see me."

With a cigarette lit, he scuffed his way through the tent flap into the tropical night air. Naked except for underpants, he urinated down the makeshift piss tube, a cardboard mortar case embedded in the dirt.

It was moments like these, getting up with a hangover in the middle of the night, that Morgan felt his years as the oldest company commander in the battalion, and the oldest in the brigade now that Harry Doyle was dead, like so many other friends since they came to Vietnam. Getting up before first light was probably the single thing Morgan hated more about the army than anything else. Invariably, as he forced himself awake to face the day, he told himself it was time he grew up and quit playing field soldiers as a company commander and settled for some sort of staff job, such as battalion executive or operations officer, which would be more appropriate for an ageing Columbia University economics graduate of thirty-six years. He had taken advantage of the ROTC program to go to university, and those carefree years now seemed a very distant memory.

He washed his face in cold water in his upturned steel helmet, then shaved in the dark by feel, using the same water. As he pulled on his fatigues and laced up his boots he tried to discipline himself to think coherently about the contents of the standby orders for an Eaglehawk operation. This would be the first time the battalion had actually implemented one of these crash contingency plans, and he wanted to be sure there were no organisational snarl ups with his own company. By the time his top sergeant arrived, Morgan was dressed and checking his gear before packing his rucksack.

"I want you to run through the Eaglehawk checklist real thoroughly while I'm at battalion orders. We're not going to have much time for company orders beyond essentials. I might have to brief the platoon leaders on the move when we board the trucks for the Beehive."

"I'll tell the platoon leaders to be standing by your jeep, sir."

"Okay. Check me over, would you?" Morgan heaved his rucksack onto his shoulders, then, stepping outside, picked up his steel helmet and sloshed the soapy water into the night before slipping in the helmet liner. Helmet on, he rubbed the bristles at the back of his neck; an involuntary gesture to ease his mounting tension at the prospect of a new operation. New operations meant new casualty lists, and the battalion had taken a lot of casualties since arriving in Vietnam. Though the casualties in his company had been relatively light, he still dreaded the thought of losing more of these boys he had trained and mother-henned so possessively through these first months of combat.

The battalion commander's briefing tent was harshly lit by two naked bulbs; the power came from a petrol-driven generator throbbing nearby. The battalion operations officer handed Morgan a white plastic mug of steaming black coffee; he sipped it gratefully, waiting for the other company commanders to arrive and the briefing to start. He lit a cigarette to ease the uncomfortable gnawing in his stomach, an all-too-familiar penalty for early rises without food.

The battalion commander, Lieutenant Colonel Paul Higgins, had only been in command for five weeks. For two months before he arrived, Major

Frank Meredith, a close friend of Morgan's, had temporarily commanded the battalion after their original commander had been wounded and evacuated back to the States. Higgins was about the same age as Morgan, but a West Pointer. A tall, thickset man with thinning hair, he was very shortsighted, so he wore horn-rimmed glasses, which seemed to need constant wiping. Because of his poor eyesight, he seemed awkward and even clumsy, but this was misleading. He had a reputation as a brilliant Pentagon staff officer and had been sent to Vietnam for command and combat experience. Higgins began to speak.

"We all know the battalion's been on Eaglehawk alert all week. Well, this is no rehearsal; this is for real. The Special Forces camp at My Trang, over here in Duc Binh province, is under heavy attack right now. You'll remember the brigade was scheduled to re-establish in Duc Binh province anyhow, so this just means we go a bit earlier, with a bit more drama. Here on the blackboard I've got a schematic layout of the My Trang area ... you'll notice I've marked the five usable landing zones surrounding the camp. The contingency plan says we'll heli-assault a relief force into one of these LZs. The initial heli-assault force will be a company group. We'll have thirty choppers in support and they're scrambling and fuelling up at the Beehive now. I've chosen you, Bill Morgan, as the battalion's senior and most experienced company commander, to take in your company as the initial heli-assault force ..."

*

The huge cattle trucks crammed with soldiers were already lined up on the main road passing through the battalion's lines when Higgins finished his briefing. The silhouettes of the trucks and the helmeted soldiers, the crackle of man-pack radios being tuned, the revving engines, the urgent-voiced officers and non-coms pacing and conferring in the dark, or within the trucks' headlights, gave the situation a palpable tension.

Morgan found his jeep and, next to it, his platoon leaders waiting anxiously for their briefing. Swiftly and forcefully he gave what orders he could.

"When will we know what LZ we're assaulting?" one of the platoon leaders asked.

"Not till we're in the air," Morgan said. "That's for Colonel Robbins, as brigade commander, to decide. He'll make that decision himself from his command-and-control chopper as soon after first light as he can see well enough to work out what's going on round the Special Forces camp ..."

The convoy headed off for the Beehive, the helicopter assembly area established on the apron of the nearby airfield. The packed figures heavily laden with weapons and equipment bounced up and down in the cattle trucks in front of Morgan, illuminated by his jeep's headlights through a thick cloud of dust. He was reminded of sheep trucks driving to a slaughterhouse.

The Beehive buzzed and roared with activity as the convoy arrived. The long throbbing lines of helicopters, their overhead rotors fanning dust and turbulent gusts of air, always made Morgan's heart race and his nerves tingle with a fresh charge of excitement. These airmobile operations made soldiering in Vietnam a totally different military experience from the trench warfare he'd encountered as a young ROTC lieutenant in Korea with the "Wolfhounds", the famous Twenty-seventh Regiment.

When the troops left the trucks there were a few moments of milling confusion, then swiftly they shook themselves out into a pattern of blobs and lines ready to board the waiting helicopters. A few minutes later Morgan received and passed on the signal to board. The company swarmed across the tarmac to their helicopters, heads bent to keep their helmets on against the buffeting rotor blasts, and hands across their foreheads to protect their eyes against the flying grit. As they reached the line of helicopters, everyone stooped at the waist to miss the spinning rotor blades, then scrambled aboard. There was a short delay while a few soldiers were put off helicopters, when pilots assessed they were too heavily loaded for lift-off. These orphan soldiers ran frantically down the lines of helicopters trying to find a pilot to accept them. A final revving and blasting of turbo jet engines, and the helicopters strained for take-off. With rising tails cocked like angry scorpions, they bucked and bounced down the tarmac before lifting off and clawing noisily into the dawn.

2

From two thousand feet Colonel Robbins saw the My Trang Special Forces camp as a small brown triangle, insignificant compared with the rubber plantation and jungle surrounding it. It nestled in a wide valley in the centre of Duc Binh province. Wraiths of early morning mist clung to the river and sat in layers of grey scattered across the jungle. It was hard to relate this scene to the battle of the night before when a VC regiment had tried to overrun the My Trang Special Forces camp, only breaking off the attack an hour before first light. Small black objects like burnt matchsticks lay across the outer barbed wire surrounding the triangle – Viet Cong corpses charred by napalm.

There was the second LZ, the Colonel noted, comparing the ground below his C-and-C ship to the map on his knee, which his operations officer had marked with the main geographic features in grease pencil.

"I've spotted all five of the contingency LZs except three alpha. Have you got it, Frank?" the Colonel's voice crackled over the intercom.

Major Frank Meredith peered intently through the plexiglass window, his muscular neck straining as he looked. He was a big, powerfully built man and his bullish good looks gave the Colonel a feeling of confidence in his judgement.

"It's still covered with mist, Colonel. It's one of those swamp grass clearings. Probably waist-deep in water; they're only good in the dry."

"Rog."

Meredith breathed deeply twice in an attempt to relieve his nervous tension. The Colonel's decision on which landing zone to use was critical; but there was no way of knowing if the LZs were ambushed. It was a gamble and if the Colonel chose the wrong one, a line company and twenty helicopters could be written off in minutes ... after all, it had happened to the Air Cavalry Division in the la Drang valley.

It had been all very well for Meredith, in the planning stages three weeks ago for what then seemed a fairly remote contingency, to write glibly in the Concept of Operations paragraph:

Based on current intelligence insert heli-borne ready-reaction forces into suitable landing zones near the My Trang Special Forces camp from which they can deploy into blocking positions and close with and destroy the enemy.

But what if the Viet Cong had envisaged exactly this reaction? Supposing the Viet Cong regimental attack on the Special Forces camp had been a diversionary attack, designed to attract a nice fat American reaction force into a web of thoroughly ambushed landing zones?

Today, to make it even more personal, it was Frank Meredith's old battalion going in first. He'd been executive officer for nearly a year and then spent two months as temporary battalion commander, waiting for the Pentagon in its wisdom to dispatch a replacement lieutenant colonel. Then, when the new battalion commander arrived, Colonel Robbins, the brigade commander, had made Meredith his brigade operations officer. But of course Meredith still thought of the battalion as his battalion, and personally – and not unreasonably – was convinced he would have made a better commander than his replacement, Lieutenant Colonel Paul Higgins.

As far as Meredith was concerned, Higgins was just a Pentagon favoured ticket-puncher – some influential politician's or general's favourite, or worse, his close relative. A posting to Vietnam for command and combat experience had no doubt been discreetly manipulated so those all-important boxes on his career file could be ticked.

Take this morning, for instance: using Bill Morgan's company to go in first seemed unwise and unfair. Morgan was getting too cautious now, and too careful with his soldiers, to make his company the best choice for an initial assault and quick reaction force. Not that there was any questioning Morgan's personal courage; in fact, he had seen much more than his share of shell and shot and still had no hesitation in risking his neck. But Morgan was older than the other company commanders. He'd lost his youthful resilience to the impact of casualties; he'd seen too many, and now they affected him too personally. He had become a canny old professional in Meredith's view – a virtue in some ways, but not from an aggressive military viewpoint. Meredith had a premonition that Bill Morgan's luck must be running out – and for all Morgan's faults, Meredith still thought of him as a friend.

He looked across at the Colonel's face, feeling a sudden sympathy for him, too – the loneliness of command. These were the times a successful commander needed good luck; perhaps even more than good judgement.

"Old Leather" was the Colonel's nickname, mainly because of his passion for highly polished leather, especially boots. He was a strikingly handsome and youthful-looking man for forty-five, blue-eyed and fair-haired, with his skin only just showing the weathering and wrinkling around his eyes and neck. With his square-cut, "All-American-boy" face, he looked his part to perfection. Of course a commander had to be ruthless, too, and Old Leather certainly had a reputation for that. In fact he had just sacked the brigade civil affairs officer a few days before. Meredith felt that had been more due to the officer's being overweight and slovenly in dress than because of any true professional failing; still, how could any brigade commander project the right go-getter image if members of his principal staff looked fat and sloppy?

The Colonel's face was drawn and the skin stretched taut across his prominent jawbones as he ground his back teeth mechanically and unconsciously. Carefully controlled, he reached into his breast pocket and pulled out a beautifully polished leather cigar case. Long use had given the case a rich whisky gloss.

Extracting a thin brown cheroot, the Colonel tapped it cleanly on his thumbnail. The cheroot suited his face – that was probably a major reason why he smoked them.

"Colonel," Frank Meredith said over the intercom, "how about we get on to the leader of the 'A' team at the Special Forces camp – maybe his Intell guy knows something about what LZs the Viet Cong have ambushed."

Slowly the Colonel took the cigar out of his mouth. Locking his jaw, he shook his head slowly and decisively – and then Meredith knew he had put the suggestion the wrong way. He should have been more indirect; he had given the Colonel too ready an opportunity for a negative.

"Clutching at straws, Frank, clutching at straws. I don't intend to pass on my command decision responsibilities to some Special Forces half-assed captain. That green beret and a pop song don't mean shit to me."

Meredith didn't reply – he was smarting under the rebuff, but knew better than to press an argument after Old Leather had used his slow head shake. A voice crackled over the radio.

"Chalky Pepper one six, this is Tired Tarantula four – serial seven complete, over."

"Tired Tarantula four, this is Chalky Pepper one six, Roger, out," Meredith answered, flipping a switch on the radio console. He checked his signals operating instructions to confirm the identity of Tired Tarantula four, and then ran his finger down the serials in the sequence of events annex in the operation order: so, the troop-carrying helicopters were on the way. He said to the Colonel, "First lift of thirty slicks is off – we should see them in about forty minutes, sir."

"Right, Frank ... Hey, Kurt?"

"Colonel."

"You got plenty of heavy stuff? Say, 250-pounders and 500-pounders in the ordnance loads your birds are carrying?"

Kurt Braemar, the Colonel's attached US Air Force liaison officer, smiled boyishly. Although he was over forty he was still in great shape as a devoted weightlifter and handball player. Until this assignment he had been flying jet missions from Thailand into North Vietnam. The Colonel found him a welcome addition to his staff with his loyal enthusiasm and cheerful professionalism.

"Yes, sir, Colonel, and we got some big cans of napalm, and plenty of CBUs."

"Well, boy, it looks as if I'm going to have to rely on you and your goddam US Air Force to shake the living shit out of some of these LZs."

"That's what we're paid for, Colonel."

"Frank, Kurt – chances are every one of those goddam LZs is ambushed, which doesn't give me a whole range of options."

"You're right, sir, but two factors you might consider, before you decide."

"Quick, Frank, what?"

As a general rule Meredith tried to avoid giving Old Leather suggestions to which he could easily say no. The Colonel had an aversion, in times of stress and bad moods, to saying "yes". Meredith irreverently referred to it as the Colonel's "no-syndrome": the art was how to capitalise on it.

"Do you think Charlie would bother to ambush LZ three alpha? He'll know it's swamp grass and water covered – and he can see the mist's blanketing it as well as we can. So he's probably confident we won't use it and therefore, he's unlikely to have ambushed it." Meredith felt pleased with himself, he'd framed that one properly. At least Old Leather had to think it through.

"What's your second point, Frank?" the Colonel asked after a brief pause.

"Taking into consideration your thoughts about the probable lack of security in the Special Forces camp, maybe we could turn it to our advantage?" That was a sly jab, and Meredith smiled: if Special Forces were out of favour with Old Leather, mocking them was in. "They've got two tubes of one-o-five millimetre artillery in that camp. If we asked them to turn those two guns onto one of the LZs, then told them that was the LZ we were going to assault, and mixed in a couple of preparatory air strikes, there's a fair chance the VC would think that's the LZ we intend to use. Therefore the VC would probably start moving their reserves in that direction. Then at the last minute we could switch all air support onto another LZ: the one we really mean to land on. We could even land on Swamp Grass?"

"Not Swamp Grass, Frank, on your own reasoning. It might be ankle-deep, waist-deep, or over-your-head-deep in water. You don't know, I don't know. We could drown every man in the first wave. But there's something in your other thought. I was thinking on the same lines. Get Special Forces on the air and tell them we're going to use LZ two. Ask them to be ready to hit it in fifteen minutes with all they can. And Kurt?"

"Colonel?"

"Before they start shelling, and to help the deception plan, let's have ten minutes of air prep on LZ two. But I want you to keep ten minutes of heavy ordnance to really neutralise LZ five – because that's the one we'll land on."

And so, Meredith thought, that's it. Of course there were no guarantees this plan would work any better than Old Leather's usual up-the-guts approach-and-destroy-him-with-our-superior-firepower tactic; but at least there was a reasoned chance they'd take less casualties. All he could do was hope he was improving the odds for his old battalion, and for Bill Morgan and his company especially.

Between monitoring calls on the brigade command net, he watched the deception airstrike go in. The Forward Air Controller was flying in a small Cessna O-1 Bird Dog aircraft, a two-seat liaison and observation monoplane. These small Bird Dogs reminded Meredith, as always, of old movies of World War I air aces in France ... those daring young men and their flying machines, invariably with flashing smiles, debonair silk cravats,

Mississippi gambler moustaches, engaged in duels in the sun with German air aces with ice blue eyes and names like Von Ribbentrop ...

The FAC was circling slowly at about the same altitude as the command-and-control helicopter. Suddenly the little plane dived, angling towards landing zone two. Abruptly the pilot hauled out of his dive and began to climb again, while a puff of white smoke began to column from the north edge of the clearing where he had fired two white phosphorus rockets to mark the target for the ground attack aircraft.

Meredith craned his neck looking for the fighters, but could not spot them; then his attention was diverted by a series of messages on the command net. Kurt nudged him, pointing down.

"See – he's dropped ordnance."

Again Meredith looked, and saw the F100 Super Sabre jet already climbing out of its dive; two carnation flashes bloomed on the eastern edge of the green clearing.

"One pass, pull ass – not bad for a practice run, Kurt," the Colonel drawled.

"We try to keep our customers happy, sir." Moments later they felt the slight impact of the shock waves and heard the deep crumps of the two explosions.

Ten minutes later, the deception plan's air preparation of landing zone two was finished; neither the strike aircraft nor the FAC reported taking any ground fire.

"What do you think, Colonel?" Kurt asked. "Maybe there's no VC down there – or maybe we got 'em."

"Don't fool yourself, Kurt. If the VC are hoping we use that LZ two, the smartest thing they could do is hold their fire – and sucker us in. Guess I'd feel happier when we prep our real assault on LZ five if your air force boys take a little ground fire – that'd mean the VC aren't in strength in that location and they're trying to scare us off to go someplace else."

Amazing, Meredith thought, the good sense the Colonel dreams up on the spur of the moment, just for the sake of disagreeing. He radioed the Special Forces team leader and told him the air-strike was finished and their artillery preparation could start.

"What's the betting on how long it takes those ARVN gunners to hit the LZ? Five gets you ten, Frank, they don't get a round on it in under six minutes."

"Okay, Kurt. You're on. Even ARVN gunners should have an edge on the US Air Force."

"One thing you both forget," the Colonel joined in, "poor old Charlie's terrified, no matter which one of them's firing. I'd defy a computer to tell me where that ordnance might land. Safest thing a line company can do when he's got ARVN guns or US air in support is call it down on his own position – that way he knows he's safe."

"Colonel, if you and Frank aren't nice to me, me and my birds aren't going to play in your war."

"All right, Kurt. We'll be nice. Give our fly boy a lolly-pop, Frank."

Kurt lost his bet. After five minutes and nineteen seconds a round from the ARVN gunners finally found the target LZ, and thereafter sporadic puffs of smoke spattered the LZ. Next, the vital airstrike on the real assault landing zone began. It was a sight the Colonel always loved. The silver birds flashing and striking like marlin; the thumping explosions of the big bombs; the billowing dragons' breath of the napalm, red caterpillars blackening swathes of jungle green; and finally, his favourite firework – like jumping jacks for a kid on Independence Day – the CBU. CBU were small bomblets which exploded to release thousands of high velocity ball bearings. Pattern-dropped by a good pilot, they exploded above the ground in a fiery sparkling carpet with lethal effect over the length of the carpet and some hundreds of feet either side.

"Who would trade jobs for this?" the Colonel exulted. A true combat command; all the air power he could use; a word to Kurt and the planes would come. Helicopters? For this operation, some forty were his playthings. And men? He was God to four thousand ...

3

"Those choppers should be real close. Can we see them yet?"

"I've had them for a few minutes now, Colonel," the pilot said. "I'll turn the ship so you can see them better."

Small black blobs against the pink of the dawn sky, they grew steadily from a trail of ants to a staggered line of tadpoles, their rotors glittering and blackening as they caught the sun. As the jet airstrike preparation of the landing zone finished with a last run of machinegun fire and twenty-millimetre cannon, the gunships skittered in low over the jungle canopy, just missing the treetops like flat stones skimmed across a creek.

The gunships were heavily armed UH-IB model helicopters, which operated in pairs as heavy and light fire teams. They were used in the last few minutes of an airmobile assault to keep the landing zone neutralised in the critical period just before and during the troop-carrying helicopters' – the "slicks" – landing.

The gunships went in for their initial pass flying crazily – slipping and twisting, bucking and yawing – machineguns spattering tracer in slashes and ricochets all through the clearing. And now, approaching the landing zone, snaking over the jungle at treetop level, flew the first lift of slicks. The gunships peeled back from the landing zone to pick up the incoming slicks and go in with them, providing flank protection.

From above, it was a fine sight. The Colonel felt justifiably proud at the smooth and professional organisation of the operation so far. The brigade had not been alerted till 02.30 hours that morning; and here, thirty miles of jungle away and less than four and a half hours later, was the first assault company. Thirty troop-carrying helicopters meant that a company of one hundred and eighty men would be on the ground in minutes. The landing zone would soon be his. He tried to suppress the sudden nightmare that, to the contrary, the Viet Cong were about to swallow this company whole. It couldn't happen, he assured himself. Hadn't they softened up the landing zone with all that heavy air? But another voice said, "If the Viet Cong are well dug in, and there are enough of them, and their heavy machineguns are well sited ..."

He concentrated intently on the scene below; it seemed too beautiful for violence: the fat lazy river, the peaceful green of the jungle, the cool of the early morning. At his height the landing zone looked like a dragonfly nest with the flashing rotors of the helicopters glinting like silver wings.

4

Morgan sat hunched forward on the helicopter seat, his stomach churning and painful with no food, too much black coffee, too many cigarettes and, of course, fear. It was always a spooky thing, being in the first wave into an assault LZ. It wasn't the sort of thing you got blasé about with experience, either; rather you felt your luck was a diminishing asset. It was like spending capital, he thought, thankfully diverted for a moment, remembering his university economics course and the dry wit of the professor, an expatriate Englishman.

"Spending capital is like a hungry snake eating its tail ..."

He had been lucky. This was his second tour in Vietnam. The first had been with Special Forces two years ago, when he'd run a Special Forces camp just like this one close to the Laotian border in the north of the country in I Corps. That tour had cost him his schoolteacher wife; the loneliness had been too much for her ... But he still hadn't been wounded. You wouldn't call those shrapnel nicks in his butt and calf "wounds", he thought. "Wound" meant gunshot, like Abe Milligan with his shoulder torn away from that huge chunk of shrapnel. "Wound" meant surgeons talking impersonally of debriding: the extensive cutting away of dead tissue destroyed by absorbing the energy of the projectile ... scooped away buttocks, jellied calf, young soldiers' horror, boys' faces stricken with shock, and the screaming. That's what wounds were: the red badge of courage.

Sweating from these Grand Guignol images, his green jacket sticking to him and black sweat splotches under his webbing harness, he forced himself to break the train of thought by looking out of the helicopter. Why in the hell did these goddam chopper pilots have to fly up each other's ass all the time? Wasn't everybody running enough risk without flying formations so tight you kept thinking you were going to be buzz-sawed with a tail rotor? What were those words again that Boswell had credited to Dr

Johnson? Something like: *Depend upon it, Sir, when a man knows he is to be hanged in a fortnight, it concentrates his mind wonderfully ...*

The choppers descended for the final approach run to the landing zone; soon they were flashing over the treetops with sudden and sickening ups and downs as air densities varied. When they humped over the crowns of the taller trees, the column of helicopters in front undulated like a roller coaster ... up, down, up, down ... Jesus, do these chopper pilots have to snag a vine on the runners before they're sure they've got balls?

He tightened up even more when he heard the clatter of the gunships completing the final preparation of the landing zone; they must be very close now. He fought to get a grip on his fear of the unknown and reminded himself, yet again, the best strategy was to concentrate on small practical details he could control. He clenched the woodwork of the Ml4 rifle between his knees and adjusted his position to get the weight of his body balanced over the balls of his feet, so he was ready to dive out the chopper side-door the moment they landed.

The side gunners in his helicopter opened fire. His mouth was dry, his heart pounding, but he was ready, gripped with the noisy and frantic excitement of the last run of the gunships as they swept over the cliff of the jungle into the clearing, spears of their tracer fire ricocheting under them.

"*Into the valley of the shadow ...*" he mouthed furiously as he lay face down in the dirt, the downdraught of the rotor blades of successive helicopters tearing at his clothing. These were the bad minutes.

If the VC had just a couple of fifty-calibre machineguns ready now, they'd knock out those birds like fat ducks ... Morgan hated to think of the cost to his company, momentarily naked in the middle of the clearing.

Still lying on the ground, Morgan fumbled for his compass and checked his bearings. He was relieved to discover that, for a change, the helicopters had brought them in to the landing zone on the planned line of approach. That would make things a lot easier and less confused in the first stage of securing the landing zone and shaking his platoons out into some sort of all-round defensive position.

The noise of the departing helicopters and the crackling of automatic fire were abruptly punctured by a violent crash at the far end of the landing zone.

Morgan peered up from under the lip of his steel helmet and saw a helicopter body momentarily suspended beneath the rim of the jungle canopy. The overhead rotor blade had vanished and the falling body looked like the fat corpse of a blowfly, helpless, with the wings pulled off. He expected to see more of the helicopters behind fall too, presuming the worst: that the VC now had a machinegun, or several, in operation.

But instead, the remainder of the helicopters lifted out safely. He got up and began to run, crouching to make a smaller target, towards the tree line where he intended to establish his company command post. In spite of the clamour of his harsh breathing, the landing zone was oddly quiet with the helicopters gone, and, best of all, there was no hammering machinegun fire cutting them down. Judging from the way his soldiers were running towards the landing zone fringes, some firing from the hip as they moved, no groups were pinned down, and he knew their luck was holding.

There was, however, too much firing by soldiers from his company to tell how much fire was incoming and how many Viet Cong they were up against. Five minutes later he was able to piece together a reasonably coherent picture from the radio reports of his platoon leaders, and relay his take on the situation to his battalion commander.

"LZ secure. Light enemy opposition. Believe local guerrillas and trail watchers only. One dead, two probably wounded, blood trail running east. Encountered several booby traps and three command-detonated Claymore mines. Own casualties: two killed, four wounded from company. Three killed, one wounded from crashed helicopter. Request Dustoff."

In the Colonel's command-and-control helicopter, Frank Meredith had monitored Bill Morgan's message to his battalion commander.

"You made the right LZ decision, sir," Meredith said to the Colonel after passing on the gist of Morgan's report. "At least the brigade's got one foot on the ground now."

The Colonel needed and deserved praise at a time like this; after all, in the final analysis he was the one who said yes or no; and he was the one who wore the results – success or failure. And, in a good mood, he was much more likely to be rational and objective about advice.

"What next, sir? Bill Morgan keep holding the LZ, put another company in to get out after Charlie, bring up a battery of guns by Chinook, then close in the first battalion? Or do you want to heli-assault another LZ?"

"Let's stick to the principles, Frank," the Colonel said expansively. He was a much relieved man, with no intention of taking further avoidable risks. "A bird in the hand's worth two in the bush. We'll develop this LZ first. I'll leave the battalion commander to do it his way. Just two riders. Make sure he understands I want those guns in early. And tell him I think it would be a real good idea to push Bill Morgan's company out to look at LZ two soon as we get another company in to hold LZ five and relieve Bill Morgan."

A fair enough plan, Meredith had to admit: tactically safe and sensible. Except for pushing out with Bill Morgan's company, it was just what he'd have done. Meredith would have preferred to see the pressure taken off Morgan's company, but ... they were on the ground, they had a chance now to recon forward and really, their casualties had been insignificant. As a combat commander, you couldn't afford to let your professional judgement be swayed by just two killed and four wounded.

And yet, Meredith couldn't help wondering about the further development of the Colonel's plan. Was he being aggressive and bold enough? Shouldn't they punch on more boldly with heli-borne assaults into the other landing zones, looking for trouble? Now they owned one landing zone, they could get their artillery in on the ground and they should welcome a big firefight. But what would he do himself if he was commander? It was easy enough to be an aggressive staff officer, because your commander was your umbrella – your own Big Daddy with his ass and career on the line.

5

When the word from the battalion commander reached Bill Morgan that his company was to push out to LZ two, he was surprised and annoyed. He'd felt certain his company would now be left alone as security for the build-up, and that the first reinforcement company would be used. He felt his company had taken enough risks and casualties for one day.

The order could scarcely have come at a worse time. His radioman had called him to the radio for the new orders when he was trying to calm young Jenkins – his favourite platoon leader – whose platoon sergeant had just been evacuated by Dustoff with his right foot blown-off by a VC booby trap.

"You've got to bear it; he's got to bear it," Morgan said, falsely callous. He had to set a hard-man example about booby traps – otherwise his whole company would be paralysed by booby trap fear. "He was a pro, like you and me. You take your chances. He's still alive, isn't he? They'll fit him a plastic foot. And teach him to walk again ..."

"Sure they will, sir. They'll give him a plastic chrome foot and a pension, and he'll make out. But that's not what gets me. You know how tough and mean he was – and mad, and brave ... To buy it like that ... that mean sonofabitch, on a goddam booby trap. He didn't scream, or yell, or whimper, or anything like that ... but fuck! When I slid him on that Dustoff in the stretcher, he was crying; that sonofabitch tough- guy sergeant crying; and not the pain. No, sir. And you know what he said? 'Sorry 'bout that, sir ... no good as a sergeant now, sir ... can't kick ass with a stump.'"

The company was sure to find more booby traps now, and booby traps were worse in many ways than an honest-to-god firefight. Morgan stopped himself thinking like this. There was a job, and either he did it or – or what? He realised he was letting the risks to his soldiers worry him too much; there was no point in self-laceration or self-pity now. That wouldn't help. Just get on with it.

He called in his other platoon leaders and gave them orders for handing over the landing zone to the relieving company and then advancing to the new landing zone. The plan was simple: an order of march and an azimuth between the two landing zones. Their route would mean traversing a combination of jungle, rubber, and more jungle.

"... And Jenkins, since your platoon's closest, you'll be lead platoon."

"Okay, sir, just one question. Worst case – what are we up against?"

"Given the VC are attacking this Special Forces camp, could be anywhere from at least a battalion to two regiments."

"That corner of rubber plantation we've got to cross. Looking at the map there's about six hundred yards of rubber to traverse in a straight line from here. If we're going to buy a firefight, that's where the VC should be. If we avoid the rubber and jungle-bash, it'll take longer, but we could surprise him from the flank."

For a long moment Morgan said nothing. He was angry with himself for failing to think more deeply about the tactics of his company's advance. But Jenkins had, in spite of the maiming of his sergeant. In just a few seconds, Jenkins had penetrated to the tactical heart of the matter. Morgan was still sitting on the ground with his map between his legs, his elbows on his knees, his body hunched forward and his head supported in his hands. Patently Jenkins was right. Morgan knew he'd been guilty of letting his irritation at receiving the order to be lead company again divert him from doing his homework properly. His plan was too obvious a reaction to the situation. Frowning, he looked up.

"Sir," Jenkins said. "I'm not arguing or anything, or questioning orders. It's just ..."

"Goddam, Jenkins. Shut the fuck up." But he hadn't meant to shout or swear. "Jenkins, you had something to say. You said it. Don't back down. You don't apologise for what you believe in. You made a good tactical point. We will go round the edge of the rubber. It'll be an extra twelve or thirteen hundred yards; but that's my problem when battalion and brigade want to know what's holding us up ... and Jenkins –"

"Sir."

"The day you don't have balls enough to tell me what you think – without apologising – I don't want you around. And that goes for you other studs. Now beat it."

Morgan was smiling again, and his change of mood was instantly reflected in the young platoon leaders' relieved faces as they took off to brief their platoons.

Loosening his webbing, Morgan sat back, using his inverted steel helmet as a stool and a log as a back rest. He knew he should try to eat; a couple of crackers and peanut butter from his C rations, or better, a tin of something; but he felt listless and just sat there, listening to the crackle of the PRC 25 radio set, happy for a few moments not to think. But his mind returned to Jenkins. He was an outstanding young platoon leader, militarily sensible beyond his years, and clearly destined to go a long way in the army. Morgan had what amounted to a big brother's jealous pride in him, and had to be careful to conceal any obvious favouritism.

Initially, Jenkins's lead platoon made fairly rapid progress, largely because his lead squad had reconnoitred well forward. The company shook out behind and followed, a long, stop-start worm. Behind them, the noise and confusion of later lifts of helicopters feeding in more of the battalion and a battery of supporting artillery gradually faded to a distant rumble. The noisy passage of the company column became the predominant sound: cracking twigs underfoot, snapping branches, clinking equipment, grunts and occasional curses. Fuck, they're a noisy bunch, Morgan fumed. And yet they were the quietest-moving company in the battalion, because he had trained them to be, and they were not moving unduly fast. Inevitably the battalion commander would be on the radio asking tersely what the hell was holding them up, but Morgan was not going to be pressured into a dangerous hurry. The other companies in the battalion had lost point scouts and squad leaders with depressing frequency because of noisy forced marches and a lack of simple jungle craft.

After a thousand yards following the lead platoon, Morgan's uniform was black with sweat. He lifted his arm to wipe his forehead with the back of his hand and a runoff of moisture welled over his eyebrows, stinging his eyes. He lifted off his steel helmet to ease his neck muscles, rotating his head slowly, listening for the inner cricks.

"Battalion wants to know where we are," his radio operator interrupted.

"Tell them we're advancing according to plan and we're located at ... then release your prestel switch so they think we're out of commo. That'll give them something to worry about for a bit."

Shortly after, Jenkins reported his lead squad had reached the rubber and he was changing direction and formation to sweep the flanking jungle edge. Morgan told him to wait until the following platoon was in position on his jungle flank; this way, if Jenkins bumped a Viet Cong ambush sited on the rubber and jungle edge, Morgan could hook in the second platoon from the rear.

The company had redeployed and been moving for no more than five minutes when the first contact was made. Two sharp pops – single shots, which could have been sniping shots, warning shots, or both. Morgan ploughed forward, anxious to find out what was going on; a fusillade of return fire answered, heavier and automatic, the noise distinctive.

What did it mean? What was the pattern? A lone VC guerrilla trail watcher? A meeting contact with a VC squad? A flank sentry to a VC ambush position sounding the alarm? How big was the enemy force? Squad, platoon, company, battalion ...?

Usually, chances were that a contact was with a squad-size force or less, but this wasn't usually. This was now, a particular case with its own background. Was it a background of the VC wanting to stage-manage the right sort of trap for US reaction forces? Was this the contact you followed up aggressively, and thereby ran down two or three local guerrillas? Or did you pull your horns in warily and probe forward with cunning and caution to measure the beast?

No longer was Morgan tired. His senses were alert; his whole body was tingling. The old war horse rides again, he laughed to himself, exhilarated, leading his company of nineteen and twenty year-olds with their fresh skin, jumping muscles and mad bravado.

6

He pulled the string on Jenkins, holding him back, ordering him to feel out on one flank with a decoy squad into the rubber, on the other, to push carefully forward. The second forward flanking platoon must press on. His plan was to deceive the VC ambush, whatever size, into thinking the decoy squad in the rubber was what they were up against, thus luring the enemy into opening fire and so establishing the size and position of their ambush.

With his company headquarters, Morgan had just reached the jungle and rubber edge from where he could watch the progress of Jenkins's left forward decoy squad when the heavy firing began. The brutal hammering of the Viet Cong fifty-calibre machineguns gashed and splintered the rubber trees, baring their milky white wood. Like rape as well as murder, he thought, watching the death of his decoy squad. How well his plan was working, he thought bitterly, watching the corpse of one of the squad jerking, tearing and disintegrating as a VC machinegunner sprayed it with a long hosing burst.

The rest of Jenkins's platoon returned fire into the general area of the Viet Cong position. Morgan ordered Jenkins to reduce this fire both to conserve ammunition and possibly to deceive the enemy as to their strength. For the same reason, he decided not to call for an airstrike yet, nor to call in more than ranging and registration artillery fire. At the same time he ordered the jungle flanking platoon to press on to determine the extreme edge of the Viet Cong ambush position so he could swing in his other platoon and assault from the rear.

While this manoeuvre took place, a survivor of the decoy squad began moaning for help. Predictably, and fatally, another two members of Jenkins's platoon sprinted out into the rubber to pull him back. With superb fire control the Viet Cong held their fire until the two men reached the wounded man and began dragging him back, then they opened up and killed all three.

At this point, the real firefight began, with Morgan's jungle flanking platoon striking heavy opposition in depth of the main Viet Cong ambush position that soon forced them to withdraw towards Morgan's headquarters. They left behind several dead and dragged back some fourteen wounded from the two leading squads.

The enemy seemed to be at least a company strong, possibly a battalion, and probably dug-in. The only sensible course now was to establish a tight defensive perimeter with Morgan's remaining troops and to hope the Viet Cong would attack, since to attack the Viet Cong in their prepared ambush positions could only mean very heavy casualties. By radio Morgan ordered his platoon leaders to close their platoons around his company headquarters in a circular defensive position and dig-in.

His troops had just begun to scratch out rudimentary foxholes when the first enemy assault wave began, heralded by a braying and tinny trumpeting, which was somehow more startling than the firefight which followed. Morgan now called for the heavy supporting mortar and artillery fire he'd been holding back. Using it prematurely could have made the VC disperse and even withdraw.

The disciplined ferocity of that first assault made him wish he'd called in heavy fire support much earlier. The first wave of VC attackers got to within fifteen feet of their perimeter foxholes before they were stopped by small arms fire and grenades. Next, their field artillery and mortars began to crump in heavily, but Morgan realised he wouldn't be able to walk their fire in close enough to break up another assault. His company's foxholes were still far too shallow to risk it.

The only effective weapons at really close range were their own small arms: rifles and machineguns especially, also both their normal hand grenades and their M79 grenade launchers with their fragmentation grenades, which could clear blunderbuss swathes through the ranks of screaming young yellow men who attacked so courageously. Fierce-looking alive, attacking like snarling cats, they lost all warrior qualities when dead and looked more like schoolboys maimed in a car accident than Communist soldiers killed in battle. During the lull after the first assault, Morgan closed his mind to the bloody and pathetic state of all his wounded soldiers; instead, he forced his attention to targeting the artillery in depth of their position and bringing in airstrikes on what he assessed as the Viet Cong's main position.

When the next assault came, on three sides this time, Morgan realised they were facing more than a company or a battalion; it had to be a regiment. There were three distinct groups: one lot in black pyjamas, another in jungle greens, and the third in khaki, probably North Vietnamese regulars. The second assault was so determined, even frantic, that Morgan thought their position must be overrun. By now, their own artillery was deafening, shells exploding constantly, and he hoped it was inflicting so many VC casualties that this would be the last VC attempt to overwhelm them.

He tried to imagine the thinking of the Viet Cong commander, initially confident that the destruction of an American infantry company was in his grasp, if only he could press home his attack forcefully enough before American reinforcements arrived. But the assault failed, finally, and the Viet Cong withdrew, leaving dead and wounded all round the small defensive island – driftwood of the battle.

Morgan knew now was the time to follow up with a quick attack, but he hesitated, afraid of more wounded and dead outside their small haven. He dreaded the thought of the detailed tally of his company's losses.

Then Jenkins slithered into Morgan's foxhole, his face red and sweating, his eyes blazing.

"Jesus, sir, aren't we going to get out after them? Kick the fuckers hard in the ass, now they're running, and they won't stop. Let me lead my platoon out in counter attack – we'll slaughter them."

Jenkins's anger and sound battle sense snapped Morgan out of his inertia.

"We are counter attacking," he said, "but not just one platoon; we've taken too many casualties. No, sir, every swinging dick who can still crawl will counter attack. Come on, get everybody on their feet – we'll all go."

With wild rebel yells and fierce exaltation, the company rose with Morgan and charged beyond the perimeter in a spontaneous assault.

That was the end of the battle: that quick attack into the backs of the temporarily beaten Viet Cong soldiers, disorganised and dispirited, and dragging their dead and wounded behind them.

*

When Morgan realised the worst was over, the first thing he noticed was his own smell, something he was rarely conscious of – a sweet vomit smell – and his skin was clammy. He stopped his hands shaking and got himself under control by lighting a cigar, then he walked around the position, almost drunkenly, patting soldiers on heads or shoulders, and incapable of speaking because of the lump in his throat. By the time the first reinforcement company arrived, the battle was long over. The whole thing had taken less than an hour and a half.

Morgan had just finished giving orders for the evacuation of the wounded and collection of enemy weapons and dead, when he was stunned to see Old Leather picking his way unconcerned towards him, arriving with a small group just after the second reinforcement company. The Colonel's party comprised only three others: a radio operator, Frank Meredith, and Kurt Braemar. They had come across blackened lifeless zones charred by napalm and smelt the obscenely appetising scent of barbecued meat; they had picked their way through a confusion of brown loam shell holes and tangled treetops spliced with shattered stumps. As they reached the company position they came on dazed soldiers staring with blank eyes at wounded and dead friends, the sitting and standing survivors somehow hollowed and drawn by the experience into a common gauntness. On the north side of the perimeter was the macabre spectacle of VC corpses strewn higgledy-piggledy, now being stacked like cordwood to simplify the body count. One young mid-western soldier held up a pair of bandy legs by the hips – the upper body was missing from the waist up – and asked his sergeant, "Does legs without top count as one or half?"

The Colonel still had a freshly laundered look, which struck Morgan as ridiculous in the circumstances, but rather wonderful; especially considering the irresponsible and improper risk he had taken by walking with such a small group through more than a thousand yards of jungle not yet cleared of booby traps, or secured from guerrillas and snipers.

"Seems like you've had one helluva firefight here, Bill – nice going. If you don't mind, I'd like to walk around and let your boys know how much I think of them. And as soon as you can, I want your casualty figures – along with your VC body count."

"It'll take a few hours to firm up the VC body count, sir. The air and artillery casualties could be up to a thousand yards out. Still, I'm sure Charlie's lost a lot more than we have. I'd guess at least two hundred body count. But my company's bled, too, sir. It looks like forty-two dead, and maybe another seventy wounded. I think we found ourselves a regiment with North Vietnamese, Main Force, and local guerrillas all combined."

"I'd say you're right, Bill. That VC regiment's got some dead to bury and wounds to lick. In fact with this battle alone, we've accomplished our mission of taking the pressure off the My Trang Special Forces camp. Another thing I want you and all your boys to appreciate, this battle wasn't just a one-shot operation. We were scheduled to move in to this Duc Binh province and start pacification operations anyway. And boy, we've moved in with a bang."

7

"I know you Americans cannot lose. But to win? I think you will turn North Vietnam into green glass with your atom bombs. And here in the South? It will be one big red dust military camp. The women will be laundresses for GIs by day and bar girls by night. And the men? They will all be military facility construction workers, or pimps. The Viet Cong will be corrupted too, and give up and go to work in the PXs – to save up for their next revolution."

You couldn't really blame the French for being cynical, Morgan thought, listening to the French planter's conversation with the chaplain. After all, they'd had a lot of practice at losing. Morgan already knew some of the Frenchman's background. He worked for a major French company that owned vast tracts of rubber plantations throughout Vietnam; as the provincial manager of that company, he was the largest employer of labour in the province, as well as the largest taxpayer, and was, therefore, a key player in the provincial power game.

Now, ten days after the My Trang battle, the brigade had consolidated at the airfield just south of Duc Binh province's capital of Canh Tri, and the Province Chief had invited Colonel Robbins and his staff officers to a party in his office. The American officers, scrubbed and clean-shaven in their freshly starched green fatigue uniforms, mingled with Vietnamese officers just as clean, but better tailored; though somehow the Vietnamese appeared more like a collection of cute dolls than real professional officers when compared with the pink and green American giants.

"But if we Americans hadn't come in after you French left, South Vietnam would be Communist by now," said the chaplain.

The Frenchman's full name was Jean Paul Junod. He was tall and slim and looked about the same age as Morgan, mid-thirties. With fair close-cropped hair, he looked more Nordic than French. He could even have been mistaken for a German. But Morgan was captivated by the Frenchman's opinionated irreverence. He hadn't enjoyed this sort of debate and posturing since his student days at Columbia University. He recognised his own stolidity in this sort of exchange, but had always been drawn to those shining students with a gift for repartee and ironic wit.

"Even so, as a religious man," the Frenchman answered the chaplain, "do you think Communism could possibly be as bad a solution – morally – as the carnage and corruption you have seen? You Americans think you are fighting a holy war, but the South Vietnamese are paying for their military salvation with moral damnation."

"You can't be serious about Communism," Morgan joined in. "I'm not saying we're perfect, and any war is a horrible and brutish thing – especially for civilians. But Communism? I served in Korea and I learnt what Communism means in that war."

"But you use the word 'Communism' as if it were a disease, like some sort of venereal infection ..."

"Communism is a disease," said the chaplain righteously.

"Look. Let me put it to you so," Junod assumed the patience of a university lecturer explaining some basic principle to a slow class. "What is more evil? America at war in two Vietnams? Or a Vietnam not at war, with no imperialist French and no military Americans: a South rejoined with the North; the men tilling the soil, the women not selling themselves in bars but keeping house and bearing their Vietnamese men Vietnamese children; a land perhaps of limited political freedom, but a land stable politically; an independent, self-sufficient, rural society? Less evil or more evil?"

"You argue a clever case. But tell me, as a Frenchman, which would you prefer? To live under the slavery of Communism, or fight with American assistance for freedom?"

The chaplain smiled a prim little smile, as if with this question he had finally demolished the Frenchman's argument. Morgan thought back to the Vietnam indoctrination and briefing sessions he'd sat through before the brigade left home: *"Because the Vietnamese are a small race physically, one should not infer they lack either the courage or determination to be free. They have over two thousand years of culture behind them, and are intensely proud of this heritage, and of their military history. From 111 BC until 939 AD they fought ten rebellions against Chinese rule, before finally winning independence ..."*

"On this one issue, I agree with de Gaulle," said the Frenchman. "We prefer to stand alone and avoid both forms of bondage. But in any case, you miss the point. My sorrow is for the Vietnamese people subjected to the American way of waging war."

"The American way of waging war?" Morgan challenged. "What's worse about our way than anybody else's? What about you, or the Germans or the Russians or the goddam Chinese?"

The Frenchman turned his attention to Morgan, noting the deep-set eyes and the intently wrinkled forehead – an honest face, but a sad face, he thought fleetingly.

"I am glad you mentioned the Russians and Chinese, because you three are so alike – so oriental."

"Us, Americans? Oriental?"

"Yes, oriental. You are an incredibly ruthless and callous nation – so careless of human life, your own especially."

"For Christ's sake ... Excuse me, chaplain," Morgan said, then added to the Frenchman, "You've got to be kidding. And what gives you the moral right to criticise the American way of waging war?"

"Because I was a professional soldier, too, in both Vietnam and Algeria, and I know, from those wars and our own brutality, how civilians suffer worst of all."

Junod's shrewd criticisms of the war now made much more sense, and Morgan was curious to learn more.

"What were you doing in Algeria?"

"Commanding a company, like you."

Now Morgan was really intrigued, and managed to extract the bare bones of the Frenchman's military past. Junod was an infantry graduate of Saint-Cyr, the French military academy like West Point. After graduating, he had served in the French war in Vietnam, and then later in Algeria.

"But how the heck," he almost said "fuck", but caught himself just in time – the chaplain was still listening with close attention, "did you end up here running a rubber plantation?"

"A long and painful story I would rather not tell now; later perhaps."

The chaplain chimed in again. "I want to take issue, Mr Junod, with this strange view of yours that we Americans are oriental, and careless of human life?"

Junod was ready with his reply, and as he expounded his views, Morgan was again reminded of a sardonic university lecturer.

"Then let us consider something as important as your American breakfast cereals – statistics. You lose about fifty thousand Americans a year in car accidents, and over the years car accidents have cost you some one and a half million dead. That is more dead Americans than you have suffered in all your wars since the War of Independence. This century you have lost some four hundred thousand Americans in domestic crimes and accidents from gunshot, which is about as many dead Americans as you suffered in the Second World War. You are a violent nation at home in peace, and in war your full potential for violence has not yet been realised. I doubt if this war has cost you even ten thousand dead this year. The American morality play is the western, and how does the hero win? He agrees with China's Mao Tse-Tung ... political power grows out of the barrel of the gun."

"Well, you French," Morgan interjected, "have certainly made your play over the last few hundred years in the military power game."

"We have indeed. But this is the American century. I am afraid of you Americans because of your awesome power, because of your willingness to die for your own emotional propaganda, and above all, because of your simple faith in violence. How will you pacify this province?"

8

The room was suddenly silent. The Frenchman's last question hung in the air like the vibrating note of the small brass gong the Province Chief had tolled for silence. A lively, vital little man, the Province Chief's name was Colonel Phan. With his slicked-back hair and sudden arm gestures, he looked like Walt Disney's Jiminy Cricket. He began his speech:

"Colonel Robbins, and officers of the principal staff of your brigade headquarters; Lieutenant Colonel Gillespie, my counterpart and my good friend, and members of your staff; Monsieur Jean Paul Junod, who soon we hope can pay all his rubber plantation taxes to us, instead of the Viet Cong ..."

There was general laughter, the Frenchman urbanely joining in. As the speech went on, all the polite, serious-faced, crew-cut heads inclined slightly to catch the Province Chief's words through his high-pitched French and Vietnamese accent.

"I have invited you all to my headquarters for a few drinks to welcome Colonel Robbins and his brigade, with its fine fighting reputation, to our province of Duc Binh. Our province has been selected for early pacification because of the importance of our rice and fruit production, and the rubber industry. Also because we have *beaucoup* Viet Cong. Too many for our Vietnamese forces, so we are very happy to have the help of our American allies to assist the economy of our province, to destroy the Viet Cong and to bring us pacification. Gentlemen, I propose a toast: to a fighting brigade."

"To a fighting brigade."

"And to a fighting people, the Vietnamese people," Colonel Robbins added, his strong voice vibrant with emotion. Morgan looked across at him warmly. The Colonel was a professional, a man you could be proud to serve under. Lightly balanced on the balls of his feet, hands controlled by sliding his fingers under his pistol belt, neck and chin thrust forward, as he began to speak the Colonel epitomised the force and purpose of his army machine.

"As the Province Chief said, our brigade has a straightforward mission: to destroy the Viet Cong in this province. It sounds simple, but I don't think any of us are under any illusions about just how much blood and firepower the achievement of that mission will cost. It's going to be one helluva fight, as we learnt in the My Trang battle. Still, none of us minds a fight and I know you're all as confident as I am that when we find Charlie we're going to tear him apart. He's good ... sure he's good ... but we're better. Now, how are we going to destroy him? It's a matter of first things first. Since we're here to stay, we need to build ourselves a base camp – a fairly permanent base camp to operate from – and as soon as the Province Chief and I can decide on the exact area, I intend to start building. But at the same time we'll have another job: protection of the rice harvest. There's nothing in the manuals about that one, but a little bit of American horse sense and I know we can solve it, and have fun solving it. Then once we've solved this rice problem, and got our base camp a-building, we can get on with our main job of destroying the VC and pacifying the province. There's nothing really new in fighting guerrillas and pacification for us Americans. After all we began playing that game in the Indian wars more than two hundred years ago.

"Finally, when the province is pacified, we swing in with our civic action and a good 'hearts and minds' campaign to get the people on side. So there it is. In broad outline: select a site and build our base camp, protect the rice harvest, destroy the VC, pacify the province ... Sounds easy, huh!"

Old Leather smiled and Morgan joined in the general laughter.

"Seriously now, even though it's a big, big job and a tough job, there's only one way to approach it – positively and optimistically. And Colonel Phan, sir, believe me, between your team and my team, we'll lick 'em all."

"Excuse me, Colonel, a question if I may?" the Frenchman said. "A selfish commercial one, but I must ask it on behalf of my owners. These estates I manage for them represent a substantial investment. How long does it take in your plan before you can restore security around our rubber estates?"

"That's a very good question, Mr Junod, and I wish I could answer it. The answer depends on how soon we can destroy the VC."

"Of course, I understand it is a little early to try to forecast. What about damage to our rubber trees caused by your Search-and-Destroy operations? Will there be compensation?"

"We'll have to look into that. I don't know. My civil affairs staff officer can advise you later."

The Colonel seemed both surprised and irritated by Junod's questions – almost as if the Frenchman was a junior officer who'd forgotten his place.

"And now, gentlemen, if there are no questions, I have the Province Chief's kind permission to make a most important presentation to my newest staff officer. Major Bill Morgan, step forward."

The Colonel gave him a warm smile, but Morgan was too aware of an audience to relax and, after stepping forward, he stood rigidly to attention, his green eyes unblinking in the deep sockets that gave his face a gaunt, almost fevered appearance.

"Colonel Phan, I wonder if your photographer could take a couple of snaps as I make the presentation."

"Of course. No problem."

"If you like," the Colonel suggested, "it'd make a very fine picture if you stood next to me while I present ..."

"If my counterpart is in the picture too. You see we Buddhists have a superstition that odd numbers in pictures are unlucky."

"Well, we certainly don't want any unlucky pictures." The Colonel laughed good-naturedly, beckoning Lieutenant Colonel Gillespie to join them for the picture.

"Until yesterday," the Colonel said to the assembly, "for those of you who don't know him, Major Bill Morgan, who is now my Civil Affairs Officer, was Captain Bill Morgan, a line company commander. Today I have the great privilege of presenting Bill with the Silver Star for his outstanding gallantry and leadership in the now famous battle his company fought in the brigade operation to relieve the My Trang Special Forces camp. It is an operation that I personally will always remember vividly – and I think you, Frank, and you, Kurt, would have pretty vivid memories too ..."

*

After dinner that night Colonel Robbins summoned Morgan to his tent for a man-to-man talk about his new job as the brigade's Civil Affairs Officer, or S5. Staff officers throughout the US Army were often referred to by such numbered abbreviations; for example, the Intelligence Officer was the S2, Frank Meredith as Operations Officer was the S3, the Logistics Officer was the S4, and Morgan as Civil Affairs and Civic Action Officer was the S5.

"The division commander, General Ivanhoe, is placing a lot of emphasis on this civil affairs program, Bill, and he directed in his memo to brigade commanders that only outstanding officers were to be considered for these S5 jobs. Now, I don't need to tell you just how well I think of you; that's self-evident ... As I see your job, Bill, civil affairs means all the liaison and coordination with the local civil and military authorities. Civic action means medical help and handing out goodies and building new schoolrooms and so on. Psychological operations mean a good 'hearts and minds' campaign.

"Now, what I want from you in your new job is ideas: real forward-looking ideas, action, and results. All this calls for experience, maturity, and good judgment under pressure. I believe it's axiomatic that a good combat-experienced line officer has these qualities. So, you've got yourself a job. Any problems, any big ideas, I'm always available ... I know there's no doubt in your mind who makes the decisions around here, but I like good sound advice – and that's why the officers I pick for my principal staff are the best. I know you won't let me down."

"I won't let you down, sir," said Morgan, "and I like the sound of the job. In my last tour with Special Forces I picked up a smattering of basic Vietnamese and improved my schoolboy French. Anyway, at thirty-six a man's getting a bit old for a line company. I lost a lot of my boys at My Trang ... those sort of casualties get you down. This civic action thing should be a good change. I like the Vietnamese people, too, especially the farmers, and the war has cost them dear. Helping them rebuild should be a real satisfying job ..."

9

The next day Morgan was back in the Province Chief's office with Colonel Robbins; this time to discuss the selection of a site for the permanent brigade base camp.

"Colonel Phan," said Colonel Robbins, "I'd be grateful if, as Province Chief, you'd take the lead and tell us what areas you think we ought to pick from for our base camp." He spoke with a formal and mannered courtesy that was almost unctuous in his quest for a friendly relationship.

Colonel Phan pointed to a large wall map, almost dancing as he jabbed, gesticulated, and volubly explained his reasoning.

"My dear Colonel Robbins, you have your brigade establish at the airfield just out of Canh Tri, my province capital. And this is good because it gives me security of the airfield and the coast road north of Canh Tri. But you are not to worry too much about this problem, because already I have one Ranger battalion from Division protecting Canh Tri and the airfield, and this task I can do. But Inter Province Route 3, which goes from my capital Canh Tri near the coast, right through the heart of my province, through my rice basin, then through all the rubber plantations till it reach the main highway north, this Route 3, I need secure. Then the villages on Route 3 and the rubber plantation can come to market in Canh Tri."

"So you'd like us to establish our base camp on Route 3 to make it more secure," the Colonel said.

"Yes, yes. That is what I like."

"What about this village here of Dong Tuy?" Morgan asked. "Where the road passes from the edge of the rice bowl into the rubber area? Isn't that supposed to be VC? It's right on our line of communications."

"Good point, Bill," said the Colonel.

"Yes, I discuss Dong Tuy now. This is a very bad place, all VC village. I think we must destroy Dong Tuy and teach them a lesson."

"Destroy Dong Tuy?" said the Colonel. "What do you mean? Re-settle?"

The Province Chief's senior American adviser, Lieutenant Colonel Gillespie, interjected. "Yes, Colonel, I go along here one hundred per cent with the Province Chief. He's explained the complete history of the place to me. It goes right back to the French colonial regime and Vietminh days. You see, places like the Duc Binh war base in the mountains, in the northern corner of the province, have been going for years. Dong Tuy has traditionally been a jump-off place for VC cadres arriving in the province waiting to infiltrate through the war base. Also Dong Tuy has been a sort of summer palace VC provincial headquarters, where the VC live with their families and take R & R if the security situation's easy enough to allow it. We've got agent reports that the village is honeycombed with escape tunnels like rat holes – one of these is supposed to be seven miles long, connecting it to the war base. The VC use Dong Tuy as a hospital, too. It's a complete VC village: all the people in it are VC."

As Morgan listened to Gillespie, he felt instinctively distrustful of the man. He was almost too persuasive, like a well-trained insurance salesman, and Morgan wondered if he had some hidden agenda apart from supporting Colonel Phan.

"Sounds real bad," Old Leather agreed.

"It is very bad," the Province Chief added excitedly. "Once the French moved all the people and tell them they cannot live there any more. But then they allow the people to go back and grow their crops, and in six months they are living there again, and a Vietminh regiment came to fight and help the people stay, and the French give up."

Irreverently, Morgan thought if Colonel Phan reminded him of Jiminy Cricket, Gillespie was a sly Felix the Cat.

"It is a very difficult problem," Colonel Phan continued, "and the people in Dong Tuy ignore the Government and pay taxes to the VC. I have dropped leaflets on this village ordering them to move and they take no notice. I take my Ranger battalion in there and we lose seven men. They shoot at us all day. It is very bad. I drop leaflets telling them when the Americans come, we will move them all out of that village and destroy it."

"What would we need to destroy it?" Old Leather asked. "Bulldozers?"

"Yes, bulldozers and bombs. We fire artillery in there to frighten the VC, but they escape into tunnels. We must destroy all the tunnels."

Colonel Phan spoke with such force that again Morgan wondered what motives were being concealed.

"Tunnel destruction." Old Leather pronounced gravely. "That could be a very big job. Maybe a B52 strike with 500-pounders would be the answer to cave them in, then tear gas and selective demolitions. I'll get my engineers thinking on it. What do you feel about this, Bill?"

Apart from Morgan's instinctive distrust of Gillespie, he disliked being pressured into decisions when there was no real urgency.

"Not sure yet, sir. Aren't we a bit premature in deciding to destroy the place? Maybe we've got other options. I mean there's a helluva lot we don't know about the place yet. How many people are there, for instance? What sort of VC are they in the village?"

"That's a different line of thought you've raised there, Bill, and I've certainly got no fixed ideas on the subject. But it does seem, after what the Province Chief and his counterpart here have said – and they know this province, they've been here a lot longer than we have – that probably this Dong Tuy village has to go. As you said yourself, it's right slap-bang on our line of communications."

"I know, sir, but speaking as Civil Affairs Officer, it seems a helluva way to start our public relations in this province by destroying a village to build our base camp. I mean what can the VC Psyops boys do with a thing like that?"

"If I could make a point here," Lieutenant Colonel Gillespie said, "I think we Americans worry a damn sight too much about public relations and what the rest of the world thinks about us. Sometimes we're too thin-skinned for our own good. We ought to take a page out of the British book in Malaya and try 'ruthless' for a change. For Christ's sake we're only talking about three thousand people in this village. They're all goddam VC. That's fact. You heard what the Province Chief said. Why the hell not move them and make an example for the rest of the province? Why take the soft option about a few VC families? By God, I was in that village that day with the Ranger battalion. We picked up women carrying grenades, and they were using ten-year-old boys as runners. As my Province Chief said, we lost seven good men that day."

Morgan felt his hackles rising. Was this half-bird lieutenant colonel, this adviser, suggesting he didn't understand what it was like to lose men? Was he inferring Morgan was soft-minded, just because he wanted to collect a few more facts?

"I'm not suggesting we should be soft for a moment, Colonel," he said, "but I'm not convinced that destruction of this Dong Tuy is the only solution. If we build our base camp just north of it, you can't tell me the VC are still going to risk using it as a hospital, or an R & R centre? In my experience – and this is my second tour, I was here before with Special Forces – the average villager's politics depends on who's the toughest guy around. If it's the VC who frightens them most, people are VC. If the Government's stronger than the VC in an area, people pay their taxes to the Government, and they'll be as loyal as you could reasonably expect."

"Well, if it was my base camp," Gillespie said gruffly, "I sure as hell wouldn't like a VC village on my line of communications, sitting right on my front doorstep, planting rice by day and booby traps by night."

"But what do you mean by VC village?" Morgan persisted. "How many men are there? How many women and kids? How many old men?"

"Well, that day we lost seven Rangers, I don't recall a single young man of military age. Did you see any, Colonel Phan, sir? I think they were all too busy firing at us. All we saw that day was goddam old men and surly women and kids. Jesus, they were a sullen lot."

The reality of Dong Tuy seemed to be as Morgan thought.

"What's the population break up?" Morgan persevered. "Is it three thousand surly old men, women and kids? What are we going to do with them all? Where do we resettle them? What about family gardens and rice fields? Do they stop work? I guess some of them were working on the rubber plantations?"

Glancing at Old Leather, Morgan sensed he had his support because he had nodded at each of Morgan's probes. Then the Colonel pulled out his cigar case and lit up.

"I have a plan for all this," the Province Chief said. "We have a place to resettle them. They can go into the other villages on the coast road. They have relatives and friends, and the Government gives them three thousand five hundred piastres to help them build a new home, and we feed them. I give them so much rice for each family. You must not worry about this. My counterpart and I have worked out a very good plan and my staff and I will execute it. All I would like from you, Colonel, to help me realise this plan, is some troops to help cordon the village and some spare trucks to move the villagers. It is very easy, I think, with your help."

"Colonel Phan, we can certainly lay on troops and trucks, if that's what you want," said the Colonel through a blue cloud of his own cigar smoke.

"Now to summarise as I see it. To help pacify the province you'd like us to set up our base camp on this Route 3 that runs through the heart of the province so we can give security to the villages on the edge of the rice bowl and in the rubber country. I'm agreeable to doing that – so that's settled. At the same time you want us to help you resettle this VC village Dong Tuy – this sort of VC province-headquarters-safe-haven – and destroy the place with all its fortifications and tunnels. That sounds fair enough to me. Now Bill here isn't sure we ought to destroy the place and he's put up some real fine arguments, but I'm inclined, Colonel Phan, sir, to your viewpoint, and I think we'll probably have to destroy it anyway. All right, Bill, I'm putting you in the hot seat. Let's be constructive about this. What's your alternative plan?"

Morgan was impressed with his colonel's rapid grasp of the essentials and crisp summary. He had no problem at all with his colonel asking him to restate his case – that was the proven and tested US Army way. Wise commanders encouraged vigorous debate and then decided. This was the system he had applied even at company level, whenever there was the luxury of enough time. In combat though, when decisions had to be made fast and executed immediately, there was no time for democracy. But every thoughtful soldier understood that.

"I'd leave it, for the time being, sir," Morgan said. "I'm concerned about destroying houses in a village where we don't yet have enough facts. Let's do a reconnaissance in strength, collect more detailed information about it, and then decide. I mean, maybe there's somewhere else we could build our base camp, or maybe we could build an alternate road and bypass it, or something."

"You'd never be able to use an alternate road in the wet," Gillespie snapped. "Anyways, even if you did, you'd have to destroy a lot of rice paddy. And this province needs rice. The whole country does."

"Yeah, but people need houses, too," Morgan said sharply.

"Okay, Bill. Let's leave it for now," the Colonel said, not unkindly but firmly pulling his major back into line. "That brings me to my next agenda point," the Colonel went on smoothly, "securing this rice harvest. I'd like to kick that ball around for a bit ..."

Old Leather then summarised briskly why his brigade had come to the province.

"As you well know, the main reason we were ordered to stay on in this province after the relief of the My Trang Special Forces camp was to protect your rice harvest. According to my brief, your rice basin is the seventh largest rice producing area in Vietnam ... and that's the major reason my division commander allocated us here on a permanent basis. So, how much rice, Chief?"

Colonel Phan seemed to enjoy Old Leather's easy familiarity, and Morgan fantasised Phan was a small bull-frog inflating with the hot air of his new best friend's attention.

"I was led to believe maybe twenty thousand tons?" Old Leather persisted.

"I don't think so much," the Province Chief said, "not with the VC and all."

"Anyways," Old Leather continued, "roughly speaking, on the basis of twenty thousand tons, Major Morgan and I did some figuring last night, and we came up with an estimate that to shift that rice harvest out would mean some eight thousand two-and-a-half ton truckloads. That's quite a few truckloads and would run us into a big continuous convoy commitment. So what I want to do is float a few possibilities. I mean we can fly the stuff out in C130s, or truck it down to the beach then ship it out. Then where the hell's it go? Saigon? How many trucks have you got? Have you got a central granary? And so on ..."

Morgan watched Colonel Phan closely as Old Leather tried to pin him down, and sensed rather than saw uneasiness.

"Yes, I understand. We must have a detail plan of protecting the rice. Let me discuss this thing with my province staff so we can work out all the facts and figures, and then we can have another meeting and make a very good plan."

"Sir," Gillespie said to the Province Chief, "I'll advise the man from USAID and the agricultural adviser to be available, too, when you have your staff meeting."

"About when do you expect the harvesting to start, sir?" Morgan asked the Province Chief. "Seven, ten, fourteen days?"

"Yes, about then," the Province Chief replied. "There is plenty of time for us to destroy Dong Tuy and shift those VC villagers before the harvest. I like to act quickly now I have my American allies and friends to help. We make quick decisions ... bang, bang, bang. We win the war very quickly."

"You know what, Chief?" said the Colonel, putting a firm brown hand on the Province Chief's shoulder. "I like your style. When you've got a decision to make – you make it. You don't horse around. You're a man after my own heart. You and I are going to get along real fine."

The Province Chief was clearly flattered. His face lit up, and he slapped a hand on Old Leather's back, saying with obvious happiness, "One of the big troubles in my country is laziness. The bonzes call it fatalism; the Taoists call it futility. They think it is better to do nothing. I am not this way. My French schooling and my military training make me different. I believe we will only make success by action. So you and I, Colonel, will work as very good friends."

"Yes, sir," Gillespie put in excitedly, "the Province Chief's real happy to have you and your brigade here. He's been so pleased to have you and your boys along; he's just about jumping out of his skin – really cockahoop, heh, sir?"

"Yes, I am very 'cockahoop'," the Province Chief said, laughing. "I have been cockahoop ever since Major Morgan destroyed the VC at My Trang. Your soldiers are very fierce and brave. It was a brilliant battle, Major Morgan."

"Thank you, sir, but it was my soldiers, not me. And your men at My Trang fought very well, too."

There was a moment's silence, then Old Leather smoothly filled the gap. "You know, when we were kids we used to seal a lifelong friendship by making ourselves blood brothers. You know, the Red Indian thing where you cut your wrists with a bowie knife and press them together to exchange blood. Well, I guess you and I are a bit old for that, Chief. But let's use Dong Tuy in the same way. You want it destroyed and resettled. Right. You're the Province Chief and you know what you want. Decision. I'm with you. Sorry about that, Bill, but that's it. A joint operation – Vietnamese troops and American troops – on with the job."

10

Driving back to the brigade headquarters at the airfield in his jeep, the Colonel was in excellent humour and very pleased with himself. He preferred to drive whenever possible, but then travelled in convoy, straddled by two MP jeeps, both carrying two well-armed MPs in addition to the drivers.

"That's the way to handle our Vietnamese allies, Bill. Friendly and straight down the line. I really go for that Province Chief. A great little guy; he's my kind of people. All this crap about the orient and the mysterious east – he's a damn sight easier to understand than my wife, you know what I mean. Christ, we're probably closer as soldiers, him and me, than I would be to a whole mess of our own American civilians. You know these bearded nuts and ban the bombers and unwashed long-haired fancy-talking intellectuals. Give me that sort of little guy any day. He'll do me for a Province Chief."

"Yes, sir," Morgan said, "you and he got along real fine. But just for the record, sir," he said, conscience-driven, "I still think you're wrong about Dong Tuy."

"Wrong?" the Colonel said in a flat voice.

"Yes, sir. I think it's too big a subject to decide impulsively. I mean, I feel there's no real rush on deciding immediately."

"No, Bill, you're wrong." The Colonel's good mood had vanished. "That was not an impulsive decision," he said. "I heard the Province Chief's views, his adviser's views, and yours, Bill. I'm glad you spoke your mind – that's good – and I held an open mind. But I had very good reasons for deciding to go along with the Province Chief. The point you miss is a political one – a human relations one. He wants the goddam place shifted; he wants it bad; he's the Province Chief, and he's the guy I've got to get along with. If he and I can't get along, I might as well pack up the brigade and get the hell out of here. For better or worse, he's the local leader – he's the one to please, not three thousand Viet Cong sympathisers. I'm sorry they'll lose their homes; sure, I'm sorry; but I'd be a damned sight sorrier for the parents of our boys the VC could kill with their booby traps as our supply convoys drive through that goddam village every day. Bill, you can afford to be sentimental about three thousand refugees. You're my S5 and that's your job. I'm commander of four thousand American boys; they're my first job. And, finally, you say there's no rush. Boy, you've got a lot to learn. In the US Army there's always a rush. It's us. It's our way of life. If our military effort isn't showing real results in a few years, the American people won't stand for this war. We've got to get results fast. We've got to hit this province with a bang and get the place moving. That's why Dong Tuy goes, and goes fast. Let's win the war first ... we can win the peace later."

"Yes, sir," Morgan said, momentarily carried along by the Colonel's rhetoric. "I just thought, I owed it to you as a member of your staff, to let you know how I felt. I mean, sir, when you lay it on the line I'll obey it. I'll follow it through all right, all the way – it's just that I know goddam well you didn't select me to be a yes-man."

"No sir. I certainly don't want any yes-men on my staff. I pride myself on always having an open mind."

The Colonel had recovered his good humour and started to hum again, drumming his fingers on the green paintwork of the jeep door as the vehicle bowled along the side of the airstrip towards the brigade headquarters.

A fat locust-like C130 transport plane lumbered down the strip to take off, blasting red laterite gravel into their eyes. Stacked pine-wood boxes of artillery shells and stores lined the runway. The brigade headquarters was a collection of olive drab tents, squat armoured personnel carriers, jeeps and tangles of concertinaed barbed wire. On either side of the airstrip were lush green paddy fields, dotted with invariably stooping black-pyjama-clad, conical-hatted peasants. Comparing their headquarters with the surroundings, Morgan thought: "Our military island in a peasant sea ..."

*

In the Province Chief's office there was a final coordinating conference for the Dong Tuy operation. Old Leather was there again, and this time he'd also brought Meredith and Braemar, as well as Morgan.

The Province Chief opened the conference by saying he now wanted to interrogate every Dong Tuy villager, because they were all Communists, relatives of Viet Cong or, at best, active sympathisers.

Colonel Robbins readily agreed and offered to provide the necessary troops to cordon off the village. Was there any other help the Province Chief would need?

"My Ranger battalion will assault and clear the village," the Province Chief said, "but if we meet hard fighting, perhaps you can help with some shock troops and artillery and air support."

"All the air and artillery your boys want, Colonel Phan. But I'd prefer you use your boys entirely for clearing the village. It wouldn't help our local image none if we have to start straight off in street fighting where we could easily kill a few villagers. Cordoning-off isn't so bad."

"Would you like me to lay on some pre-attack airstrikes, sir, to soften the place up?" Kurt Braemar, as air liaison officer, asked the Province Chief. "Before you send your Ranger boys in?"

"Yes, that would be very good. This is a very bad village – all bunkers and tunnels, like ... like ..."

"A rabbit warren, or a honeycomb, sir," Gillespie helped out.

"If those bunkers and tunnels are really deep, maybe I should try and lay on a B52 strike with 500-pounders to cave them in?" Kurt suggested, echoing Old Leather's earlier thinking.

"For Christ's sake, sir," said Morgan, scarcely able to contain himself, "let's not do any air or artillery strikes till we get those villagers out. We can try starving them out before bombing them out."

"If we had the time, Bill, we could do lots of things," the Colonel said. "But I agree, air and artillery strikes should be a last resort. Still, let's not lock ourselves into pussy-footing around ... we'll bomb 'em if we have to."

"What troops do we use for the cordon, sir?" asked Meredith. "The three battalions?"

"Hell's teeth, I hope not. I want to keep one battalion at least back at base camp as protection. And one in reserve, so we can swing it in any-where. I think we should get by pretty nicely with one battalion, making full use of our tracks and jeeps in the open stuff. We could barrel in at first light with our tracks loaded with infantry and lay the cordon down in a big arc for their sector; then the tracks could push on to their own sector. Maybe we'll need to drop a part of the cordon by chopper. Anyway, I'll cer-tainly be up in my C-and-C ship to control the cordon; and we'll have your Bird Dog up, Kurt, which can tell us if they try to make a break. Then, if they do, the tracks can redeploy to head 'em off at the pass, eh? How's that sound, Chief?"

Old Leather bent forward and slashed a few grease pencil lines on the Province Chief's acetate-covered map to illustrate his plan.

"I like your plan, Colonel Robbins. It is very swift. At first light you lay the cordon and then with my Ranger battalion we pounce and take them by surprise."

Old Leather nodded vigorously and with his right hand did a swooping gesture onto his map with his fingers extended like an animal trap. "Zot!" he said, smiling, and clenched his hand, presenting his closed fist to the Province Chief as if he had caught a fly.

"Any questions or comments, gentlemen," Old Leather asked, with a sweeping look at his staff officers, "on the broad outlines of the plan?"

There was a long moment of silence, which Morgan finally broke. "One or two suggestions, sir."

The Colonel looked at him keenly. "Shoot, Bill. Always glad to hear out any constructive ideas. After all, that's what these coordinating conferences are all about."

The Colonel's reaction was encouraging. "Two points, sir. I can't see us getting surprise. They know we're coming, we're like goldfish in a bowl; no matter what we do, we telegraph every punch. Second, I don't think we've got enough troops in that cordon: it'll be full of gaps you could infiltrate a company through. I think we should include the other two battalions in the cordon. After all, that village covers six map squares, which means we have a perimeter of about six miles to cordon. If we want to have any chance of making that cordon effective, I think we'll need to do a night move as well, and have the cordon in position by first light."

The Colonel slowly shook his head, his lips pursed. "No, Bill. I think you've made some very fine points, but you've overlooked what to me are the determining factors. First, we do live in a goldfish bowl. That's why I want to move in fast. I can't disguise my intentions, but I can surprise him with when – if I'm quick. Second, a night move like you suggest would be just too complicated to work ... fellas stumbling, and cussing, and getting lost, and stepping on booby traps, and waking up dogs. Hell, it just wouldn't work. It'd be like feeding time at the zoo. And as I said before – I don't have three battalions for this cordon – one it is. What we lack in troops on the ground, we've got to make up with the speed of our tracks, our fire power and air observation. Still, they were good points, Bill, and I'm surely grateful to you for suggesting them."

11

As soon as the operation started, the comedy – or tragedy – of errors began.

Morgan had got permission from the Colonel to travel with the Province Chief's command group when the Ranger battalion entered the village. He spent the night before the operation with the US advisory team in their headquarters at Canh Tri. At four in the morning he was woken, and the ten truck drivers who were transporting the Ranger battalion to Dong Tuy – some forty troops per truck – began revving their engines. The milling Vietnamese soldiers slithered by Morgan in the dark, looking for their assigned trucks; small as American early teenagers, slight as girls, chattering and giggling as if off for a picnic.

At the head of the column of trucks, Morgan found Lieutenant Colonel Gillespie. "I'm riding in the first jeep at the head of the column with the Province Chief," said Gillespie. "You can come along in the second with my Ops and Intell officers."

"Why are you and the Province Chief riding at the head of the column? The road could be mined."

"Listen, Morgan, this Province Chief's got balls. He wants to lead his troops into combat – I say, great. I'll ride along. A few more like him around and they wouldn't need any help from us."

"Sure. I agree, you're both being very brave, sir. But the quickest way to lose the good guys is unnecessary risks. Who commands this outfit when you two get blown up?"

"That'll be enough from you, Major."

"Sir."

An hour later, with the convoy stopped just five hundred yards before Dong Tuy while they waited for the cordon to get into position, it happened. Several of the tracked armoured personnel carriers had bogged down in paddy-field mud; in the dawn half-light, they looked like boulders dotted across the plain. Morgan was listening to a heated exchange on the command net between the Colonel and the armoured company commander when an explosion tore the earphones from his head.

Up, up, went the Province Chief's jeep, seeming to float for a moment like a hovercraft before turning sideways and ejecting the passengers like rag dolls. Dust mushroomed and the shockwave temporarily blinded Morgan. It must have been a command detonated mine, he thought, scrabbling out of the jeep and leaping to the side of the road. He took up a fire position in the paddy next to a bund and fired a long burst into a clump of bamboo a hundred yards away, which could have been the hiding place for the Viet Cong who had detonated the mine. After several minutes, when there was still no answering fire, he ran forward to the overturned jeep. There he found the Province Chief unconscious, and the Vietnamese driver dead. Fortunately Gillespie was unhurt, although he had been badly shaken and was still white and trembling with shock. Five minutes later, when the Colonel came down in his C-and-C ship, the Province Chief was still unconscious. On the instant the Colonel decided to evacuate him in his own helicopter, and took off immediately.

The Ranger battalion commander had now come forward with his adviser, a chunky captain with a football player's bull neck. As the noise from the Colonel's departing helicopter faded, Gillespie turned on the adviser, "Let's stop half-assing round, Captain. Let's get this show on the road. We've all got our missions; little explosion like that doesn't change one goddam thing."

The troops in the leading two trucks were still sitting there. Morgan was appalled. Those from the remaining eight trucks had got out and formed a horseshoe around the mined jeep. None of the most rudimentary soldierly precautions against another mine or ambush had been taken.

Five minutes later the convoy started up again and drove in a column into the heart of an apparently deserted village. It stopped near the Buddhist pagoda, where a large cloth banner was stretched across the road. In Vietnamese and English it read: "*Welcome to Dong Tuy, home destroyers, murderers of old men, women and children.*"

The truck engines were switched off, the troops were silent; the only sounds were distant bird noises. It was a depressing moment, and Morgan found himself afraid, too; a superstitious fear that to destroy a village would be sure to bring bad luck, some sort of moral retribution. Their careless tactics – sitting ducks in vehicles on the central village road – pleaded trouble.

The troops had just begun to climb out of the trucks when the second explosion went off, this time at the rear of the convoy. Later, when the confusion had settled and the dead and wounded had been sorted, Morgan worked out the cause of this second explosion. A Vietnamese Ranger had been carrying half a dozen grenades hooked loosely onto his webbing harness. One of these must have been scraped from his harness in the press of climbing out of the truck. The explosion had killed four Rangers and wounded another eleven.

Above the stone wall of the pagoda courtyard rose a thin column of blue smoke. With his interpreter, Morgan walked over to see what was causing it. Even before they entered the courtyard, he recognised the incense smell of burning aloes. Inside the courtyard was a small rectangular lotus pool and on the other side of the pool the saffron-robed figure of a bonze was feeding a small brazier with gold and red crepe paper – the votive paper money normally used by mourners at funeral ceremonies.

"Ask him where the Viet Cong are," Morgan said to the interpreter.

Stripping off his sandshoes and removing his cap, the interpreter crossed the courtyard and knelt in front of the altar, where he performed the gassho three times, knelt, and lowered his head to the floor three times. When he returned he told Morgan, "He says the Viet Cong ordered all the people to leave last night and instructed him to say prayers for the death of the village."

"Does he know how many Viet Cong are left in the village?"

"He could not say ..."

Morgan felt he was being stared at. He looked up sharply and saw a boy hiding behind a pile of rubble in a corner of the courtyard. The boy looked more curious than frightened and continued to stare at Morgan.

"I thought all civilians were supposed to be gone – by VC orders. Why is he here?"

But already the monk was explaining the boy to Morgan's interpreter.

"He has grandmother – very sick. His mother stay and him – to look after grandmother ..." Gradually Morgan extracted the essential details. The boy's name was Trinh, his mother was eight months pregnant and his father was dead, executed by the VC as a traitor because he had been conscripted into the Popular Forces and returned home to see his family. Trinh was effectively the major source of food for his mother and grandmother, picking fruit from their family plot and working for other families for handfuls of rice. So Morgan arranged with the Ranger battalion adviser, an infantry captain called Leo Purvis, to collect Trinh's mother and grand-mother and put them in the courtyard too.

*

During the next three hours, booby traps and snipers accounted for another five Rangers killed and six wounded. Then, just before ten o'clock, the Rangers began to reassemble near the pagoda. Shortly after, they began boarding the trucks.

"What the hell's going on?" Morgan asked Purvis.

"Screw me, sir. Captain Doan, the battalion commander, says he just got a secret message from the Province Chief ordering him to return to Canh Tri with his battalion immediately."

"But what about the operation, and finishing the job of clearing and destroying the village here? When will they be back?"

"Search me, sir, that's all I know. But we've picked up Trinh and his mom and grandma ..."

"Helluva way to run a war. You know anything about this, sir?" Morgan asked Lieutenant Colonel Gillespie who had joined them.

"Only just heard about it myself. I thought the Province Chief's staff were all acting odd and suspicious – like they were ashamed, or something, and didn't want to tell me. It's not like the Chief to order things like that without discussing it with me first as his counterpart."

By now the battalion were mostly reloaded on the trucks; only the command group and a small protective screen of sentries along the road were left. This redeployment of the Ranger battalion must have been ob-vious from the air; even as Morgan attempted to make radio contact with Old Leather to tell him what was happening, the C-and-C helicopter spir-alled down to land outside the pagoda. The Colonel's face was a controlled mask, his lips thinned to white lines of gristle.

"What the hell's going on?" he demanded, embracing the troops in the trucks with an interrogative sweep of his hand.

"Province Chief's ordered them to pull out. We don't know why," Morgan said.

"That's not good enough for me. I want to know what sort of why – now. Even shell shock doesn't wash. This sure strains the friendship ..."

12

On regaining consciousness, and as soon as it was clear he had no other serious injuries, the Province Chief insisted on returning to work in his office. When the Colonel, Gillespie and Morgan arrived, they found him propped up on pillows on a steel hospital cot installed by the window. A Vietnamese nurse was dressing abrasions on a bared shoulder. His skin was sallow beige; he looked small and thin, like a spatchcock served on the white sheets. An orderly stood at the bed-head passing files for signature; a second orderly monitored a radio at the foot of the bed.

The sight of the Province Chief, so frail and brave and already back at work, defused Old Leather's anger in an instant.

"Colonel Robbins, my dear friend," said the Province Chief, "I am glad you come to see me. I wish to explain a new development in our plan to you."

"Like your ordering the withdrawal of the Rangers? I'm very interested in that."

"Before we talk business, excuse me please ..."

The Province Chief gave rapid instructions to his orderlies; there were then several minutes of social obligation time-wasting, Morgan thought, while chairs were arranged and the orderlies passed cigarettes and poured everyone, except the Province Chief, half tumblers of Scotch whisky. The Province Chief had a small bottle of locally produced fizzy orange drink instead.

"Good luck," he said raising his glass, his white teeth gleaming like dice. "So far our operation is very successful, my dear Colonel. Though I am blown up, I am already better. The villagers all left the village, which saved us much work. We have had some casualties, but not so bad. Now we can go to Phase Two, and here I beg your help, because of a new circumstance."

"What sort of help?" Old Leather asked suspiciously.

"To destroy Dong Tuy so your base will be safe from booby traps and mortar if the VC go back to their homes."

"I've agreed already. We'll help with engineer advice, explosives, and dozers if necessary – and the cordon is still in place."

"No. You don't understand. I have not explained properly. There is an important political conference in Vung Tau to discuss the constitution and future elections. Many very important politicians and generals will be there." The Province Chief puffed out his little chest to mime self-important politicians and generals. "Very important VIP people – you know. The division commander directed me to withdraw the Ranger battalion to go to Vung Tau as part of the special guard. They will be picked up by your air force in C130s and Caribou this afternoon. At first I am very angry because of our operation; but now it is successful, it is all right, and I only beg one cooperation from you. Please finish destroy the village because I must lose my battalion to guard the big brass."

When Colonel Phan finished his explanation, Old Leather sighed heavily and shook his head slowly from side to side. "It's a helluva time to hold a conference," he said resignedly. "Still, if that's the way the cookie crumbles ... When did you find out about this conference?"

"Two days ago, but I take no notice. Often these things are cancel."

"Hmm. Now I see," said Old Leather, putting a hand to his forehead. "Seems like we're screwed every which way, Chief – both of us. Doesn't seem anything else for it. So Bill, let's get constructive – about being destructive."

"If I could make a suggestion, sir, in light of this new development. Perhaps we don't need to destroy Dong Tuy after all. We've got the villagers out; now we could search it thoroughly, and then destroy the tunnels and fortifications. Maybe later we could let the villagers return after we've screened them and sterilised the village."

"You know what, Bill? I'm just about inclined to go along with you. I certainly don't like the idea of the publicity of American soldiers personally destroying a Vietnamese village. Vietnamese soldiers doing the job was a different proposition. When'll your Ranger battalion be back, Chief, from guarding the brass?"

A compromise was reached eventually: the Colonel agreed to send in his engineers to destroy any bunkers and tunnels, but any further destructive action was left to the Province Chief when his Ranger battalion returned.

That afternoon Old Leather withdrew his cordon having decided, with the villagers gone, it was pointless to maintain it. A line company of infantry was then tasked with protecting the engineer company whose job was to destroy the bunker and tunnel network. Morgan watched the armoured personnel carriers as they dismantled their loose cordon: like snails on a billiard table, their long looping tracks crisscrossed the surrounding paddy as they withdrew. That afternoon only two infantrymen and one engineer were wounded. The heavy casualties came the next day.

*

The engineer company and the protective infantry company re-entered the village uneventfully at about seven-thirty next morning. Small reconnaissance groups of engineers, with infantry squads and half squads as protection, began to radiate through the village. At eight o'clock the engineer headquarters group was suddenly attacked by a platoon-sized VC force. Eleven US soldiers were killed, including the engineer company commander. Simultaneously several other engineer parties were attacked and sniped at by small groups of guerrillas.

On hearing the news, the Colonel immediately ordered the remainder of the battalion providing the protection company to proceed to Dong Tuy in armoured personnel carriers. Meanwhile, the remainder of the original engineer and infantry force in Dong Tuy had called for heavy air and artillery fire support: the artillery responded in minutes with an initial crashing salvo from every gun in the artillery battalion.

"That's what those bastards want, that's what those bastards get," Old Leather yelled at Morgan above the din as they boarded his C-and-C helicopter.

Until the airstrikes began, there was little evidence in the village of Dong Tuy – as seen from the helicopter – to suggest the battle below. Many of the artillery shell explosions were hidden by the green blanket of fruit and banana groves. The drifting white smoke might have been from household cooking fires. At first, the reinforcing armoured personnel carriers drove straight up the road to Dong Tuy as if asking to be mined. But a sarcastic blast of obscenities from Old Leather immediately sent them lumbering off into the paddy fields to fan out like black spiders to encircle the village.

"Do we still leave this place, or do we destroy it, Bill?" the Colonel asked. They had landed outside the pagoda again where the relieving battalion commander had set up his command post; the area was also being used as a collection point for the recent American dead. The corpses were laid out in a rough line, twenty-three of them waiting to be loaded onto a "slick", a troop-carrying helicopter, by a black crew chief and a pimply young white door gunner.

The crew chief said to his door gunner, "They won't bite you, boy. They're all-American, and they're all dead. The faster we load them, less chance the flies get."

The Colonel stood watching the corpses being stacked into the helicopter, then muttered angrily, "See those dead GIs, Bill. You were wrong – dead GIs wrong. This village should be razed: a dustbowl in summer, a swamp in winter. The whole thing will have to go ... defoliate, burn and bulldoze ... Scrape it off the map."

All that day and night the artillery thundered; the next morning bulldozers and tracked carriers began methodically pushing down the vacant peasant houses; tearing and grinding at them until they were reduced to piles of red tile rubble – like scattered blood drops, viewed from the Colonel's helicopter.

The soldiers themselves seemed angry with the village, as if the place itself, rather than the VC, was responsible for killing and maiming their buddies. There was savage and childish glee on the faces of bulldozer drivers as houses were tumbled by their massive and uncaring blades. A new breed of hero became famous too: small, scrawny men who crawled, pistol and flashlight in hand, through the Viet Cong tunnels; a claustrophobic and filthy job for which they were christened "the tunnel rats". Morgan thought it an aptly chosen name when he saw one rat-faced soldier emerge from a tunnel slimy with black mud, his chest heaving, his eyes wide and relieved at the light.

"The return of the black turd," someone shouted.

The casualties continued to mount, in ones and twos but, infuriatingly, with scarcely any Viet Cong bodies to show in compensation. By clever use of the thick natural cover in the village, together with the tunnels and bunkers, the VC fought a skilful withdrawal. And, to make matters worse, the intelligence picture (as gleaned from a haversack full of captured documents and the various contact reports) suggested the VC numbered not more than forty at most. Furthermore, as the engineers compiled all their tunnel data on one master plan, it became obvious that apart from one major tunnel with a few minor branch systems, the village was not really extensively tunnelled. What at first had been thought to be tunnel entrances under almost every house were now known to be merely entrances to individual cellars or air raid shelters.

All this only served to strengthen Morgan's original conviction that the village need not have been destroyed. It was a rich fruit-growing area; the peasants would still have to be given land and houses elsewhere, and the bunker and tunnel network, as now established, could have been surgically destroyed without seriously damaging the majority of the houses and crops. However, Morgan realised there was no turning back. Both the Colonel and the Province Chief had committed themselves to a policy of laying-waste.

The most frustrating development of all occurred when Morgan went to see the Province Chief to get his signature on the official request form to defoliate the total village area with chemical defoliants.

"Sir, if I could just have your signature on this letter under the brigade commander's, confirming you want Dong Tuy defoliated. The area referred to is this one here that I've ringed in grease pencil on the map."

"Defoliate? It is very good we destroy Dong Tuy ... no more peoples there, no more houses, boom-boom all the tunnels, but Dong Tuy is very rich in fruit ... ready for harvest soon. I do not want to lose the fruit. Does defoliation damage the fruit?"

"Yes, sir. It certainly should. The best technique of defoliation is to spray on aerially a chemical which will brown and kill the leaves on all vegetation. Then later you can napalm and burn."

"We must not hurt the fruit. Saigon, Vung Tau, Bien Hoa, this province, all needs fruit."

"But I thought from our original discussions you wanted Dong Tuy totally destroyed?"

"Yes, yes. Destroy the village, but not the crops. The province must grow crops to eat. Otherwise everybody is hungry."

Morgan managed, with an effort, to control himself, but was completely taken aback by the Colonel's reaction when he returned and briefed him.

13

When Morgan got back to headquarters, Frank Meredith told him the Colonel had just finished briefing a group of Congressmen on brigade operations. He found the Colonel alone in the special-purpose briefing tent used for daily briefings and visiting VIPs so the operational business of running the brigade could continue unhindered.

The Colonel looked relaxed and very pleased with himself as he lounged back in one of the VIP chairs, smoking a trademark cigar and sipping from a mug of steaming sweet black coffee.

"Bill, my man. And my highly regarded S5 – I've just been singing your praises to a garrulous bunch of Congressman. Sit yourself down and join me in a cigar and coffee ..."

Morgan was reluctant to deflate the Colonel's relaxed good mood with the sorry tidings of the Province Chief's inconsistency. But when Morgan finished briefing him, it seemed today Old Leather was impervious to Colonel Phan's intrigues.

"Just goes to show, Bill. East is East and West is West, and naturally we don't always speak the same language. I just finished two hours briefing those Congressmen and they were seriously interested in the job we're doing, and impressed by the way we're going about it ...

"As I told them, getting the people on side is our main mission – apart from destroying the Viet Cong. So food is vital. I briefed them on how we're going to protect this rice harvest; that really got their attention. Maybe we can haul in the Dong Tuy fruit crop at the same time. I also emphasised how vital it is to have a good friendly relationship with our Vietnamese counterparts ... like me and the Province Chief.

"You've got to compromise occasionally, Bill. Anyways, I'm pleased with our Dong Tuy operation. I know we've shed some blood, a lot of blood, but as I told the Congressmen, we've destroyed the VC province headquarters. We've got control of a key food supply installation. We've resettled three thousand or so villagers. And most important of all – we did it in close cooperation with the Vietnamese.

"In another day or so, we'll finish blowing up tunnels and VC houses and we'll be in great shape to start building our base camp and hauling rice."

The Colonel's capacity to put an exaggeratedly favourable interpretation on events – events which Morgan saw as minor disasters and classics of muddled planning – came as an uncomfortable revelation. Morgan tried to rationalise away his doubts by telling himself he was too emotionally involved with the Dong Tuy operation to be capable of objective judgment. After all, he had to admit, looked at from the Colonel's viewpoint, there was nothing actually false in his interpretation of events.

*

Nevertheless, Morgan was to hear a very different interpretation of the Dong Tuy operation when, five days later, he encountered that cynical survivor of the French regime, Jean Paul Junod. Morgan was working in his tent preparing a civil affairs summary of the operation when he received a field telephone call from the MP controlling the Route 3 checkpoint.

"Sir, there's a French guy here who says he runs all the rubber north of here. He wants to go through and I told him he can't, and he asked I should call you. Name of Junod."

"He's okay, but I want to come see him. Can you fix him a coffee?"

"Already have, sir."

It was a short drive from the airstrip through Canh Tri and across the bridge to the checkpoint, and Morgan was there within fifteen minutes. The checkpoint was on Route 3 at the southern edge of Junod's company's rubber plantations. The brigade MPs had commandeered an existing checkpoint with a small hut by the roadside and a red and white striped boom pole, counter-weighted with a rough cylinder of concrete. The checkpoint was jointly manned by brigade MPs and a group of Vietnamese soldiers sent by the Province Chief because they spoke rudimentary English. Morgan gestured to Junod to get in Morgan's jeep and drove about thirty yards further into the rubber, so they were out of earshot of the MPs.

"They tell me I cannot go through because of your operation in Dong Tuy," Junod said.

"We're not letting anybody through just yet," Morgan replied.

"I wanted to inspect our plantations and try to do something about the labour shortage your resettlement of Dong Tuy has caused."

"I guess you do – a reasonable request. But we're still drawing fire in Dong Tuy."

"But not from the villagers, surely? I heard they all evacuated from the village before your operation started."

"Yep. They'd all gone before we got in ..."

"I gather you had some disappointments with this operation. It has not been as easy as anticipated."

"Disappointments – yep – you could say that." It was a finely honed understatement, the irony sharpened by Junod's twisted grin.

"As a former army officer, I am intrigued by your operations. How on earth did three thousand villagers avoid your cordon?"

"Don't think it was too difficult – the cordon was stretched awful thin, and I'm sure they knew we were coming."

"Forgive me being blunt – but it made your brigade look foolish. Old men, women, and children giving the mighty American military machine the slip."

Morgan knew Junod was right, but he still didn't like to hear criticism of the brigade from an outsider – especially a Frenchman. As the Colonel had said, "Losers hate winners' guts, and the French will never forgive us for winning World War II any more than they'll forgive us for not losing here."

"Not losing" – the Colonel had put his finger on it there; and perhaps it was the most realistic thing you could say about the present state of the war.

"Surely you realised when you planned this operation you would have no secrecy if you included the Vietnamese in your planning? You know as well as I do that Viet Cong agents have penetrated every level of this Government."

"Just like I know you surviving Frenchmen pay your VC taxes and give information to both sides."

"One must survive. It is the first rule. But please, I am not so devoid of sentiment and racial prejudice that I would ever tell the Viet Cong anything useful – anything they did not already know. But Dong Tuy?

"Perhaps I am underestimating your Colonel? Was it deliberate to let the VC know you were coming? A thin cordon to allow the villagers to escape, to save you the trouble of trucking them away? If so, congratulations on a cunning I must respect."

"Thanks," Morgan said wryly.

"You know most of the Dong Tuy villagers have moved to My Trang and Ap Moi," Junod went on. "Ap Moi is that village about three kilometres west of Dong Tuy at the foot of the hill with the Special Forces camp. But because the road from Ap Moi to my rubber plantation passes through Dong Tuy – and you have blocked the road for your Dong Tuy operation – my rubber tappers cannot come to work. Of course, it gives the poor trees a rest from the daily bloodletting, but there is no profit ..."

"How come you speak such good English, Junod?" Morgan asked, to change subject. It would have been too disloyal to the Colonel and the Province Chief to say what he really felt about the botched resettlement of Dong Tuy. "You go to college in the States?"

"No. My mother is English. I spent three years in an English boarding school, and now I have been in Vietnam so long with so many Americans that I am, in fact, a very suspect Frenchman. I even have American friends, and I have learnt to speak passable American too."

Morgan smiled and was reminded again of how entertaining Junod could be. Beneath the cynicism, so typical of most French expatriates in Vietnam, there was considerable charm. In Saigon or Paris he'd make an amusing and lively companion. Conscious of his own dourness, Morgan was drawn to iconoclastic friends like Frank Meredith to provide the sparkle he felt he lacked.

"And must we be so formal? I am used to surnames from my English boarding school, but I prefer Jean Paul."

"Then call me Bill." Morgan put out his hand; Junod shook it with a firm dry grip.

"Perhaps, Bill, you could join me for lunch some time soon? I have a small villa quite close to Colonel Phan's office."

"What about the VC and your personal safety?"

"As long as my company, by whatever arcane means they employ, pay the VC their taxes, or bribes, I am perfectly safe."

"Should I wear uniform or civilian clothes?"

"Uniform, I think, to avoid even a hint of the clandestine. It is a given my servants report to both Colonel Phan's men and the VC."

"I'll check my diary and call."

Even in the shade at the edge of the rubber plantation, it was already uncomfortably hot. Morgan took a swig from his water bottle and offered it to Junod, who accepted and asked Morgan a seemingly irrelevant question.

"Have you had a chance yet to examine the land tenure system in this province?"

"Not really, but I guess you're going to tell me."

"I tell you for two reasons. One, my own vested interests, and two, because I like you, and you have a huge and challenging job … It is going to be very difficult, if not impossible, to resettle those Dong Tuy refugees you have created. Everybody in this province, and most of Vietnam, live in closely worked and developed areas. There is virtually no spare land, apart from jungle, in most of Vietnam. Those refugees from Dong Tuy will have to live on American charity and hand-outs unless they can go back and farm their own plots. Most of them only have smallholdings in Dong Tuy, where they grow excellent fruit, and many of them worked on our estates, too, for extra cash. Now it seems they can do neither, especially if you build your base camp just north of Dong Tuy. Almost the whole of our southern rubber estate would be devoured to build a big enough camp for your four-thousand-man brigade."

"Where else do we go?"

"I really don't know. Of course now I am a capitalist civilian and I just say: 'Don't destroy my company's rubber trees.' Or in my other identity as a greedy Frenchman, I cackle like Shylock, rub my hands and say: 'Ah good, this rubber plantation is very difficult to operate. I must risk my life and my company must pay high taxes to both the VC and Government to work it. Nobody in his right mind will buy it. But wait … American soldiers must have camps. Perhaps they will take over this difficult investment and pay compensation for all the trees they destroy to build their camp. Then we can extricate some of our capital investment. Thank heaven for Uncle Sam with a bomb in the left hand and a bag of dollars in the right.'"

Morgan laughed harshly. "Seriously though," he said, "what the hell else can we do?"

"Build your base camp in the jungle. But that would mean you don't protect the road so much. In my other identity, as ex-soldier Junod, I suggest your brigade is the wrong organisation for this war. Perhaps you should chop it up into company groups – one to each village – protect the people, instead of blundering through the jungle on your impressive but extravagantly futile Search-and-Destroy missions."

"At least we're killing plenty of Cong."

"That doesn't mean you are winning. Though on the surface, you're not obviously losing. Tell me, Bill, what did it cost to destroy Dong Tuy?"

"You mean dollars, lives, psychologically ... or what?"

"Let us take lives first."

"Is this quiz the lead-in to another lecture?"

"Not at all – just a continuation of the present one," but Junod smiled so impishly and persuasively Morgan could not take offence.

"Around fifteen Viet Rangers dead, twenty-three wounded; forty-two US dead and just under seventy wounded was the count at the brief this morning."

"And dollars? It doesn't matter exactly, but it must be millions. You have all that welfare to pay to dead GI families. Still, it is chickenfeed to the US, I suppose. Probably, though, the cost of that operation alone could have paid all the villagers for two years, bought all their land and houses, paid for a school and a hospital, and perhaps even an electric dishwasher for each family, with a vibrating toothbrush for all children under seven ... Do I need to point out what it means psychologically to those whose houses you destroyed?"

"I know, you're asking, 'Was it worth it?' But it's not my job to answer that. As soldiers we've got to do it. My question, Jean Paul, is how would you do it?"

"My answer as a Frenchman is: we couldn't; and now, we wouldn't."

"That's a very evasive non-answer, Jean Paul."

"I'm sorry. I did not say that just to avoid the issue. I am only being honest. You see I have no solutions. When we left in 1954 the problem was clearly of a magnitude beyond French resources, and now it is even more difficult. I am a pessimist at heart, but a friendly one. When you come to lunch, perhaps I will be more inspired."

Junod began to clamber out of the jeep and grabbed his knee to make it easier to extricate his long legs.

"Before you go, thanks," Morgan said. "You talked a bunch of sense."

"And I have enjoyed talking to you, Bill Morgan. These days, running a rubber plantation is a lonely occupation, and a man becomes hungry for human contact and conversation."

"Opposite for me. Our Colonel's a driven taskmaster, and I've got a big new job in front of me. The rice harvest's coming in."

"Ah," said Junod. "You will learn."

"Learn what?" said Morgan warily.

"Oh, just some facts about rice," said the Frenchman airily. "Like rubber, it is a very interesting commodity."

14

The next brigade operation was, in fact, to protect the province' rice harvest. The background directive the brigade received from the Saigon planners stated:

> *The Duc Binh province rice basin is the seventh largest rice producing area in Vietnam. Last year this harvest fell into the hands of the Viet Cong. In order to prevent the harvest (estimated at some twenty thousand tons) falling into the hands of the Viet Cong this year, the brigade is to provide protection over the harvest period and secure the crop ...*

The Colonel ordered Morgan to work out a plan for the operation. As a first step, Morgan asked Kurt Braemar to take him on a reconnaissance flight in his Bird Dog over the rice basin. They flew north-east after take-off from Canh Tri, then followed the coastline. Three lines of breakers crumbled below onto a deserted beach; a line of sand dunes and hillocks acted as a windbreak for the extensive spread of paddyfields which formed the rice basin. From four thousand feet the basin formed an intricate chequerboard pattern of varying greens, occasionally pocked with bomb craters, silvered now into circular pools.

"Can you take it lower, Kurt? I'd like to get a good look at the coastal road and the villages along it. Then I'd like to check out the jungle and rubber edges."

"We might take some ground fire up north from the VC Duc Binh war base, but it'll be worth it if we spot the elephants."

"Elephants?"

"Seen them a few times. If you look close you'll spot their tracks through the elephant grass. I don't think this part of the basin's ever been planted with rice – a lot of it's just elephant grass. And a lot of other parts don't look planted this year. VC must have scared the peasants off ..."

As they dropped lower Morgan could easily see for himself that extensive areas of the basin were not planted with rice. They dropped even lower, to no more than ten feet above ground, and skimmed across the paddies. The propeller blast temporarily flattened the rice below and left a long yellowed trail. A line of peasants, stooped to weed, looked up, startled, clutching their conical hats as the little Bird Dog roared over.

Eventually Kurt tired of this game and regained height to head back to the base camp airfield. It was then that Morgan saw something.

"Hey Kurt, half right – I can see a track through the grass and a grey shape. What do you reckon – buffalo or elephant?"

"I've got it. That's no buffalo, that's an elephant. I'll dive lower so we can see better. Elephants are a herd animal, so there's probably more."

Morgan was as excited as a small boy to see an elephant in the wild – and he had spotted it first. Braemar put the Bird Dog into a steep dive heading for the lone elephant. Morgan felt the G force squeezing him back into his seat, even pressing his eyeballs further back in his skull. He tried to focus on the lone elephant and ignore the G forces – and halfway through the dive, he saw the rest of the herd, barely visible through the high grass.

"I've spotted the rest of them," Morgan shouted excitedly.

"Me too," Braemar's voice crackled back laconically. "We'll take a few passes over before we take them out."

"What do you mean – *take them out?*"

"Just that – elephants are VC trucks. They use 'em to carry the heavy loads all up and down the Ho Chi Minh Trail. US Air Force Intell says they also use the old ones as a high protein food source. "

"But you can't just take out those elephants – they're wild." Morgan was so shocked at Braemar's apparent lack of feeling, he was speechless.

"Might be wild now, but if the VC find them, that's a whole fleet of VC trucks."

"Kurt, as Brigade S5, I'm in charge of civil affairs in this province and I don't want you to take out those elephants."

"Bill, I brought you up as a favour. You've got your job on the ground, but your brief sure don't include telling the US Air Force what to do. You fight your ground war, we fight our air war. Sorry about that, but I've got a job to do."

Kurt switched off the intercom and called in standby ground attack aircraft with cryptic brevity for this random target of opportunity.

Braemar then flew his Bird Dog back to its normal height to avoid the risk of ground fire while they circled and waited for the attack aircraft. Morgan was seething with outrage at what was about to happen, but his inner voice argued treacherously that Kurt was right. Braemar's ruthless military logic was unfortunately correct, and if Morgan pressed the issue further, he'd not only lose a friendship, but a very important professional asset. Kurt Braemar was invariably good natured and cooperative, and very relaxed about taking him up to check out roads and villages and even hard-to-find rice. Now Braemar had bared his teeth and barked, so Morgan reluctantly decided he just had to watch the elephants die.

Within twenty minutes the attack aircraft arrived and Braemar put his Bird Dog into a steep dive to mark the target with a white phosphorous rocket known as a Willy Peter.

Morgan watched, transfixed by the G forces and horror, as Braemar fired his Willy Peter and hit an elephant squarely in the flank. The elephant stood frozen for a split second, then raised its head to trumpet its agony as the phosphorous rocket hissed, burned and smoked in its side.

As they regained height, Braemar was already talking to the attack aircraft and spelling out his instructions. "... no heavy ordnance – just two passes: one with cannons, one with machine guns – and that should do it ..."

After they landed, Morgan drove straight to the American agricultural adviser's office. He was a tall, leathery-faced, slow-spoken man from Louisiana.

"About this rice harvest," Morgan said. "I've just flown over the basin and there's paddy after paddy overgrown. I'm very suspicious now of that Saigon harvest estimate of twenty thousand tons."

"Well, something else you may not have figured on. These little characters haven't done a whole lot of weeding this year, and that really matters ... sort of strangulates the rice. Then again the VCs spread a real nasty rumour about my chemical fertiliser. They said anybody who ate fertilised rice and then had kids, the kids would be born blind. That's great propaganda, but it means I've still got two hundred and forty-three tons of fertiliser cluttering up my warehouse. Those farmers just wouldn't touch it."

"Then how much rice do you reckon they'll harvest?"

"That's hard to say, but I wouldn't guess more than three and a half, maybe four thousand tons. And that's paddy rice, of course, not polished rice."

"What's the difference?"

"The paddy rice is what we'd call unpolished rice – dirty rice we call it in Louisiana. I suppose you could take off about five hundred tons from either figure to get the polished amount. Of course that's real rough figuring – I could be a few hundred tons out either way."

"But that's crazy – twenty thousand tons reduced to three thousand tons. One of the biggest reasons the brigade was sent to this province was to protect an allegedly vital rice crop surplus. I can't see much surplus at all."

"I'd agree, Major Morgan."

To clarify the situation, Morgan set up a coordinating conference with the Province Chief, his staff, and the relevant American advisers.

"First problem I'd like to clear up, sir," Morgan said to the Province Chief, "is just how much rice you expect to get from this harvest, and how much surplus you expect after allowing enough to feed the province. Twenty thousand tons was the planning figure given us by Saigon, and that means eight thousand two-and-a-half ton truckloads, which is an awful lot of trucks."

"Not twenty thousand tons – not so much. I say so to Colonel Robbins before."

"Then how much, sir? Your agricultural adviser here thinks only three thousand tons."

"Yes, I think about that."

"In that case, sir, how the hell did Saigon come up with a figure as wrong as twenty thousand?"

The Province Chief shrugged his shoulders and turned up his palms in a Gallic gesture.

"Perhaps they make it up in Saigon from the statistics. In 1954 no rice is grown here, the rice basin is a swamp, and the Government put in refugees from North Vietnam. By 1960 the refugees work very hard and make ten thousand tons. Now it is a few years later, so perhaps in Saigon they think we produce another ten thousand tons. Ten and ten – twenty. Next problem, please."

Everybody burst out laughing and the Province Chief grinned happily.

"I think this solve your truck problem, too, Major Morgan."

"It may well, sir," Morgan replied. "Do you have any figures on how much the province itself needs? Then we can calculate the surplus."

"I've got some figuring on that," the agricultural adviser joined in. "Last year's harvest, I've discovered, was about five thousand tons, and that's the bare minimum for a province this size to feed itself and have enough over to seed the next crop."

"In other words," Morgan said, "we'll have to bring rice in to the province."

"Yes, sir, about two thousand tons."

"Jesus wept," Morgan said, unable to contain himself, "so instead of trucking out twenty thousand tons to Saigon, now we'll have to truck in two thousand tons of US Aid rice to save the seventh largest rice producing province from famine ..."

*

Morgan returned to brigade headquarters and explained the whole story to the Colonel. "In my opinion, sir, we're the butt of a pretty smooth confidence trick. I wouldn't be at all surprised if the Province Chief himself was behind those Saigon estimates to give the impression Duc Binh province is such a vital rice producing province it deserved special national priority ... which would mean American troops, which means us wasting our time here."

"Now just a minute, Bill," the Colonel said sharply. "Don't get too carried away ..."

15

Morgan was torn when he arrived at Junod's villa. Torn between looking forward to Junod's witty and cynical take on the war, and annoyed because he felt Junod could and should have warned him in far more detail about the Province Chief's manipulation of the rice harvest.

Junod's villa was a single-storey cream-painted bungalow with a narrow strip of concrete for a front yard. Green wooden shutters covered the front windows – no doubt for security, Morgan thought, but it must be a house of bachelor-gloom to live in. He knocked on the door and a Vietnamese woman, middle-aged and expressionless, opened it. She led him to a large living room at the back of the house overlooking a well-maintained tropical garden.

"My dear Bill," Junod said, rising from his cushioned cane easy chair and stepping forward to meet him with outstretched hand. "As punctual as expected ... I can offer local beer, absinthe or whisky."

Junod shook hands firmly, his face alight with transparent pleasure. Morgan was disarmed and his annoyance now seemed trivial compared to the warmth of his new friend's welcome. He glanced about; a typical provincial French colonial villa, simply furnished, dim lighting, window-fitted air conditioner barely controlling the midday heat; and Junod's chair angled away from the window, where he'd been reading a book and smoking.

"I'll join you with absinthe – acquired a taste on my first tour. Just water and ice."

"Any challenges with the rice harvest?" Junod asked mischievously.

"No more than I'm sure you anticipated," Morgan said, "and thanks for the useless cryptic warning – although at least you prepared me for surprises."

"How did your Colonel accept his surprise?"

"With surprising calm."

Junod leant across and offered Morgan a Gauloise pack. Morgan shook his head. "Prefer a slow American death." He pulled out a pack of Lucky Strikes and lit one.

"My Colonel treats the Province Chief like some sort of favourite but errant teenage son. He's forgiven, or made light of, far more Colonel Phan bullshit than I'd have thought possible. It all started with that fuck up with the Duc Binh refugees – and now this imaginary rice ..."

"I knew what was coming. Our province's agricultural adviser comes from Louisiana and is Cajun French. So we talk ..."

Morgan decided to let go his annoyance with Junod over the rice harvest. There were far more interesting things to talk about and Junod intrigued him.

"You were going to tell me more about your military past and that Algerian war ..."

"I was indeed." Junod agreed and then gave Morgan a shortened version of his military past. After graduating from the French military academy in 1951, and finishing his regimental training, he had served in Vietnam for two years as a young platoon commander and was wounded twice – the first time with minor shrapnel wounds in his back from a booby-trapped French artillery shell. The second time was more serious: a bullet through his stomach. He was invalided back to France, and made a complete recovery. He then spent two more years in France as an instructor, preparing troops for the insurgency in Algeria. He was promoted to captain and sent to Algeria as a company commander with the French Foreign Legion.

"So what caused the war there?"

"The old story of the end of empire – a de-colonisation war for Algerian independence, complicated by a civil war and very dirty tactics on both sides. It lasted from 1954 to '62 and ended in failure for France, independence for Algeria, and finished my army career."

"Heh – slow down – too many unanswered questions. You said a civil war?"

"Between those Algerians loyal to France, aided and abetted by French colonists who'd made a good life there, and Muslim terrorists in the so-called National Liberation Front, which you've probably heard of as the FLN ... It was a very nasty and brutal counter-insurgency war and I'm certainly not proud, in hindsight, of my small part in adding to the general misery."

Junod drained his yellow absinthe and water and poured himself another two fingers at least – then added water and ice. Morgan was surprised at the depth of feeling Junod had revealed; it was such a change from the cynicism and biting wit he normally hid behind.

"Enough of me and my ancient military history – tell me more about how your magnificent Colonel plans to pacify this province."

"I don't think he's actually decided yet – and even if I did know, I could hardly tell you, a self-confessed VC informant."

"My dear Bill, as I told you before, I only talk to them in the broadest generalities. I'm not asking about operational details – I meant operational philosophy, broad strategic thinking. Just something else to talk about before we switch to the joys and pitfalls of Vietnamese women."

"Last time we met," Morgan said, deliberately moving the conversation away from current operational planning, "you promised to tell me why you left your army and ended up here."

"I remember," Junod acknowledged, exhaling twin streams of Gauloise smoke. "A sequence of events that radically changed my life ...

"When our regiment first arrived in Algeria, I was ludicrously proud of the toughness and skills of my Legionnaires and naively confident that, with troops like them, we could not lose that war. It was only a matter of time and patience before French professional military skill and our superior planning and logistics crushed those amateur Muslim fanatics.

"But I was so wrong ... I thought the professionalism of my regiment ranked far above the great underlying currents of history. The primal drive, especially after the Second World War, for self-rule and independence was a noble and terrible spur to Algerian self-sacrifice. I had too narrow a view of the war back then, and too small a torch; it was my company, my Legionnaires, right or wrong ..."

Junod paused for a big swallow of absinthe and to light another Gauloise. He was talking very freely now, the booze loosening his tongue; clearly he was reliving his war.

"Did the FLN torture our Legionnaires if they got lucky and caught some? Yes, and horribly. Did we also take revenge and torture them and their sympathisers? Yes. And with the same self-righteous lack of humanity, sanctified by operational necessity ..."

Junod's servant with the expressionless face told him lunch was ready. They ate in an annex overlooking the zealously maintained garden. The annex was shaded by a large mango tree.

"I became an aficionado of couscous in Algeria, but mostly with lamb or goat. Today we have to make do with buffalo stew instead, but the vegetables are fresh. Wine?"

Morgan nodded. Why the hell not? He had always handled liquor well – and very much to his advantage in his periodic all-night poker games. After all, this lunch with Junod was arguably a working lunch, since Junod's company was the largest employer in the province.

"You were telling me what made you quit the army," Morgan prompted, and swallowed a mouthful of Junod's imported French red.

"At the beginning of 1962, you may remember, there was a referendum in France about the future of Algeria, and a majority voted that Algeria should have the right to self-determination. Some popular generals and colonels disagreed – including some involved in the 1958 coup that helped De Gaulle become President ... Anyway, there was a major sense of betrayal by many in the army fighting in Algeria. So a group of generals and colonels decided to act. In France now, it is known as the Algerian Putsch.

"On 21 April my regiment, of about 1000 Foreign Legion paratroopers, was given the job of seizing key strategic points in Algeria. My company took over the radio station in Algiers, and the regiment seized all its objectives. It seemed at first that the Putsch had succeeded ... But our Putsch leaders completely underestimated De Gaulle and his self-righteous cunning. I'm sure he actually believes he is the French Messiah – God-given and God-anointed ... So that's how the shit hit the fan, and I was a mere company commander pawn swept up in the purges that followed ... So now I am simply a rubber man."

"21 April '62," Morgan said, thinking back. "That was just four days after the CIA Bay of Pigs invasion of Cuba – and during my first tour here. I remember the date well because it happened on my mom's birthday. So events in Algeria seemed pretty remote. All my focus back then was on Cuba and whether we'd end up in a nuclear war with Russia."

"I understand – but back then my universe was Algeria and France."

"Were you court martialled along with the rest of the Putsch guys?"

"It was a military justice sausage machine – many units were broken up – crazy rumours and threats running wild ... It was my good fortune not to live in earlier times, when I would have been hanged or shot."

"I'll drink to that," Morgan laughed with unusual gaiety. "If you'd been hanged I wouldn't be enjoying this fine French wine."

"Still – in my premature retirement, I have the best of both military worlds: French professional training at Saint-Cyr, then battle service in Vietnam and Algeria. And now – I am a compulsive armchair critic of the mightiest military power on earth."

Junod raised his glass in mocking salute to Morgan, who raised his glass, too, but fully aware of Junod's pain and sense of loss at the premature end of his chosen career.

Junod drained his wine glass with a flourish and refilled it. He looked enquiringly at Morgan, who shook his head. Although Junod still wasn't slurring, he was patently well in his cups.

"Enough of me," Junod said. "I'm yesterday's man. Let's go back to where you don't want to tread. How will your brigade pacify this province? And don't bother to look worried – I'm not going to ask; I'll just make some guesses at your Colonel's options.

"After you secure your home base, the most urgent thing to do is destroy the VC Main Forces, but that will be almost impossible if you can't lure them to risk battle ... because, in the long run, just survival by the VC could be enough for victory. How long will your American voters tolerate the casualties and financial costs of your American way of fighting a counter-insurgency war?"

"What's so different to our way of fighting counter insurgency war and yours? Apart from us not getting whipped in a big set-piece shit-fight, like you Frenchies at Dien Bien Phu?"

Up to this point, Morgan had enjoyed lunch with Junod. He had been especially interested in Junod's military career and the seismic French political upheavals that had finished it. But then Junod went too far.

"Your naive national arrogance, your simple-minded faith in firepower and overwhelming logistical plenty, your gross national insensitivity to the strengths and wisdom of smaller powers –"

"Hey, hold it right there, Jean Paul. You just used a heap of words that I take offence at, but as your guest ..."

"Oh for God's sake, Bill, I'm talking generalities – none of what I say means you personally ..."

But Morgan was looking at his watch and now feeling guilty for such a long and self-indulgent lunch. He saw it was almost 4 pm.

"But when you call my country 'naive' and my army 'simple minded', I do take it personally. Look, I enjoyed lunch till now, but I've got a heap of reports to do. I really should be going."

Morgan pulled back his chair and stood, ignoring Junod's renewed apologies and his pointing out that both the absinthe and wine bottles were still half full.

As Morgan walked back to the Province Chief's compound where he'd left his jeep and driver, he felt flat and disappointed with himself. Why had he terminated such a pleasant lunch and a new friendship so abruptly? Was he really so sensitive about his country? Or was he masking some deeper personal malaise in dealing with outsiders, of any sort, to his own closed-world of the US Army, right or wrong?

16

It was two weeks after the confidence-trick of the rice harvest, but, for an evening, Morgan could forget all that. Similarly, he had largely suppressed his guilt and rationalised his actions on walking out so abruptly on Junod.

It was dusk in Vung Tau, and he and Frank Meredith strolled past the beachfront bars knotted with GIs and occasional Australian soldiers. Groups of black US servicemen dominated the sleazier bars on the ocean side of the beach road and, as the two white officers approached, the black groups closed up, radiating a morose hostility.

Meredith and Morgan were only in Vung Tau by accident. They had been stranded at the Vung Tau airfield when the helicopter they'd used that afternoon to attend a regional operational planning conference had broken down. Since the repairs would not be finished until morning, they'd scored a night off. After hitching a ride into Vung Tau with a US Air Force captain, they'd booked into a hotel, showered, and were now walking through the town before dinner.

"We're wrong side of the tracks," Morgan muttered.

Meredith smiled, and changed subject. "This must have been a fine resort in the old French days ... Cap St Jacques, wasn't it?"

"Yeah. But since then, between the Vietnamese and us, we've made it a slum. Still, even slums look good at sunset."

A horse-drawn taxi jingled by, the bells conjuring images of more peaceful times. French colonial influence was still architecturally dominant, with tree-lined streets, outdoor bars and cafés, and rambling villas along the point.

Two schoolgirls rode by on bikes; with the streaming tails of their white *ao dais* and their long black hair, they looked like swallows. One of them pulled over a few yards ahead and tried to lift her bike over the kerb. Meredith strode forward to help and easily lifted the bike onto the footpath. Then a young Vietnamese woman – obviously a bar girl – stepped out of the darkened entrance of an adjacent bar and began to shout at the schoolgirl in high-pitched, excited Vietnamese.

Sheepishly, the girl took her bike from Meredith and wheeled it through a gate the bar girl opened for her and down a narrow alley beside the bar.

"My sister – too young for soldiers. Still at school. I bad-mouth her. You have drink with me in my bar. Very high class, officer bar. Majors number one; drunk GIs, number twelve ..."

"You serve American beer?"

"Bud, Schliss, Barmi Bar, Bierre Larue, all beer ... What you want?"

"You. You in a big, bare-assed glass." Meredith laughed and tried to pinch the girl's ass. She slapped his hand away.

"Be nice. Be nice. Don't touch me. I think you number one Cheap Charlie. Touch, touch, touch ... ugh ... all the time. You buy me Saigon tea?"

"Okay. I buy you Saigon tea. C'mon, Bill, let's have a beer..."

They walked up two steps from the street into the bar and sat on high swivel stools next to the bar counter, their backs to the street. A finely featured Eurasian barman, about thirty years old, took their orders.

"Some French planter's bastard?" Meredith muttered, as the barman moved away after serving their beers.

"Maybe. Big sister could be part French, too," Morgan said as she came back and stood between them, one hand on each of them – on their thighs. Instant lust stirred Morgan's groin. How long since a woman?

"Where my Saigon tea?" she demanded. "You all promise, but no buy. Very Cheap Charlies."

Kurt called to the barman. "Two Saigon teas for the lady – one from each of us."

Coquettishly she put her arms around their necks, and said, "My Vietnamese name is Phan Thi Tu. My American name is Maria. What your names?"

"I'm Frank. He's Bill."

"Please to meet you, Bill, Frank." She shook hands with them in turn; her hands and fingers were long and fragile. Easily crushed, Morgan thought; then noticed the barman sliding away, having left two beers and two small liqueur glasses each containing a thimbleful of watered crème de menthe, or Saigon tea.

"Cheers!" the girl said to Meredith and drained one glass. "Cheers," she repeated to Morgan and drained the other glass. The barman slid back with replacement glasses of Saigon tea.

"How old you?" she said to Meredith, running her hand up his neck and tickling the short hairs of his crew-cut. "You look very young, very handsome. You no Cheap Charlie, eh? *Thieu ta?* Major ... you very rich." She fingered Meredith's badges of rank: the golden oak-leaves stitched to the collar of his jungle-green fatigue jacket. "You *Thieu ta* too," she said, turning back to Morgan, holding his shirt lapel with one hand and stroking his cheek stubble with the other. Squeezing between his legs on the stool, she tweaked his nose, and pressed her small breasts into him. Then, leaning forward, she drained another Saigon tea in a gulp. As she finished, Morgan gripped her buttocks, one cheek in each hand – ripe small melons – through the silk of her trousers.

"I want you. Two thousand P. Okay?"

"Huh? Two thousand P? What you think I am? You go buy old, fat cow for two thousand P. You very Cheap Charlie." She wriggled free and sniffed in Morgan's face to emphasise her sense of insult. She turned back to Meredith, and drained the Saigon tea. "Buy me drink. You number one, now."

"No," Meredith said. "Say please, first."

She looked at him coldly, then slid away, moving lithely down the steps and into the street. There, two more Americans, but in civilian clothes, were peering into the bar, trying to penetrate the gloom and see what sort of action was on.

"Hullo, you!" she said, taking each of them by an arm. "What your names?"

"Ed and Charlie."

"Civilian? You work RMK?" RMK was a major American civilian contractor – and its civilian employees were much prized as boyfriends by the bar girls, because they were well paid, often had villas, and mostly stayed put – with minimal risk of being killed.

"Uh-huh."

"You got girlfriend?"

"Not yet."

"I be girlfriend. You like drink?"

The two civilians came in and within fifteen minutes Maria had vamped them of five Saigon teas each. When they left, she came back to Meredith and Morgan.

"Play card!" she said, slapping a deck in front of them.

"What happened to your civilian boyfriends?"

"No civilian," she pronounced it *sybillian*. "Pretend they have villa. Cheap officer Charlie like you. Play card. I cut you. You lose, you buy me Saigon tea."

"You buy me Saigon tea if you lose?"

"Cut," was all she said in reply.

Morgan drew a seven of clubs, Meredith a nine of diamonds; Maria won with a queen of clubs. Almost immediately the barman slid over two more Saigon teas. Maria was happy again. She sat on Morgan's knee and dealt herself a patience hand. Then Morgan saw her schoolgirl sister at the end of the bar, staring shyly but intently at Meredith. Meredith moved quietly up to her end of the bar and Morgan heard him say, "Need any help with your homework?"

The girl laughed; a high tinkle. Several Saigon teas and hands of patience later, Maria was still on Morgan's knee. Meredith and the schoolgirl were also playing cards – kids' grab – involving endless dealing and hand-slapping and her giggling for every pair. The barman moved into a central position between the two Americans. Once, Morgan caught his eye and sensed intense dislike, in spite of the man's expressionless mask.

"He any relation?" Morgan asked Maria later when the barman was looking away.

"He nothing. Just work here."

Three young Americans in civilian clothes came into the bar. Maria excused herself from Morgan, squeezing his thigh as she left, and began to talk to the newcomers. After sitting alone nursing his beer for over fifteen minutes, he began to feel restless and hungry. Paying the bill for both of them, he walked up to Meredith. "Hungry time, Frank. Let's eat."

The schoolgirl sister looked shattered that her rich handsome prince was being torn away. Then Maria remembered her big sister duties and scolded her schoolgirl sister in a flood of angry Vietnamese. Then turning to Morgan she seamlessly switched roles. "You come back later with your friend. Maybe she finish homework then ... have some drink, okay?" And hugging Morgan with one arm, she squeezed his genitals with her free hand.

"Maybe ... take it easy."

As they walked away Meredith said, "Thanks for paying. How much?"

"Too much."

"We'll split it."

"A hundred P a beer, one-fifty P a Saigon tea, and who was counting? Any complaints – forget tail."

"You're dreaming about tail and getting laid with Maria. That bartender guy was her husband; Orphan Annie, my new favourite schoolgirl, is her half sister – she told me."

"What a great liar – she swore he was no relation. Poor guy must love us – pawing and propositioning his wife while he sets up the drinks."

"Can't all of us be winners. Market economy in action ... But there's more – good news and bad news."

"Good news first. So I suffer more with the bad."

"Big sister is available for the right price."

"What a way for a family to earn a living. Poor fucking Vietnamese ..."

"At least you got the 'fucking' right. And not just Vietnamese. It's a very ancient and honourable dishonourable profession, pimping and wife-peddling. At least her screwing isn't breaking up the marriage. She earns a buck and it probably holds the marriage together. Remind me to write and tell my wife I've found a new business opportunity for her."

"Seriously, how would you like to be a Vietnamese male? If you join up to fight the VC, there's every chance some other Vietnamese who's bribed his way out of fighting will fuck your woman. If not, she won't have enough cash to get by, so she'll get a job in a bar and be screwed by GIs, because they pay more. But she'll only fuck the worst of us, the fat ass blubber-guts with a safe job in Saigon, who draws his combat pay because daily he risks death by traffic accident ... Or, if a Vietnamese male has enough money to bribe his way out of fighting, he'd belong to the Cercle Sportif and Club Nautique set – with a lot of rich French guys and smooth American MACV staff colonels who soft-talk and fuck his woman anyway. I swear, Frank, just by being here, so goddam many of us, with too much money and too many PX goodies, we've castrated the Vietnamese male. See, they've all turned into a pack of queers."

Two Vietnamese soldiers were walking by, lean hips swaying in tightly tapered green fatigues, little fingers linked; their red berets tucked under their shoulder tabs and their hair carefully combed and brilliantined into glossy Presley ducktails.

"So what? Should I feel sorry? Our women have castrated us, too. At least an American soldier in the Orient gets back his masculinity – and wears the pants with Asian women. And those guns we carry! Man, we're an army toting phallic symbols ..."

"Easy there, Frank, remember what the general said, 'Any man who cheats on his wife, cheats on me.'"

"That's a big plus for all you divorced guys. I get a dose – I'm a disloyal officer."

17

They ate at a restaurant suggested by the Air Force captain who'd given them the ride from the airfield. It was run by an elegant, middle-aged Frenchwoman. They sat outside in a roof garden at tree-top level. A light on-shore wind carried the sharp tang of sea and fish. After eating, they leaned on a waist-high wall to look through the crowns of the trees at the street below. Listening to the food hawkers and watching the crowds, chattering and vibrant, the atmosphere was that of a weekend vacation at the seaside, not war.

"Great to escape – even for just one night," Meredith said. "Time out to relax and recharge the batteries."

"Wish I could relax the way you can," Morgan said, "but destroying Dong Tuy and that rice harvest screw up still get me."

"What you've got to learn, Bill, is how to laugh at situations you can't change. Don't get so personally involved. One way or another, monumental screw ups and all, we're still going to win this fucking war."

"Win? Depends what you mean by win. Still, let's save that debate for the next bar. What's really screwing me up is the Colonel. Sometimes, you know, I don't think he's the guy I thought he was."

"Maybe he thinks the same about you?"

"Maybe. We sure don't get along as easy as I thought we would. The biggest thing I'd always felt about him was, he'd back a guy to the hilt."

"He surely would. If it suited him."

"I liked to think of him as a bigger man than that. When I told him about those screwed up rice estimates, I said I thought the brigade was wasting its time in the wrong province. I said I figured there must be more important national priority provinces that needed pacification more urgently.

"Well, he chewed hell out of me. Wasting our time, were we? He was commanding this brigade. He was paid to be the judge of that. He made the decisions. This was a superior brigade and he intended to keep it that way. Then he came out with all our casualty figures, and the number of VC in the province. Then he asked me when I was going to start building some schools and hospitals and producing some real positive civic action results, instead of trying to make a fool of the brigade and him with a whole lot of negative statistics. And for Christ's sake, all I was trying to do was let him know the facts so the brigade won't look foolish."

"Good old Bill. Honest Bill Morgan, blundering in with embarrassing news where wise staff officers fear to tread. Imagine how news of a fiasco like that would affect the division commander. The Colonel only releases bad news very reluctantly in that direction. You've got a lot to learn about Old Leather."

"Are you trying to tell me I shouldn't have told him? Bull-crap the facts? Sugar the truth?"

"Yeah. That's what I'm trying to tell you." Meredith was silent for a moment, letting the full import of his words sink in. "If you can't learn how to do that – if you can't learn how to handle Old Leather – you won't survive. He'll sack you."

Morgan was stunned. He had instant dry mouth and couldn't swallow. "Horseshit," he croaked.

"You don't really think that," Meredith said evenly. "I've scared you because you know what I'm saying is true."

"It might be true if I'd fouled up. If I was wrong, I'd deserve to be chewed-out, but not sacked. He's never going to sack me for being right, or telling him the truth. He mightn't like the truth at first – and I know I'm not the most tactful guy in the world – but he's a bigger man than that."

"Bill, why won't you accept the Colonel for what he is, instead of pretending he's some sort of nice military uncle? He's a self-seeking, self-justifying political animal from way back. Look at his background. Maybe that'll help you understand what makes Sammy run. He was born in Junction City, Kansas, near the Fort Riley cavalry post. The family sure wasn't rich. And from what I've heard, they mostly lived on the edge because of his dad's boozing and gambling. His dad was an ambitious, ineffective ward-heeling State politician. Old Leather, or Young Leather back then, went to Junction City High School, and a lot of his friends were army brats. His best friend's dad was a bird colonel and a West Pointer. He took a shine to Young Leather and treated him like a second son ... So going to West Point and an army career was his new escape from the sleaze of his own dad's delusions of wheeling and dealing ... And he hung on to that friend-ship like a limpet. Then his dad lobbied hard for appointment as a Circuit Court judge but missed out. And as a sop, Young Leather got a Congres-sional appointment to West Point."

"So his father was an alcoholic loser and political lightweight – so what? How does that help?"

"You're missing the point," Meredith said. "What I'm getting at is noble altruism wasn't part of Leather's upbringing. He's a child of wheeling and dealing compromise, and backroom arm-twisting. He knows in his bones the price of political failure. Leather is a driven man and his goal is the power and perks of at least a three-star general. He's German stock, too, so ruthlessness comes easy. My advice to you, Bill, is never disagree openly – especially if there's anyone else around. You've got to learn to play him very, very cool."

Morgan flashed-back to the Colonel at the Province Chief's welcome, when the Colonel pinned on Morgan's Silver Star – the Colonel deeply emotional over what Morgan and his men had achieved. That took him back instantly to the end of the My Trang battle and the Colonel appearing like an improbable mirage with no proper infantry escort – just Frank and Kurt – and the Colonel, so dapper and unfazed ... Then he remembered the Colonel talking to him so warmly and confidentially in his tent: "*Bill, I need proven line officers on my principal staff; guys with balls who know what it's like to be shot at, and guys not only with ideas but the guts to carry them through ...*"

"You're wrong," he said to Meredith. "You're just not being fair to him. He's a much better man than you paint him."

"Come on, Bill," said Meredith. "You're a big boy now. The Colonel hates to be told he's ever wrong. He needs staff officers for just two reasons. First, so he can say no to most of their ideas, which makes him feel firm and decisive. Second, for them to approve his own ideas, so he feels warm and confident in his own infallibility as the great white father figure of the brigade."

"Okay. Okay, Frank. Now you're getting carried away. One thing I'll never be is a yes-man. Is that what you're trying to tell me you are?"

"Yeah, kind of, but I bide my time. When the Colonel's mind is made up, no matter how wrong you think he is, you'll never shift him right then. So why disagree? You only make him mad and more stubborn."

"He always hears me out – even over destroying Dong Tuy."

"Sure. He doesn't know himself he can't take criticism. He'd hate to think that. The best time to work on him is before he's made up his mind. His decisions are almost sacred to his sense of self-worth as a decision-maker. Therefore, you've got to take advantage of his enjoyment of saying no. If you've got an idea, suggest the opposite to him. He'll probably say no and react by suggesting your original idea. If so, you should disagree, giving a few minor objections so he can get stubborn and like it all the better. Finally you should capitulate graciously and agree with him on the soundness of what was in fact your original idea."

Morgan laughed. "You're a devious sonofabitch. I can almost believe you do operate like that. But that's not me, and I don't believe it's really him."

"It's your Efficiency Rating – not mine," Meredith laughed in frustration.

They left the restaurant to walk to the big Officers' Club, where the Air Force captain had said there was a floorshow, including a visiting Filipino stripper.

"You want girl? My sister young, clean ... she number one boom-boom." A grinning urchin danced backwards in front of them making an obscene pumping action with his small hands. They were now walking down a dimly lit back street.

"Number one boom-boom ... you look?"

"Why not?" Morgan said. The boy led them up the outside stairs of a nearby house, then into a cluttered hallway where two old crones were squabbling over the contents of a black pot.

"Cigarette?" one asked, making a puffing motion with her right hand, the fingers in a V, and sucking with her lipless old mouth.

"Girl?" Morgan asked, giving her a cigarette. "We look."

She crab-walked past several curtained-off alcoves, chuckling and cackling as she pulled the curtains apart to peer inside.

"Girl," she announced at the third alcove, beckoning Morgan and Meredith across, and sweeping back the curtains. Reclining on a bed of grubby yellowed sheets was a fat Vietnamese woman of about thirty-five, holding the sheet up to her chin with one hand. One slack breast lay uncovered, hanging from her chest like a spare arm or flipper. Morgan made a sweeping gesture with his right hand to indicate pulling the sheet away. The old crone grabbed the sheet at the foot of the bed and clawed it to herself in a bundle, leaving the girl in the bed uncovered like a dimpled pig, staring placidly at them.

"Too young," Meredith said.

The crone looked incredulously at him for a moment, then began to laugh, baring her toothless gums and betel-stained mouth and pointing to herself. Meredith gave her the remainder of the cigarette pack, and they left.

On their way to the Officers' Club they passed bar after bar crammed with bar girls and soldiers. The prettier bar girls were stationed on the steps at the entrances to entice customers, and just inside, the bar wallflowers waited in sad hope.

Reaching the Officers' Club, they looked for a table, picking their way through the crowd drinking at the bar on the outside terrace. Morgan was glad to see Kurt Braemar, sitting alone at a corner table near the bandstand and stage.

18

"Hey, Kurt? What the hell you doing here?"

"Down here to brief myself and my FACs and catch an eyeful of this stripper. FACs tell me she's something else."

"Tough life the Air Force has," Meredith laughed.

"Yes, sir: gentlemen of the skies. We deal out death by day and dolls by night."

Insistent thumping and shouting started at a nearby table:

"Where's the stripper?"

"Bring her on."

"Let's see her take her gear off."

"We want a strip – we want a strip – we want ..."

All heads turned to focus on a table of Australian officers – obvious from their longer hair, occasional moustaches and different jungle greens – shouting boisterously, laughing and banging their table. With them was the US Air Force captain who had given Morgan and Meredith the lift, and regularly flew as one of Kurt's FACs. His name was Captain Eddy Francis; he was in his early forties, of average height, with thinning black hair, carefully combed back, and a small beer drinker's paunch. Francis caught Morgan's eye, waved, and came across to their table.

"Those Aussies are great guys," Francis said, sitting down. "That's a bunch of their officers from the Aussie battalion that had the big firefight couple of days back. I was flying close air support. Boy! Did we drop some ordnance that afternoon and night – and did they zap some Cong."

"They're sure noisy," Kurt said.

"Yes, sir, but that's what I like about them. I was there, and New Zealand, in World War II: Auckland, Melbourne, Sydney, Brisbane ... Say, look at that crazy sonofabitch. What the hell's he doing?"

One of the Australians had climbed onto his table, which was directly beneath a heavy-bladed overhead fan. He'd stripped off his shirt to reveal a hard-muscled, suntanned chest. With hands on hips he squatted on the table, gradually rising from a deep knee-bend towards the spinning fan. Staring at it, his head thrown back, his neck muscles corded, he rose closer and closer to the fan. The other Australians began a steady drumming on the table, gradually increasing the tempo. Drinkers from all over the club clustered around.

"What's the goddam fool gonna do?"

"Give himself a crew-cut," one of the Australians shouted back. The man's hair was thick and curly, streaked with grey. A nurse began to scream.

"Stop him, somebody. It'll tear off the top of his head."

"Don't worry, dear," an Australian officer said. "Not a brain in his head. Your only problem's splinters."

With his head only inches from the whirring blades, the Australian tilted his head forward so that his thick-haired crown, rather than his forehead, aimed at the fan. His eyes strained upwards to judge his progress; from below he seemed to have no pupils, only bloodshot staring whites.

"No!" another nurse shouted as the Australian straightened, pushing the crown of his head up into the blades. With a reluctant *brrrrr* noise, like a stick slapping a picket fence, he stopped the fan with his head.

Of course, it was a tried and tested trick. Morgan noticed the cutting sides of the fan blades were tilted up and realised how the trick had been done. The Australian had slowed and stopped the fan by pressing his head against the hub and the apparently dangerous edges were safely angled up.

Grinning and grimacing under his moustache, the Australian straightened his head above the level of the halted fan blades, resting his chin on the edge of a blade, and rolled his eyes like a madman with his head canted forward on the fan blade as if he'd been guillotined. As a finale, he gave a bloodcurdling yell and leapt sideways from the fan, snatching a foaming bottle of champagne from one of his friends. Squatting on the table, he began to drink from the bottle, the foam running down his chest.

"Wild bastards," Francis shouted with glee.

"Crazy."

After the melodrama of the Australian and the fan, the Filipino stripper was almost a let-down. Her large and widely flared nostrils reminded Morgan of a Pekinese dog, and her stiffly lacquered hair was like a poorly made wig. Everything else she wore – from necklace and earrings to dress, scarves, veils and shoes – was green.

"Come on. Get your gear off. Get your gear off like me," the fan-stopper shouted, standing and pointing at his bare chest. Two of his friends pulled him back down into his chair.

"Pull your head in," one of them said.

Then the girl began to dance and undress: first the scarves, veils and dress, then her bra and stockings. She moved into the crowd, sitting on knees and flitting to lecherous but embarrassed officers for assistance. She persuaded two officers to climb on stage with her for a few awkward bumps and grinds. Then, wearing only a green G-string and pasties, she jumped onto the Australians' table and began to dance to a raucous chorus. She bent over the fan-stopper, rotating her breasts and their tassels in separate directions simultaneously. He poked out a finger and stopped one of the tassels twirling, then made a grab for her breast. She evaded him easily and won laughing applause; then cheekily poked out her tongue at him from upside down, her legs framing her face. She then went to the far end of the table where she bent forward again, rotating her ass and asked another Australian to take off her earrings. Suddenly the fan-stopper Australian stood up and fired a champagne cork which hit her on the ass. He followed up by spraying a geyser of champagne foam into her crotch. The stripper fell forward in shock and surprise, scrambled off the table and, with the Australian chasing after her, ran back to the stage and vanished behind the curtains. The Australian tried to follow her, but his friends caught and held him. So he turned the remainder of the champagne on them, spraying them as well as other officers at nearby tables. A final jet reached Morgan's table and splashed Kurt Braemar in the eyes.

"Stupid, childish motherfucker," Kurt muttered, mopping his eyes.

"He don't mean nothing by it, sir. He's just having fun ... letting off steam," Eddy Francis said.

"Grown man ought to drink it, not spill it."

There was a crash and tinkle of smashed glass above Morgan's head. He felt a sharp sting on the back of his right hand and his cheek. He noticed Kurt was holding his hand to his face, too, and realised the Australian must have hurled the empty champagne bottle away, smashing it above their heads. Cursing, Kurt got to his feet, but already Captain Eddy Francis was out of his chair. He put a restraining hand on Braemar's arm.

"Forget it, sir. I know them. I'll speak to him."

He moved over to the Australian group standing near the stage and Morgan saw him tap the half-naked Australian on the shoulder. The Australian looked mid-thirties – Francis early forties.

"Pardon me, but that bottle you smashed … some of my friends got cut by the broken glass. I think you owe them an apology." Francis held the Australian lightly by the elbow as he spoke.

"Take your hands off me, Yank," the Australian snarled.

"I'm no Yankee," Francis replied, exaggerating his soft Southern drawl. He smiled as he added, "Of course we don't fight no more over that. Now be a good fellah and –"

"I said take your hands off."

Francis dropped his hand from the Australian's elbow and said reasonably, "Come on. All they want you to say is sorry." Involuntarily he replaced his hand under the Australian's elbow to guide him to the American table, but even this harmless contact inflamed the Australian again. With a single punch he knocked Francis sprawling.

Morgan and the others at the table stood up to intervene, but Francis got back to his feet, wiping his mouth, and walked back to the Australian saying, "That was uncalled for, Aussie. I got no quarrel with you. All I asked you to do was apologise to my friends for smashing that bottle."

"Go on, you yeller dog, you're scared to fight."

"No, I'm not scared. There's no quarrel between you and me."

"Come on, fight, you bloody dingo."

Although the Australian had shaped up like a boxer, his fists were unclenched and his fingers were extended and rigid like a karate fighter's. He made a swift lunge and slapped Francis on the face with an insulting backhander. Francis automatically brought his hands up to protect himself, then made a wild and angry swing to the Australian's head. The Australian slipped the punch and karate-chopped Francis viciously in the ribs. The hit made a hollow thump and Francis sank to his knees, gasping.

"Come on, who's next?" the Australian yelled.

But a big and balding Australian major stepped in front of him and said acidly, "That's enough, Marsden. You've gone way too far. Apologise."

"I'm buggered if I'll apologise to that Yankee bastard. Bloody big-time interfering busy-body bloody Yanks."

"I won't argue. That's enough. Get out of here, you can report to me in the morning. I'll decide what to do about you then."

"You can't tell me what to do; we're not on duty now."

"You're being very silly. Do you want to be put under arrest? Take him outside and sober him up."

At that, the Australian's drinking friends calmed him enough to take him outside.

The major walked over to Morgan's table where Kurt had eased Eddy Francis onto a chair.

"On behalf of all of us, I'm very sorry about what just happened. It was ugly, and completely bloody unnecessary. You people give us the run and hospitality of your club, and he abused it like that. I'll personally ensure he gets what's coming to him. The CO will probably send him straight back to Australia."

"Hey, don't do that, sir," Eddy Francis wheezed. "Jesus – all he had was a few drinks too many. Just because the guy knocked me down, I don't want his career on my conscience."

"I could understand that sort of behaviour from other ranks, but from an officer ..."

"Oh, come on, Aussie," Kurt interjected. "Maybe the fellah just doesn't like Americans – period. Sure he was a loudmouth and thought he was a tough guy, but it probably wasn't anything personal – just the booze. Maybe he thinks we deserve it anyway. Maybe he just found out his mother screwed one of our boys stationed in Australia in the last war while his dad was fighting Japs in New Guinea. C'mon, have a drink with us. He's gone now. Forget it."

"Why don't you all join us instead?"

"Maybe we'll do that. But you have a drink with us first," Kurt Braemar insisted.

19

"How long you been here, major?" Morgan asked, while Kurt got a drink for the Australian.

"By the way, my name is Charlie Hunter," the Australian said. He was a powerfully built man, well over six feet and around 210 pounds, Morgan guessed, and looked like a farmer or a footballer or both. He had an educated voice and the easy authority of a natural leader.

After the introductions and preliminary small talk, Charlie Hunter said, "I just can't get Marsden's stupid and bloody obnoxious behaviour out of my mind. I think you're all being far too reasonable and tolerant. Although it's one of your nicer national failings, I suppose, being too altruistic and decent for your own good."

"What exactly do you mean by that, Major Hunter?" Kurt asked.

"Just call me Charlie, please," Hunter said. "We're all more comfortable with informality."

"Okay, Charlie," Kurt agreed automatically, "but same question."

"The ungratefulness you've reaped from those you've helped: the Russians, the French in particular, and then all the underdeveloped nations in Africa, Asia, and South America ..."

Morgan guessed, from the confident and relaxed way that Hunter spoke, that he must have had long experience as an instructor at some major military training establishment in Australia.

"Bloody Marsden's behaviour back there was typical. Well-meaning and friendly, you gave him hospitality; he abused it. You rebuked him mildly; so he rationalised his own bad behaviour as your fault. That made it necessary to insult you, and fight Eddy Francis, to clear his conscience. There's the behaviour pattern of Russia, France, Indonesia, Cambodia ..."

"What's your solution, Aussie?"

"Bugger them. If they don't appreciate the aid, don't give them any more."

"Would you say the Vietnamese appreciate what we're doing?" Morgan asked, curious to hear Hunter's take and compare it to Junod's.

"A lot do. Especially the building contractors, the bar girls, the taxi drivers, the souvenir hawkers, the senior army officers, and the employees of all your building firms and civil and military aid agencies – I think they're all grateful."

Hunter was being disarmingly frank, which struck Morgan as passing strange – most American officers he knew would be far more guarded in a similar situation.

"On the other hand, I don't think the Viet Cong appreciate you very much, and they're rather outspoken about it. You're probably not very popular either with the refugees your big operations create, or with a large percentage of young Vietnamese men whose wives and girlfriends have been seduced by your soldiers' dollars."

"That's a very depressing picture."

"We share the image," Hunter smiled agreeably. "For most Vietnamese, Australians are the same as Americans ... big red-faced bastards with long noses."

The Australian reminded Morgan of Junod: the wry humour and irreverence were similar.

"Back in the States we've got a lot of bearded beatniks and left-wing intellectual pacifists who think we shouldn't be here. You got the same problem in Australia?" Kurt Braemar asked.

"Yes. But not so widespread. Although I think our pacifists are much more dangerous to our security than yours. After all, an American can put up a good case for never getting involved in Vietnam. The American isolationist case is much sounder than an Australian version."

"You saying you don't think us Americans should be here?" Eddy Francis asked intently. "Jesus, I thought at least you Aussies agreed with us on that."

"If I was an American, knowing my country had a great nuclear arsenal and an immensely powerful navy and air force, I think I'd be swayed by General MacArthur's advice to Jack Kennedy: 'Son – don't ever get yourself involved in a land war in Asia.' What would it really mean to the security of fortress America if the whole of mainland South-East Asia became Communist?" Hunter had them in the palm of his hand, all listening attentively for his next quirky observation.

"Another fifty million or so Asian Communists added to seven hundred million Chinese ones – so what? Militarily, the problems of governing, peacekeeping and developing those extra countries would weaken China through over-reach. You didn't think it was worth the cost of a shooting war to fight in Hungary or Tibet. Similarly, I'm surprised you thought Vietnam was worth it. This war is just ludicrously expensive for you, considering what you stand to get out of it."

"If you don't think we ought to be here, what about you Aussies?" Meredith asked.

"Our Communist Party argues it's Diggers for Dollars. I can't agree with the financial soundness of that argument – after all we pay our own way in this war – unlike our Korean friends who are just lavishly paid US mercenaries. No – this war costs us. But I'm sure American investment dollars are far more likely to be attracted to our economy for profit, rather than sentiment. But Diggers for Dollars in a crude way symbolises the longer term reality."

The Australian paused, possibly sensitive to dominating the conversation for so long.

"Go on," Meredith said, "you've got us all intrigued." Hunter took this as a mandate to continue holding the floor.

"Australia is no fortress. We're only twelve million people living in a couple of corners of a great empty continent almost as big as America. If you shook Australia, we'd rattle like a handful of golf balls in a forty-four gallon drum. We've got a small navy, a small air force, and a small army. After the fall of Singapore in 1942, we realised the British wouldn't, in fact couldn't, help us. The Japs could have walked in if you Americans hadn't won the battle of the Coral Sea. We couldn't go it alone against a major power like Japan, or Communist China."

Hunter paused to drain his beer, and Eddy Francis beckoned a waiter for refills all round.

"If the Chinese did take over South-East Asia and decided to build the air force and navy they'd need to invade us, Australia would be theirs. And it's not just a theoretical threat to us. China really does have population problems, and to them Australia must look attractive – fat, rich and empty. So we're realists."

Hunter paused to light a cigarette from an Australian pack Morgan didn't recognise.

"We admit we'd need a big brother if bully-boy China tried to invade. You're the only brother big enough to help. So although in the short or long term, it really doesn't affect Australia's security if Vietnam is Communist or not – the power reality, of whether you'd help defend us later on against China, matters a hell of a lot. And obviously, a zone to our north of friendly, independent, or neutral buffer countries is in our best interests – American support or not. So, supporting you in this war is sort of like taking out an insurance policy to strengthen our alliance. Dead diggers now are a down payment on that policy."

"The way you put that, you don't give a goddam about the Vietnamese people themselves ... what they want, or don't want. All you're here for is your own strategic vested interest," Morgan said.

"Stripping the Australian commitment of any moral rationalisations – yes."

"At least you're honest about it, but ..."

"That's one of the things I find hard to understand about you Americans – your capacity for self-delusion. Remember McNamara's promise that your advisers would mostly be home for Christmas 1964? That ability for self-indoctrination with your own propaganda at even the top levels of government ... perhaps that's why harsher critics think of American foreign policy as half-baked and bumbling."

The clinical harshness and directness of the Australian's logic was almost as shocking to Morgan as the karate captain's drunken aggression. Glancing around at his American friends, he sensed they were as surprised as he was.

"Let me tell you something, Aussie," Kurt said in a slow drawl, breaking the awkward silence after the Australian's blunt observations. "We know you Australians are pretty good. You've got quite a reputation, for a country with such a small population, as soldiers and sportsmen. You've produced some real fine swimmers and runners, and you own that Davis Cup just about. You play real fine tennis; yes sir, you're great little tennis players. But soldiers – how many here? Ten thousand? No? Five thousand, is it? Uh-huh, five thousand, and you do an outstanding job, I'm sure. Now as you said about we Americans, there's nothing brilliant about us. No sir, we're more often than not, 'half-baked and bumbling', I think you said. I mean where you Aussies, or British, or say the French, do something with one brilliant athlete or scientist – we ain't so clever. We're just ordinary folks, so it takes lots of us ordinary folks to do the same thing.

"I mean, you take sport, what you Australians are so good at. We have to have thousands of colleges and universities all over the country working at sport; so that with a big mass effort we can finally pick our Olympic team. Even then quite a few of our best still get beaten by some of you remarkable Aussies and clever guys from other little countries – at say swimming, or mile running or something. But of course when you tote up the overall score, the odds are stacked against the little nation with just a few big-hearted real outstanding athletes. Overall, a big nation of ordinary guys just sort of overwhelms the little nation, by sheer volume of mediocre talent."

"Look, don't get me wrong," Hunter interjected. "I'm no anti-American, but there are certain things about you Americans ..."

"Let's take science, Aussie," Kurt said, silencing the Australian with a hand gesture. "You know how critical all the world is of American degrees compared with, say, Oxford, the Sorbonne or Heidelberg; or maybe even Sydney? Hell, you can get a degree in most anything somewhere in the States, people say: paper-bag making, cream puff stuffing, nuclear physics, biochemistry, metallurgy, surf board riding ... You take the atom bomb. There's a kind of example of what I mean – the Manhattan Project. Maybe some brilliant British or Aussie scientist might have made the whole thing alone in his own backyard out of Bunsen burners and bits of string. But in our own mass production, 'bumbling and half-baked' way, we said, we're not that clever as the Aussies or British. Let's make it a massive joint project, and we put thousands of guys to work on the problems in New Mexico, and finally they managed to solve it, too."

"I'd rather you didn't compare us Australians with the British. There's a lot of un-British Irish blood in Australia."

"Okay, British, Irish, or Australian – but you're still different to us. Now, I don't know if you read Li'l Abner, but according to that cartoon series, we're a nation of schmoos. Now schmoos are nice, reasonable, identical, average guys, and there's an inexhaustible supply of them. You can use them to make or do anything. You could even eat them. Schmoos are slow to get angry, but when we do it's kind of frightening. Remember what happened to the poor old Germans and Japs in World War II. Thousands and thousands of clean-cut schmoos, fair hair, crew-cuts, scrubbed white skin, fuelled on ice-cream and sentiment, began pouring out of America. Like robots it must have seemed, or big soft locusts. You could slaughter them in thousands, like the Japs did in the Pacific, but they kept increasing till the thousands became millions. The more you killed, the more you made. Terrifying. You know there were twelve million US soldier schmoos by the end of World War II, and we were just getting cranked up. Other thing about schmoos is, when they finally start, they don't stop till everything they touch is schmoo'd. So now you've got schmoo impregnated women and part-schmoo children in Europe and Japan – and even in little old Aussie-land. Everywhere now, there's schmoo gadgetry – jeans, Coke, juke boxes, TV and even ten-pin bowling."

"How about you schmoo up for a bit, Kurt, so we can all get another drink?" Meredith drawled.

"Just a minute. Let me finish," Kurt said tersely. "I want to set the record straight for our Aussie friend, Major Charlie Hunter." Morgan and Meredith were seeing a totally unexpected side of Kurt Braemar.

"You see, Aussie, schmoos in mass are impersonal and callous once they fight. See, they lose so many themselves – it's their way to suffocate an enemy with sheer weight of schmoos – they ain't afraid to destroy whole cities to build new and better schmoo ones. So these schmoos dropped bombs on Japan – atom bombs. Hiroshima, Nagasaki ... puff goes the weasel ... and if it was a matter of schmoo survival – atom bombs would be dropped again."

Morgan was surprised by Kurt's passionate eloquence, and the Australian was obviously surprised too.

"You see, Aussie, there's a lot of common misconceptions about us Americans," Kurt went on remorselessly. "A lot of the world hates us, but mostly that's just jealousy, because we're richer and we do so many things better. Not much of the hatred is based on fear; but do you know what, boy? It ought to be. People don't realise just how tough-minded and ruthless we Americans can be. Most of us even have ourselves fooled into thinking that basically we're nice guys, and that's another reason we're so dangerous in war. We see ourselves as the good guy, the one riding the white horse, wearing the white Stetson ... knights in shining armour ... If I was a North Vietnamese, or a Chinese, and I knew what I know about Americans – I'd be terrified. If this war don't go well we could easily drop a few li'l old A-bombs, and if we don't use A-bombs we could still bomb the crap out of North Vietnam with conventional ordnance, like we did to Germany. There's a mean streak in us. We Americans aborned both the Ku Klux Klan and the Black Muslims. We Americans have both our own Nazi party and Communist party. Hell, some Americans call John Birch a left-winger. We're the land of lynching and tar and feathering; we're the land of gang warfare and teenage violence; the land stolen from the Indians; the nation born in revolution, blooded in Civil War, and that assassinates its presidents. Boy, we're mean and cruel. *'When you see us comin', better step aside, a lot of men didn't and a lot of men died.'* Don't underestimate us, Aussie."

20

"All right. I'm impressed. You're not nice at all. Underneath, you're meaner and nastier than anybody else. Good on you. Now what about a drink?"

"I'm not drinking right now, thanks, Major Charlie Hunter, and you're laughing. But Aussie, let me tell you – you ought to listen, and listen good. Maybe you've heard of the John Birch society, and you think 'fringe crazies'? But there's a lot of people think we ought to get tough with Communists, especially North Vietnam and China – real tough, and now. Maybe you saw *Dr Strangelove* and laughed at the thought of the US pulling off a pre-emptive nuke strike. I've got news. What we ought to do, and there's a lot of people think like me, is bomb North Vietnam off the map – nukes and all, bomb the crap out of her. And if the Chinese object? Fine business, we fly over and knock out those Chinese nuke sites, and industry, and bomb her back ten thousand years into the Stone Age. And do you know something? We'll do it if we're forced to. We'll burn 'em up. You're smiling again, Aussie. You think I've drunk too much, or I'm some kind of nut. No, I'm just an average, run-of-the-mill, Air Force officer, ready to be promoted to lieutenant colonel just like another few thousand US Air Force major schmoos. Look, Aussie, we're so goddam big and powerful, and rich and ruthless, we could take on the world. Hell, we don't need your pissant five thousand here. If we wanted Australia, we could take or destroy it tomorrow. Christ, what are you compared to us? You're not a country, you're a tennis court."

"I suppose that explains why we keep beating you at tennis." The Australian's joke broke the tension and everybody laughed.

"I'm sorry, Aussie," Kurt said, "but sometimes we have to take off our sheep's clothing. Our disguise had you fooled – just like it had your Captain Karate fooled. I hope you don't underestimate us in future."

"It's all been very instructive, but quite unnecessary. I like Americans."

"Listen, Aussie, you don't have to patronise us. I couldn't care less whether you like us or not. I'd prefer you didn't. Just a little healthy respect and fear will do fine as a substitute for 'like.'"

The Australian stood abruptly. He was no longer smiling or even trying to be good-humoured. "You have frightened me. Suddenly I'm very afraid. As a citizen of a small country I've just realised how vulnerable we are. Now I understand why the Viet Cong fight so well – I almost feel a brotherly sympathy. And I almost hope you lose this fucking war."

"Sorry about that, Charlie boy," Kurt laughed, "we've never lost a war yet, and we're sure not about to start learning ..."

After the Australian left the table, Meredith said to Kurt, "What got into you? He was being friendly – and it was him who stopped Captain Karate."

"I guess suddenly I'd just had enough smug criticism of what's wrong with us poor old Ugly Americans ..."

*

Later that night Morgan and Meredith walked back to Maria's bar. A light sea mist made the streets darker and encircled the street lights with globular rainbows.

"Kurt was way out of line," Morgan said.

"He was just blowing off steam to make up for not having the guts to go in and take on Captain Karate. So he took it all out on the Aussie major instead. Anyway, what the hell ... He went and bought Major Charlie Hunter a drink after a bit. And you know Kurt – later he felt so guilty, he promised to take the Aussie up in his Bird Dog tomorrow."

"I'm glad about that. When Charlie Hunter walked away, Kurt had him really hating Americans."

"In a lot of ways, though, I agreed with Kurt," Meredith said. "It's a sign of foreign relations maturity when we stop worrying so much whether people love us or not. The main thing is, do they respect us?"

"But we can't just ride roughshod over the world. It's important the smaller countries believe we respect them too."

"You're right, old buddy. Of course you're right. But just now, all I want is to skip the respect and enjoy some depraved schoolgirl screwing ..."

When they got back to Maria's bar it was crowded. There were now four additional bar girls as well as Maria. But there was no sign of her schoolgirl sister. The barman served them with no sign of recognition, and initially Maria looked right through Morgan. But after twenty minutes or so, she came over and promised to return soon. Another fifteen minutes went by before she finally joined them.

"I have drink?" she said, pressing close to Morgan and whispering in his ear. Then, as soon as he nodded, she pulled away, and yawned behind the back of her hand.

"Where's your sister?" Meredith asked.

"Sleep. She go school tomorrow."

"Can you wake her?"

"You mad. She baby, schoolgirl ... go way."

"I'd very much like to see you tonight when you finish work," said Morgan.

"Not tonight. Too tired: work, work, all day."

"But I've got to leave in the morning."

"Okay, you see me next time you come."

"Don't know when I'll be back."

She looked at Morgan, a flat calculating stare. "Buy me Saigon tea, or I go. He get angry," she pointed to her husband. Morgan put both hands on her flanks, feeling her lean hips through the silk *ao dai*, circled with the fine elastic ridge of her panties.

"I'd like to make love to you."

"Don't touch me," she said, pulling away. "All you Americans the same. *'Hullo you, what your name? Buy one drink. I love you, you sleep with me.'* Bang, bang, bang. No love, no respect. You think dirt."

"I've bought you a lot more than one drink."

"Ugh, you think you buy me?"

"I'll give you three thousand piastres."

"Go away ... Wait. How much you got? Show me wallet."

Morgan pulled out his wallet, wondering how much he did have left. He saw he only had five thousand piastres in total, although he had another hundred dollars in military payment certificates.

"You give me all that. Then maybe I come with you."

"You crazy? I could get ten girls in Bangkok for that."

"How much you pay for girl in Bangkok?"

"Ten dollars – flat."

"You married?" she asked.

"Not any more."

"Why?"

"Divorced ... after my first tour here with Special Forces."

Jolted, Morgan thought back. It seemed so long ago; but he was long over the pain, and there were no kids. If there had been kids, the loneliness would not have been so bad for her. Whereas he'd had the challenge and excitement of the Special Forces camp. After her shattering letter telling him she was having an affair and wanted a divorce, he'd dulled the pain with overwork and risk-taking. That was a big advantage of the army: it could demand and give as much as father, mother, wife and mistress all combined.

"Okay. If Bangkok girl ten dollar, twenty dollar I go with you. Give me ten dollar now and two thousand P. I give bar one thousand P, and one thousand P taxi. Okay? You wait your hotel. I see you there later. You go now."

She reached for Morgan's wallet and began extracting notes, until he closed his hand on hers and his wallet.

"Hold on. If I give you money now, how do I know you'll come?"

"You give me no money and I go; how I know you pay?"

"How soon can you leave?"

"Soon. When bar close."

"You don't need me to fight it out," Meredith interrupted, and stood. "If I don't get some place else before the bars close for curfew, I won't get me a girl tonight." He waved and grinned at Morgan, then left.

Morgan went on bargaining with Maria and finally, after he handed over a thousand piastres and ten dollars MPC, she agreed to meet him on the corner of the block. She'll sucker me for sure; she won't turn up, Morgan thought; but after a long ten minutes, she arrived and immediately asked him to buy her two bread rolls from a street vendor. Morgan was hungry and ordered one himself. A drunk Australian stumbled past and muttered, "You'll be right, mate. Buy yourself a homer on a hepatitis roll."

When the Australian was out of earshot, Maria, mouth still full, muttered to Morgan, "You get taxi and go your hotel. You wait. Very bad if people see me talk you. They think bad girl, American soldier girl. You go, quick, quick."

"But I've got no guarantee you'll come."

A cruising taxi slowed down as it drew near and Maria signalled it to stop. She pushed Morgan towards it and suddenly, pressing herself close to him, she reached down and squeezed his genitals.

"You go. I come quick. Very soon we have number one jig-a-jig."

Momentarily convinced she meant to follow, Morgan got in the taxi, which took him to his hotel. After waiting half an hour, during which his confidence that she would come had steadily ebbed, he saw an American military police jeep approaching along the deserted street.

"Excuse me, sir, you got a curfew pass?" one of the white-helmeted MPs asked.

"No, I haven't."

"It's after curfew, sir, so if you're waiting for a girl I reckon she's stood you up."

"I'm not waiting for a girl, sergeant. Just waiting for Major Meredith." He mumbled Meredith's name, ashamed of himself for deigning to give such a corny excuse.

Morgan returned the sergeant's salute, ignoring his knowing grin, and walked up the few stairs into the hotel foyer. A sleepy night porter, dressed only in baggy pyjama shorts, began closing concertina metal gates across the entrance. The metal scrape on the concrete floor set Morgan's teeth on edge, but he stayed to have one final look. The grille framed his face like a prisoner as he looked out on the empty street. Scraps of paper blew about in a wind gust; then a rat, fat and dignified, walked slowly across the top step.

Finally Morgan admitted he'd been had. She wasn't coming and never intended to. It was all so predictable and he'd left himself wide open. As he climbed the steps to his room he smiled wryly, and gave her reluctant credit for a fine night's work.

21

As the small two-man helicopter spiralled down to the brigade headquarters landing pad, the sun glinted on the plastic bubble enclosing Morgan and the pilot. From a distance the helicopter might have been a science fiction mutation, some freakish flying ant.

Morgan had just finished double-checking the brigade civic action projects which the Colonel was inspecting that afternoon. It was over six weeks since he and Meredith had their accidental night off in Vung Tau. In that time, development of the brigade base camp had been spectacular. It sprawled over a circle perhaps two miles across, centred like a huge chancre in the surrounding rubber estates and rice paddies. Circling and criss-crossing roads, like long red slashes between the huddles and rows of tents and tin-roofed huts, linked the brigade units. But everything was made starker by the dying rubber trees now losing the last of their leaves.

Some fifty square miles of rubber estate had been defoliated and destroyed by the same accident that had denuded the base. Indirectly, an encephalitis epidemic had been the cause, and Morgan still vividly remembered the medical officer's briefing at one of their first evening conferences after moving in to the new base.

"Seven more cases of malaria last week, sir, and three encephalitis ... Two malaria not serious, but the rest – serious. And all three encephalitis are serious. We'll have more if troops don't use repellent, keep shirts on and sleeves rolled down – especially after dark."

"Now look here, Doc," one of the battalion commanders objected, "it's all very well for you, and even me, to keep shirts on. But when my boys are out there digging and sweating, it makes more sense to work shirts-off."

"It does, sir, if you don't mind your troops turning into vegetables. We've got three in hospital we're barely keeping alive in alcohol baths – they'll never recover – vegetables for life."

"You say this is caused by bites from the same mosquito as the malaria carrier, Doc?" the Colonel asked. "The anopheles mosquito?"

"Yes, sir."

"Well, gentlemen, I see this as a real serious threat. Our medical casualties last week were three times our battle casualties. Man takes sensible precautions, like digging a foxhole to avoid being shot; it seems elementary horse sense to wear a shirt to stop ending up a vegetable, as the doc puts it. I sure as hell hate to think of American mothers' sons not even having the honour of dying from decent gunshot. Hell of a thing for these young tigers of ours to be turned into idiot vegetables. I'm going to hold every commander here personally responsible to ensure shirts are worn at all times."

"What about showering, sir?" Meredith asked, smiling.

"This is no laughing matter, Frank."

"Sorry, sir, but isn't there something else we could do, like aerial spraying and man-pack spraying on stagnant pools?"

"The doc and me are way in front of you, Frank. He's organising aerial spraying; we're having the whole camp and a big area round it done, soon as the aircraft's available. Should be within the week."

"Does this spray affect the rubber at all, sir?" Morgan asked. "Like aerial spray defoliation does? After all, those rubber trees are worth about eighty dollars each."

"What's the answer to that one, Doc?" the Colonel asked.

"To the best of my knowledge – no, sir."

"Fine business," the Colonel said. "Any more questions?"

Within a week the spraying had been completed, and as a result of the emphasis now placed on personal anti-mosquito measures – such as the new and unpopular shirts-on rule, plus more strict supervision of the taking of chloroquine – the rate of new malaria and encephalitis cases began to decline. It was only weeks later, when the foliage all through the camp and around it began to brown, that the mistake was realised. To make it more embarrassing, it was the divisional commander, on one of his regular visits, who was the first to guess at the truth.

Just before the divisional commander's briefing on recent brigade operations began, he turned to Old Leather and said, "As I flew in here, I noticed your base camp and all around it starting to brown off. I hadn't realised you planned on defoliating. I know a lot of units have, but it seems a real pity to lose that shade."

"We aerial sprayed, sir, but that was anti-mosquito spray we ordered, not defoliant."

"Well, your whole base area looks just like some of those big swathes we sprayed in War Zone D when the defoliant was kicking in. Maybe this anti-mosquito spray defoliates too. Pity about that. You'll have a real dust-bowl ..."

In the witch-hunt that followed the divisional commander's visit, it was finally confirmed that a mistake had been made – defoliant had been used. Fortunately for the doctor, the error had been made by the US Air Force. "Some kind of clerical screw up ..." Kurt defensively justified his own service's blunder to the Colonel. Unfairly, it was the doctor who became the butt of most of the headquarters teasing on the subject. The younger staff officers, remembering the doctor's now famous briefing, perpetuated the error by describing the camp as the "Vegetable Farm", or shouting to the doctor, "Death before defoliant."

Junod was at his caustic best with Morgan, presenting him with an astronomical claim for the extensive area of destroyed rubber trees.

"Now I understand your brilliant commander's tactics. First, destroy unfriendly villages. Second, destroy unfriendly vegetation. Third, I suppose, convert the province into desert, because your brigade equipment and organisation is better suited to desert than jungle warfare. The logic is impeccable."

In the helicopter a crackling through his earphones and a cryptic message from the fire control centre brought Morgan's attention back to the present.

"H-and-I fire commencing in squares ..."

The pilot nudged Morgan and pointed out the area on his map. "Harassing and interdictory fire" was to be shot into Dong Tuy village. Morgan saw the red smear and white puff of the first round at the edge of a banana grove, and then the helicopter descended too low to see more.

Even though Dong Tuy had been declared a forbidden twenty-four-hour curfew zone, many of the villagers had continued to return there, attempting to salvage something from their destroyed homes and to harvest what they could of their ripened fruit crops before rot destroyed them. Intelligence reports from local agents said that guerrillas were also entering the village area to collect food, observe the brigade base, and set booby traps. Contact reports from brigade patrols confirmed the Viet Cong were using the village. So, the Colonel ordered the H-and-I artillery program, to try to keep the Viet Cong out.

The artillery may have had some deterrent effect, but the only demonstrable result had been a patrol's discovery of a badly wounded old woman with her right arm blown off, together with the corpses of her husband and a grandson of about ten years old. The three had been fossicking through the debris of their house. Understanding the compelling human reasons of lost homes and hunger that drove the villagers to return, Morgan felt strongly that the best solution would be to allow them to do so, but under stringent control and curfew restrictions. So far, however, he had refrained from raising the matter with Old Leather, afraid he would reject the idea out of hand, as if such a solution would be evidence that his earlier decision to destroy the village had been wrong.

When Morgan landed on the headquarters helipad, he saw the Colonel's C-and-C helicopter was already warming up, and the Colonel's jeep was fast approaching.

"Civic action projects all inspection-ready, Bill?"

"Yes, sir."

"Then let's get airborne."

The Colonel's love of dash and hurry, the aura of urgency he gave to his job of commanding the brigade, were characteristics Morgan enjoyed. Working on his staff was exciting, and in spite of their disagreements and Meredith's cynical appraisal, Morgan was still captivated by the style of Old Leather.

The C-and-C helicopter landed in the Special Forces company compound in the village of My Trang in a flurry of dust and scattering chickens. The local District Chief met them, together with his American adviser, a Ranger captain. An honour guard stood to attention for the Colonel's inspection. The young Vietnamese soldiers in the honour guard looked smart enough, in spite of their oversized weapons, but Morgan's eyes wandered around the camp itself. Ramshackle tin and cardboard roofed bunkers, a small child cuddling a mangy cat in the shade of a bunker, grass growing in the perimeter barbwire ... A flag pole and a faded yellow flag identified the District Headquarters building – a bullet-pocked, yellow-painted bungalow.

"Bill," the Colonel called, "the District Chief has hit me with a request already. He asked if we could provide flame-throwers to clear that grass in the perimeter wire."

"I've already spoken to his adviser on that, sir. I've given them diesel fuel, and they've got a hundred pairs of hands here and plenty of matches."

"So?"

"I think they should help themselves – if they can – before they ask our help on a thing as fundamental as clearing their own fields of fire."

"Well, you've got a point there – a real good point; but in this case, since he's asked me direct, I'd rather give him what he wants for the sake of good relations."

"Yes, sir," Morgan said, trying to follow Meredith's advice on how to handle the Colonel, but his irritation at being over-ruled must have been obvious. The Colonel stared at him sharply – almost eager for confrontation. But wisely, Morgan let it go.

22

They climbed into jeeps to tour the civic action projects in the remainder of the village. My Trang had been made the priority village for civic action. It was the nearest major village to the brigade base apart from Dong Tuy; it was also the seat of the district headquarters, and it had a population of some five thousand, which had been further increased by the flood of refugees from Dong Tuy – perhaps another two thousand.

Utilising brigade medical and dental staff, Morgan had been able to organise combined medical and dental teams to treat patients in the village for several hours every day of the week. In the jargon of the war, these were known as MEDCAPS and DENTCAPS –Medical and Dental Civic Action Projects. Watching these teams at work was invariably a moving experience: the earnest, fresh-faced young doctors and medics, giant and hulking in their jungle greens, yet touchingly gentle as they examined, bandaged, needled and pilled suddenly silent children, wide-eyed girls and stoic old men and women. Afterwards there was always comic relief when, ordeal over, bandages and treatments were proudly compared.

The Colonel and Morgan stood watching for some minutes as a young Vietnamese sergeant interpreter helped a doctor with his diagnosis of a voluble old woman. The next patient was an old man with a hugely swollen foot and an ugly ulcer almost two inches across. Then a baby was needled in the bottom with penicillin while the mother helped hold her steady. A boy followed, with a harelip and cleft palate.

"What do you do about that, Doc?" the Colonel asked, shaking his head with a mixture of sorrow and revulsion.

"Send him to the Korean hospital at Vung Tau. They do a real fine job on harelips."

"Why the hell haven't we got more civilian doctors from Stateside over here? Jesus wept, these people need help."

As they walked to the jeep, the Colonel added, "You've organised a fine thing here, Bill. I'd like to see a lot more of it. What's next?"

"We're adding two classrooms to one of the village schools, building them a Vietnamese-style latrine and sinking a water well. It's an Artillery Battalion project, sir."

From the MEDCAP, they drove half a mile along the village's main street, then a few hundred yards more down a right-angled branch track. On the way, children ran to wave and shout their newly acquired English.

"Okay. Okay."

"GI number one."

"Okay, goodbye, goddam."

The more precocious kids made puffing V signals and shouted, "Cigarette ... you give Salem cigarette ..."

But very few adults smiled or waved; mostly they stared impassively, or turned away to avoid acknowledging the passing jeeps.

"Even the kids didn't wave when we first drove through," Morgan said.

"At least that's some progress," the Colonel said. "I surely hope we don't have to wait till those kids grow up before adults wave."

The final track to the school was a long green tunnel, the trees interlacing overhead. A sickly smell of rotten fruit hung in the still air. Morgan suffered an acute attack of sniper paranoia; not for himself, but the Colonel ... At last they were through and into a pool of sunlight, reflecting from packed yellow earth circling the school.

A team of brigade engineers were pouring concrete – the foundations for two new schoolrooms. The Colonel spoke a few words of praise to the soldiers for their "fine humanitarian work ..." Next Morgan led him to the original classroom, where a cluster of very small children were being taught.

The teacher, a shy and pretty girl, stopped the lesson immediately she saw the District Chief, the Colonel and Morgan peering through the door. The District Chief introduced the Colonel to her and the children. A brigade public relations cameraman snapped busily, and then suggested the Colonel and teacher sit together at one of the desks. The children near the chosen desk shrieked with laughter. But the boy next to the Colonel went rigid with embarrassment and fright. The Colonel put a paternal arm around the boy's frail shoulders, to reassure him and make a better picture, but the gesture only frightened the boy more. The cameraman salvaged the situation professionally with a high shot, capturing the fatherly arm and two bent heads studying the textbook: the Colonel's crew-cut, the boy's black mop ... it would make a fine PR mirage of brigade civic action.

After the school, Morgan took the Colonel and his party to a nearby house with a typical fruit and vegetable garden.

"You'll notice, sir, apart from the traditional thatched palm-leaf and tile roofs, there's a handful roofed with tin. That shows at least some of our aid is getting to the villagers ... And here's one walled with uncut beer-can tin."

The tin walls, printed with dozens of red and blue labels, clashed oddly with the areca palms surrounding the house – a bizarre embodiment of the clash of civilisations.

"This next house, sir, we fixed the harelip of a little boy ... his grandfather would be very proud to have you be his guest."

He led the Colonel through the small vegetable garden in front, and pointed out the deep water well. The old man came out and greeted them with the traditional gassho, his palms together. Punctiliously, Morgan responded in kind and was delighted to see the Colonel self-consciously try the gassho himself.

"This red paper on the door here, sir, and these mirrors, are to frighten evil spirits away and prevent them entering his home ..."

The old man ushered them to a wooden bench, the legs driven into the packed earth floor. He offered them a dusty bottle of beer, but Morgan explained they would prefer tea, and the old man hobbled off to prepare it. By now a collection of young children and other members of the family were shyly peering into the room.

"Just to the right of the pregnant girl, sir, is the family shrine and ancestral tablets ..."

Briefly, Morgan explained the display of candlesticks, scrolls, tapestries and incense burners, and how the sacred tablets contained the names of ancestors through the fourth generation.

"The ancestors watch over the family. Nearly all Vietnamese, whatever their religion, still venerate ancestors. It's the Confucian tradition surviving after a thousand years of Chinese occupation ... And a small tip, sir, don't pat children on the head; a lot of rural Vietnamese still believe patting the head is an attempt to steal the spirit. See that little boy over there with the earring: that's to fool the evil spirits into thinking he's a girl ..."

"Thanks for the tips, Bill. I declare these Vietnamese are almost as foreign as the British."

Morgan smiled politely and the old man came forward with the tea. Outside again, they continued the tour. A couple of fowls clucked and flapped away from them to resume pecking under a guava tree.

"Chickens, Bill!" the Colonel said suddenly. "Have you thought of chickens? It's what these people need and could handle themselves. Hell, we could fly in a few planeloads of chicks, and teach these village folk how to look after them. All they'd need is incubators, and a few simple technological aids. We could get them started with a real useful local market commodity. It'd feed them too, and when they began to get more efficient, they could market in Saigon ... Even in the brigade, we could take big orders ourselves. What do you reckon?"

"I'd like to think on it a bit, sir."

"Well, there's the idea, boy. You work on it. What you need in this civic action is ideas and drive."

"Yes, sir. But I've got to be practical about it. If I rushed in half-assed to fly out planeloads of chickens, I'm just as likely to end up with a whole lot of dead chickens."

"That's your job as a staff officer, Bill, to make sure things don't get done half-assed. But you've got to be visionary too, and utilise your imagination. Now just these few things you've shown me this morning have given me a lot of new ideas. Obviously what these people need is productive economic activity. You don't find fat rich men turning Communist. As I see it, that's the nub of our problem: these village people need new pressure-cooked economic incentives. I see our role as providing the pressure cooker: security. And the heat for cooking? The incentive of new ideas. You following me? Take laundries: I know a lot of village women take in troops' washing, but how hygienic, how efficient are they? We ought to be able to design a real simple laundry layout with a few slabs of cement, forty-four gallon drums cut in half as washing tubs, and adequate clothes line capacity. You could then train these women into red hot laundry teams, say ten or so to handle the washing of a line company. That'd inject a lot of business and new piastres into the village."

"But what about afterwards, sir, when we leave? What then?"

"Hell, who says we're leaving? We're still in Korea. And these people have a problem now. Let's start solving that one first. Another job I've thought of that these villagers could tackle is brush clearance. I know the Air Cav did it – in fact I'm surprised you hadn't thought of it already. Round our perimeter, the edges of our L of C, and along Inter-Provincial

Route 3. We could hire a lot of people on that ... improve all this poverty. Bill, what these people need most of all is our business."

"Sir, I understand your points, but I'm not with you all the way. You see if we make these people dependent on us ..."

"Bill, you're being stubborn, a stick-in-the-mud, too conservative."

"I don't think so, sir. That sort of dependence on us ..."

"Okay, Bill. Let's drop the subject for now. What's next on the program?"

23

Morgan realised what a near thing he'd risked: he'd only been saved from himself by the Colonel closing the subject. But if he couldn't express deeply felt opinions to the full, or confront the Colonel with uncomfortable truths ...? He answered the Colonel's question.

"A visit to the Dinh and the market, sir."

"What's this Dinh thing, Bill?"

"A kind of combination temple and community centre, sir; the housewives use it for special prayers and offering food to the guardian spirit, the *thanh loang*. The *thanh loang* is supposed to be able to give protection against natural disasters."

"I don't think the housewives here are all that different to those back home. And after the market?"

"We're meeting the Province Chief at the refugee camp on the north edge of the village, sir. Mostly refugees from Dong Tuy."

"That should be real interesting, Bill."

"It is, sir. But the VC have still got a strong hold. It's the same in this village and all the other villages in the province. Security. Till we provide real security to these villages, the VC infrastructure just keeps working away below our radar. And really, we're getting nowhere. All our civic action's just a waste of time if we can't weed out that VC infrastructure."

"I can't disagree, Bill. Solid sense in what you say – but local security, destruction of the VC infrastructure – that's ARVN's job, not ours. Our primary job is destroying the VC Main Force so ARVN can get on with their job under our umbrella. Our first job is real honest-to-God soldiering. This civic aid and civic action's still a sideline; people like USAID, JUSPAO ... those civilian agencies are the main boys for that job."

"Well, I disagree, sir. I believe you've got to look at total strategy in this province."

"Bill, you're always disagreeing. You teaching me to suck eggs? Maybe I ought to send you back to your line company?" The Colonel laughed harshly and patted Morgan on the back. "Bill, you ought to relax, you're too intense. A man in his mid-thirties is a bit old to be an angry young man."

As they walked through the market with its small stalls of vegetables, fruit, fly-clouded meat, fish, cloth, assorted clothing and hardware, the Colonel said, "There's not a whole lot of difference in these small village markets from South America to South-East Asia or even the Middle East. You've seen one market – you've seen them all. Unhygienic, inefficient gossip hives ..."

When their jeep stopped at the refugee village, the Province Chief darted over to shake the Colonel's hand and welcome him enthusiastically.

"Colonel, my number one good friend. I am so happy to see you again."

"That's my boy, Chief. You're looking in pretty good shape, eh? Great to see you looking so good and full of go."

"Go man, go!" the Province Chief said, clicking his fingers.

Everybody laughed, especially the Colonel's black driver.

"Come, and we will inspect these refugees," the Province Chief added. "Then I must listen to their complaints. Refugees are always full of complaints."

It was a sad and depressing spectacle, oddly like an old and yellowed black-and-white film of refugees in other wars. The main image was desolate family groups, huddled under makeshift shanties of mixed burlap, cardboard, tin and atap. The family clusters were made more poignant by salvaged family treasures: a huge cedar bed, a brass-bound chest, an old sewing machine, a calendar, a bike ... And worse, there were no young men; the heads of the huddled families were all women. There were grubby-faced babies being suckled; just-walking tots, invariably naked and pot-bellied; young girls; very young mothers; old crones and clusters of old men – everybody dressed in black pyjamas, picking their way through the shanties and mud like unkempt crows.

Midway through their inspection of the Dong Tuy refugee camp, a Vietnamese boy grabbed Morgan by the arm. The Colonel and Province Chief sauntered on, the Province Chief talking volubly – clearly trying to sell Old Leather some new and dubious commercial scheme

"I am Trinh. You are good man. Save my family from VC." Morgan was astonished; it was the boy who had been hiding in the temple the day of the abortive Dong Tuy cordon operation when the Province Chief had been blown up and then pulled out his Ranger battalion. The last time Morgan had seen Trinh was with Purvis, the Ranger battalion adviser, as the Ranger battalion headed off in their trucks, abandoning the Dong Tuy clearing operation.

Morgan's interpreter came forward to help. It appeared that Purvis had semi-adopted Trinh and his family and made a special effort to ensure the pregnant mother and sick grandmother did not starve. Trinh now had a baby sister and Purvis had also arranged for Trinh to have a job as a gopher with his close friend, the captain running the Special Forces camp nearby. Trinh was clearly an extremely bright boy and had already learnt rudimentary English. Morgan gave Trinh the small change in his pocket, but Trinh refused to accept it. The interpreter explained Trinh was not begging, but just expressing his thanks because he now had a job. Morgan was stunned at such a response from a boy barely into his teens. He solemnly shook Trinh's hand, and headed off to rejoin the Colonel.

24

"Don't see too many menfolk around to produce all these babies," Old Leather said, after they'd walked through the refugee lines.

"All R & R babies, sir. VC or good guys." The Colonel laughed, and Morgan went on with his briefing. "The war makes a helluva manpower shortage ... Conscription into the RVN army, air force and navy, plus the regional forces, the popular forces, the special forces guards, and now, these revolutionary development cadres. Then there's VC manpower demands. Main Force, province troops, guerrillas and porters for all ... And finally, all those fellas have been fighting and killing themselves for years. I tell you, sir, this place is bleeding."

"You leave some out," the Province Chief interjected with infectious good humour. "What about policemen? And interpreters for US forces and labourers for big US construction companies like RMK? Many young men have left the province to work in Vung Tau and Saigon. The old men, women and children must grow the rice. That is what all those old men are telling me."

Morgan and the Colonel looked across to the group of old men the Province Chief indicated.

"They are a delegation. They say all the bad VC who were living in Dong Tuy have fled to the jungle, or were killed by the Americans. They say all that is left to become refugees are old men like themselves, and women and children. They say they had to do as the VC told them, because they were afraid, because many VC were living in the village among them. But now the Americans have come, the village VC are frightened and have run away, and now these people have nothing. They have lost their homes and their belongings, and they cannot work their land and get their fruit because of the curfew. If they go back they are shot and killed by bombs. While they stay here, they have nothing except what rice we give them each month – but no land. So they beg me to let them return to their land and build their houses again, now the VC are gone."

"I certainly feel sorry for them, Chief. What do you think?"

"Dong Tuy was a very bad VC village, but all these refugees are a very expensive problem. Each month we must feed them until they are resettled, but where can I resettle them? There is no land except jungle, which is very difficult at first to farm. And I have no troops to protect them. But now if they go back to Dong Tuy, there are no VC, because you are close and you can protect them."

"Now just a minute, Chief. The whole reason we destroyed that village and cleared it was so I wouldn't have a VC village on my doorstep."

"But it is different now. You killed the VC or they have run away from Dong Tuy. These are only old men, women and children. The VC will not hurt them if they go back."

"No, but they'll use them."

"Not so much, because the VC will be afraid with you so close."

"I'll tell you what, Chief. I might change my mind and come to the party if you provide a regional force company, or popular forces, to protect them."

"Okay. I try and find RF or PF to protect them. But can you help with barbwire? Then we can build a big fence around that village to keep VC out."

"And that fence would keep the people in, so they didn't get shot up by my patrols," the Colonel said. "What do you reckon, Bill?"

"I've thought that way all along, sir. There'll still be problems, of course, but ..."

"So we agree at last, eh, Bill? You know, Chief, this S5 of mine is very independent-minded."

After all the argument and drama that had led to the destruction of Dong Tuy, Morgan was staggered at how readily and painlessly the Colonel and Province Chief could rationalise their turn-around.

"We make a good team, Colonel, my friend. Not too much talk-talk. You and I make quick decisions."

"Only way to operate, Chief."

*

Next was a joint aerial reconnaissance of the province by helicopter, with the Province Chief sitting next to the Colonel. Both chattered on the intercom the whole flight. Finally there was a wrap-up meeting in the Province Chief's office.

"Chief, you mind if I start this rolling with our best guess of what VC we face in the province? I know you know ... but this way we'll see if we agree straight off, without losing time on a heap of staff officer briefings."

There was no doubt, Morgan admitted, the Colonel knew just how to handle the Province Chief; equally, the Province Chief knew just how to handle the Colonel. He smiled then at Frank Meredith's new nickname for the pair – Batman and Robin.

"As I see it," the Colonel began, "we've got one, sometimes two Main Force VC regiments basing up in the province; one mainly up here near the Vinh Duong province boundary, and the other up in the corner here in the Duc Binh war base area. We've also got the usual VC province mobile battalion, VC district companies and guerrillas. My strong hunch is, without the psychological support of those Main Force regiments, the rest of the VC in this province would be a much easier problem. I see the Main Force as the brain, the heart and the whip that keeps these local VC going. If my brigade could destroy the Main Force, I think the rest would wither on the vine. That would leave you free, Chief, to protect the villages with your provincial forces and make fast progress with your pacification role. What do you think?"

"Yes. I like your plan. You destroy Main Force. My troops pacify. Simple plans are best."

"Bill? Any comments?"

"Providing we can find the Main Forces, sir, and bring them to battle, it should work fine."

"I'm touched to have your agreement, Bill," the Colonel said in a sarcastic but friendly tone. "Here's the broad concept of my plan to destroy the VC Main Forces ... First thing we need is a good name, something fitting for the death of the VC in this province – Operation Tombstone City."

The Province Chief clapped his hands in approval. "I like it. And a very bad omen for all VC."

"Well, Chief, that's it – all I had to talk about. One last thing – you got any problems in the pacification and civil affairs area?"

The Province Chief murmured to his orderly in Vietnamese, who went to a filing cabinet and returned with a map.

"I have discussed your idea, Colonel, to employ local labour from the villages to work in your brigade camp. My staff think this a very good idea, and I direct my chief of police to make security checks and passes for all you ask for – four hundred civilian labourers. Okay. I agree with you. This will bring much money into my province and help the economy. Next thing. My staff suggests this to help business in the province ..."

The Province Chief began to unfold and spread his map, which was an enlargement of the provincial capital of Canh Tri.

"This area here I can set aside for your troops for local leave. You know, restaurant, barber shop, souvenir shop, massage parlour, bar: all those things I would centralise here, on the edge of town. This way your soldiers can have fun and spend their money in one small area we can make secure. Then they do not have to make fun in the rest of the town."

"I get your message, Chief. And I'm the first to admit it. Our boys are young tigers, and with all the good intentions in the world, if we turn 'em loose through your town, some of them could do the wrong thing. Only needs one rape, and your whole town is terrified. Your idea's real sensible. It boils down to our own brigade red light area – but between you and me, patrolled, controlled and supervised. Of course, Chief, I can only go along with this officially provided there's no brothels involved; but as men of the world, I think we understand each other."

"Yes, my friend. You nod and I wink. And, for extra security, I tell none of my staff about Operation Tombstone City." The Province Chief put a finger to his lips and winked theatrically: "Our secret ..." Then, chuckling delightedly with the Colonel, he escorted the Americans outside to their helicopter.

25

Operation Tombstone City was an ironically apt name. But the Colonel could not know that when he briefed the divisional commander on the role his new Long-range Reconnaissance Patrols would play.

The divisional commander, General Clayton D. Ivanhoe, with his forbidding nickname of 'The Iceman', looked deceptively youthful and even kindly on first meeting. Unlike so many officers in the US Army, he did not have a crew-cut, but had a parting through his well trimmed and greying hair. Another West Pointer, he was born in Virginia in 1918 and graduated in 1940, just in time for World War II. He first saw combat in North Africa as a baby-faced platoon commander; later he commanded a company in the advance to Germany and won two Silver Stars. In the Korean War he commanded a battalion and earned his nickname as the Iceman. After Korea, he proved himself as a formidably logical and pragmatic staff officer. His nickname served him well in the Pentagon and he was widely tipped as a rising star. According to senior officer gossip that Old Leather had passed on to Meredith, General Westmoreland had specifically asked for him as a replacement divisional commander when his predecessor was killed in a helicopter crash.

"Our biggest problem, as you know, sir, in these Search-and-Destroy operations is actually finding a big body of Viet Cong," Old Leather began. "Their trail watchers usually spot us coming. So, we've devised two new tactics to solve this problem. First, I put out small feelers, my Long-range Reconnaissance Patrols, or LERPS the guys are calling them. Only six men in each, moving stealthily enough for a successful and undetected recon. Their mission is very simple – confirm Main Force base areas."

"What if a LERP gets into a firefight and takes casualties?" General Ivanhoe asked.

"We extract."

"Could be kind of difficult in deep jungle with no LZs," the Iceman countered.

"All LERP men are volunteers."

"Okay. But still a big problem if they get sprung."

"That's why they're all volunteers."

The Iceman understood the Colonel's deeper meaning in an eye blink and gestured for him to go on.

"Second part of the concept is decoy and lure tactics with company groups. We insert the decoy companies near the LERP-confirmed VC bases. If the VC take the bait and try to swallow a decoy company – we close the trap. We react with massive firepower, both artillery and air strikes. Next, we swing in the rest of the decoy companies, and insert our heli-borne reserves. Then destroy him utterly."

"And what if he's too big and quick, and swallows the bait?"

"No, sir. One of our line companies and the firepower we can bring to bear would tear him apart. My S5 here, Major Bill Morgan, proved that in the My Trang battle."

"Should be a real interesting operation – providing it goes as planned," General Ivanhoe said in a way that readily explained his nickname.

Morgan's first reaction to the Colonel's plan was also sceptical, but progressively he was converted by the Colonel's enthusiasm and capacity to reduce such a complex military operation into deceptively simple and convincing steps. The broad strategic concept had a boldness, a reasoned detachment about casualties, and a military nerve, that commanded respect for the Colonel as a fighting leader. Morgan was so converted, he even recommended Jenkins, his favourite platoon leader from his old company, as the best young officer to organise and train the LERPS. Often, too, Morgan wished he could still play a more active part in the operation. Comparing the tensions and unsettling problems of his new civil affairs job with the much simpler demands of commanding a line company, he looked back to that period as the good old days. Back then, he made the decisions, he was the boss two hundred soldiers looked up to and admired as "the old man". Whereas now he was slowly appreciating the unpleasant truth of Meredith's advice that a successful staff officer needed to be more of a scheming court flatterer than a straightforward combat officer.

The long-range patrols were inserted deep into the Duc Binh jungle by helicopter three days before the battalions and fire-support base artillery. Morgan's first scare with Jenkins's patrol came at lunchtime on the second day, when the duty officer from the Tactical Operation Centre interrupted the Colonel at lunch.

"Sir, Jenkins's patrol says they located a base camp with two to three hundred VC wearing khaki uniforms and steel helmets. They circled the base and found a whole mess of tracks heading east that could lead to another camp. They're following a trail now that looks like some fifty men have used it, but his patrol has heard voices the last half hour and he swears they're being followed. Wants to know if he should extract now they've been compromised, or should he stay?"

Morgan knew it was none of his business, but couldn't help feeling Jenkins had achieved more than enough already. Jenkins must have thought he was in real trouble, or he wouldn't have asked for guidance.

But the Colonel saw it differently. "Fine business," he said calmly, looking up at the nervous young duty officer as he wiped his mouth with a napkin. "Fine business, finding that camp. Seems he's getting skittish now though; voices following him ... Tell him to stay."

After the duty officer left, the Colonel elaborated to those members of his principal staff eating with him.

"Over-excited is all – just needs somebody to tell him he's doing a fine job – which he surely is. Could be he'll turn up another camp."

Yes, the Colonel's view was the correct one, Morgan had to admit. He'd been letting personal feelings cloud military logic. After all, when six men found a major VC target that could result in a battle in which hundreds might be killed on both sides – there was no room for being squeamish about losing a small squad. But what a lousy philosophy, Morgan nagged himself, yet knowing full well there was no other way to win battles.

The next phase of the operation went smoothly and the brigade was helicoptered in to several different landing zones, broadly surrounding the VC base camps Jenkins had found. Little contact was made with the VC at first, apart from the usual booby traps and sniping trail watchers. However, two Viet Cong trucks were discovered and thirty tons of rice hidden in nearby caches. Then, at 0130 on the fifth night of the operation, Jenkins radioed a compelling message.

"Intensive activity along the trail ... Over three hundred porters using torches and flares have passed north since midnight. We think the VC are bugging out, or preparing for a major battle ..."

The Colonel was still in the operations centre when Jenkins's message came through and he said to Meredith, "Let's hope Charlie's aiming for one of our decoy companies. I want all three battalions ready to move at first light ..."

Just before first light, A Company of Morgan's old battalion radioed they were being mortared.

"Twenty-eight rounds of incoming mortar fire so far. Too many casualties to move without help. We are digging in and consolidating ..."

Later it was established that A Company had not dug-in at all, thinking the chances of being mortared were remote in a one-night bivouac. That decision not to dig-in cost the company four dead and seven wounded.

As first light filtered through, A Company began to clear an extraction landing zone for their casualties. At the same time, the rest of the companies in the battalion began to close in on A Company in case the mortaring was the prelude to a full-scale attack, and to provide security in depth for the extraction.

Shortly after seven-thirty the Viet Cong launched their attack on A Company, just after a squad of engineer lumberjacks were winched in to help improve the landing zone for the casualties. By then the company had learnt their lesson from the mortaring and had dug rudimentary foxholes, which saved them from being overrun in the first onslaught.

The battalion's other companies, which were trying to close in, faced intensive sniper fire and booby trap harassment; their rate of advance was so painfully slow, it was unlikely they'd get to A Company before nightfall.

Meanwhile A Company was repeatedly attacked, and called for constant artillery and air support to avoid being overrun. With one other long-range patrol still in the general area, and the other companies drawing in closer and calling for fire support too, the control and coordination of the fire program began to get out of hand, and it was only a matter of time before a major accident.

Morgan was in the Tactical Operations Centre following the progress of the battle when Jenkins's voice, angry and afraid, snapped out:

"This is one three ... Our own artillery's falling all round us. For Christ's sake stop it ... switch it ..."

They heard the explosion, and Jenkins's scream sharp and close over the radio, though where he died was miles away. Morgan walked outside, shocked and numbed, thinking of Jenkins's father, a retired Marine colonel, and his mother, a gay sparkling woman Morgan had met just before the brigade left for Vietnam. Jenkins had been an only son. Morgan tried to shut out his grief, telling himself Jenkins was only one casualty; you couldn't mourn them all and retain your sanity. He was surprised then to discover that all was not silent and still, as it had been in the intensity of his sorrow; the noise of the artillery barrage was deafening, and he looked up surprised at the strength of the sun and the blue of the sky.

26

The second accident was a major one, occurring late that afternoon shortly after Morgan's old company finally reached A Company. Early in the afternoon, the Viet Cong had eased off the pressure, probably to collect their dead and wounded, as they must have taken heavy casualties too from the constant air and artillery fire support. This made it relatively easy for Morgan's old company to link up with A Company. But then, just as the newcomers were going through the muddled and confusing business of taking over a sector of the perimeter, with A Company partially disorganised by the relief and excitement of the reinforcement company's arrival, the Viet Cong put in another major assault. In the operations centre at brigade headquarters they heard the A Company commander's radio report:

"...being attacked again. It's a bad one; they've caught us in the middle of reorganising the position. Request all artillery and air support available ..."

"You've got to pay the Viet Cong," the Colonel said to Meredith and Morgan. "Those guys are real professionals. Their timing couldn't have been better – or worse for our boys."

"Yes, sir," Morgan said, "But the odds are with us now. Two US infantry companies, even disorganised, can lay down a powerful weight of fire. Main thing I learnt at My Trang, as long as the troops don't panic, our automatic small arms fire sure carves up an assault."

Morgan was right and, soon after, the VC assault was turned back. Then the A Company commander, a newly appointed young captain fighting his first major battle, called for an immediate airstrike on his northern flank where the Viet Cong seemed to be massing for another attack.

"Should be calling for artillery, not an airstrike that close to his position," Meredith said.

"Hope he doesn't learn the hard way," Morgan said, "but when the VC are that close and you hear the planes overhead, you feel instinctively an airstrike should be more accurate than guns firing miles away. With jets over jungle, artillery's always a safer bet. But I know the temptation."

They walked over to the air force part of the operations centre to listen in to Kurt coordinating the airstrike from his FAC plane circling the battle.

"... Right on, right on ..." they heard Kurt's rasping voice. He then gave minor corrections for the next strike. "The forty millimetre and cannon fire was dead on target. Now, let's have a run of CBU on the same line, but fifty yards north."

Tragically, the second pilot misjudged his run by seventy-five yards.

"... You cock-sucking, mother-fucking idiot," Kurt screamed over the radio. "You're way off line. You let go into good guys ..."

Those seventy-five yards of pilot error, dropping his lethal carpet of CBU bomblets, cost the two companies seven more dead and thirty-seven wounded. But the VC must have suffered heavy casualties too, because that was their last major assault of the day.

At dusk, the last company from the battalion, together with battalion headquarters, closed in to the position. To evacuate the large number of casualties it was vital that work on the landing zone begun by A Company was finished as soon as possible. There were far too many casualties to be litter-carried on foot to a more convenient landing zone.

So, in spite of mortar and small arms fire through the night, work continued to clear the tall timber and carve out a large enough clearing. As a direct result of the exposed LZ work, there were many more casualties. At the same time the Viet Cong took the chance to clear their own dead and wounded, but simultaneously prepared for their next and last attack; a wild assault launched in the dark and half-light of a deep jungle dawn.

The Colonel and his key staff stayed up all night in the Tactical Operations Centre monitoring radio reports of the battle.

"The fight you'd been looking for, sir," Frank Meredith said shortly before dawn. "Your concept has worked beautifully. Now the battalion's all tight and closed-in, our worries are over..." Morgan cringed at Meredith's blatant flattery. How could he pour it on so thick? But Frank was still at it. "... Soon as we extract those casualties tomorrow, we can start feeding in more troops – A Company suckered those VC in like flies to a honey pot. We must have killed hundreds."

"Yes, Frank. They must surely have. We've really torn those VC apart ... hundreds, yes, must be hundreds of VC killed in a firefight like that ..."

But Morgan was surprised at the Colonel's appearance and his voice. He looked so tired, so uncertain, frightened almost; and his voice lacked its usual crisp authoritarian tone. It was as if he was drawing strength and comfort from Meredith. The way he'd said, "We've really torn those VC apart" was so lacking his usual tigerish tone, it was more like a hurt child's formula to ward off insults: *Sticks and stones may break my bones, but words will never hurt me ...*

Next morning, even though washed and shaved and looking more like himself in fresh fatigues, the Colonel still looked subdued – even humbled.

Morgan was especially touched when the Colonel asked Meredith and him to fly in his C-and-C helicopter to the battalion position as soon as the LZ was cleared. It was a thoughtful gesture, appreciating Morgan's concern for his old troops. And that gesture largely cancelled out his harsher feelings against the Colonel.

Taking his C-and-C chopper in first to a battalion still in a firefight was one of those signature acts of bravado which so endeared the Colonel to his men – especially later, when it was learnt the helicopter had been hit several times while descending. Adding to the Colonel's legend, his pilot then declared the landing zone approach too dangerous until more trees were cleared. It took another hour and a half of feverish tree-felling before the descent was deemed safe enough for the med-evac choppers.

The pathos of the sight at the bottom of that dark lift-well descent was something Morgan would never forget.

"Dante's inferno," Meredith whispered huskily.

Morgan was reminded vividly of Goya's war paintings when he saw the surviving soldiers' faces – haunted and haggard with shock.

Lieutenant Colonel Paul Higgins, the battalion commander who had replaced Meredith in the job, was a transformed man too. When he had first taken over the battalion, a few weeks before Morgan's My Trang battle, Morgan had been wary that Higgins was too much of a staff officer and not enough of a soldier. But Higgins had been seasoned and toughened in the brief months since taking command. He had now weathered two major battles with his men and grown into his combat chieftain role.

One of Old Leather's first questions to Higgins was, "What's your VC body count?"

"Not that many so far, sir," Higgins answered levelly, wiping his glasses and carefully replacing them. "I think about twenty-three ..."

Morgan was impressed by Higgins's honesty. Many battalion commanders would already be trying to cover their ass by vague-ing up the body count.

"What do you mean you think twenty-three? What sort of an answer's that? You've reported one hundred and fifty-three wounded of your own and sixty-three dead. Fucking hell – with the firepower we've applied and the firefight you've had, you must have killed hundreds of VC."

"Yes, sir, I'm very damn certain we must, but twenty-three bodies are all we've actually counted so far ..."

"Then you'd better organise a more thorough and comprehensive body count pretty damn quick."

Old Leather led Higgins away, and Morgan didn't even try to eavesdrop. He was far more concerned about talking to survivors from his old company and seeing how they were. But it was no surprise to Morgan there were so few VC bodies. After all, the VC had had a whole night to collect their dead and wounded, and weapons. Similarly, if the VC commander had called for an American body count based on the number of American corpses actually recovered by the VC, the figure would be zero – even though there were in fact sixty-three dead Americans stacked in long lines at the edge of the LZ, waiting to be flown out.

Later, when all the American dead and wounded had been evacuated, Morgan was surprised to overhear Meredith and the Colonel arguing.

"...But Colonel, why extract the whole force now? He's been firing at us all day. He's still close and he'll be slowed right down with all his casualties. If we only found twenty-three VC bodies, he must be moving awful slow, probably still burying his dead and litter-carrying his wounded."

"What do you mean, only twenty-three dead?" the Colonel snapped. "Three hundred and twenty-two is the re-assessed VC body count. We've had recon patrols out all round recounting. Three hundred and twenty-two is the current official figure ..."

"Three hundred and twenty-two," Meredith repeated, and Morgan read his mind, even though Meredith's poker face and voice gave nothing away. "Then, sir, that recount only confirms my judgment ... if we counted three hundred-plus dead, then he's got to bury all the other VC dead we didn't find – and maybe a thousand-plus wounded must need litter-carrying ... Right now is surely the time to pour in everything we can and follow him up. Aggressively pressure him, and capitalise on this battle. VC must be hurting real bad ..."

"No. I disagree, Frank. VC Main Force will have broken contact. I'd say this morning's attack was just a cover for his evacuation. This is just stay-behind guerrilla harassment stuff, this firing now. He's gone. And anyway, the fight's all gone from this battalion. Look around."

"But we can throw in two fresh battalions, sir."

"No. I want to extract ..."

Morgan agreed with Meredith's military logic, that two fresh battalions might well hunt down many more VC, but he also understood the Colonel's reasoning and the Colonel's fear. The alarmingly heavy casualties Higgins's battalion had suffered, the touch-and-go situation where two entire companies had almost been overrun, the possibility of the Colonel's fear of a disastrous defeat if he gambled all on chasing the VC with his last two battalions. Finally, underlying all, the chance that the Colonel's big lie about the VC body count would come out. No commander could expect to hold his command long with a disastrously unfavourable body count ratio.

*

Next day, with the entire brigade pulled out from Operation Tombstone City and back at base camp, Meredith and Morgan went to listen to Higgins's after-operation analysis. The battalion motto was inscribed on a placard above the briefing map: *When the going gets tough, the tough get going.*

Morgan's old company had suffered heavy casualties, although not as many as A Company. It was a deeply sad and moving experience when a group of his former non-coms came up to shake his hand.

"Real nice to see you again, sir ... hell of a fire-fight it was ..."

"Oh man, were we bleeding."

"We were missing you, sir – really hurting."

"Real sorry about Lieutenant Jenkins, sir."

Morgan's throat was choked with pride and sorrow as he listened to Higgins going through the good and bad points of the operation. There'd been so many dead, everyone in the battalion was still numb. The de-briefing finished with a statistical summary.

"...Including resupply, an average of eleven hundred and seventy rounds of rifle ammunition was expended per man. Brigade artillery fired five hundred and forty-two tons of ammunition over the total operation. Five hundred and fifty-three tons of ordnance was dropped by ground-support strike aircraft. Current casualty figures: we now have sixty-six dead and one hundred and fifty-three wounded – nearly eighty of our wounded, though, are minor shrapnel and will be returned to full duty within the week. Viet Cong body count was three hundred and twenty-two ..."

"That works out about three tons of explosives and three hundred small arms rounds to kill each VC. Relatively speaking, I'd say that was cheap," Meredith murmured to Morgan.

When Higgins finished, they stood and circulated among old friends, and were stunned to find out how readily the grossly exaggerated body count figure had been accepted by the battalion. It was almost as if there was a giant conspiracy, but Morgan decided Meredith was probably right the way he explained it:

"They'd hate to believe a figure like twenty-three – make them look real weak sisters. The higher the figure, the more they like believing it. Anyway, goddam body count's a load of crap."

"So, does that justify Old Leather lying about it?"

"I think – truly think, it does. Old Leather's lie could be far more accurate on actual VC casualties than the misleading truthful body count. And think of morale ..."

"Maybe. But a lie like that diminished Old Leather in my eyes. I can understand his line of reasoning, but I can't respect it."

27

Later that day, the divisional commander, General Ivanhoe, and the Vietnamese corps commander, plus a large press contingent, arrived for a briefing on Tombstone City. The Colonel decided to give the briefings himself: the VIPs first, and then the press. Fronting his audience in immaculately tailored and starched fatigues, his spit-polished boots gleaming, his trim athletic figure poised, he radiated confidence and epitomised a brilliant and successful combat commander. What a different man he seemed to the tired and frightened figure Morgan remembered from the long second night of the battle.

Colonel Robbins made the operation sound so simple as he sketched the enemy threat and outlined his "long-range patrol" and "decoy and lure" concepts. He jabbed at the map with expressive hands to show the airmobile assaults, and concluded with an impressive feat of memory on detailed statistics. Old Leather was so persuasive, Morgan even half-believed some of the slick exaggerations; and probably Old Leather did too.

"How come you recovered only seventeen enemy weapons?" General Ivanhoe asked in his clinical Iceman voice, "but claim three hundred and twenty-two VC dead by actual body count. I mean is that actual body count, or an estimate?"

From the way General Ivanhoe asked this question, Morgan sensed more than scepticism – even personal dislike. But the Colonel handled the question plausibly and smoothly.

"No, sir. That's actual body count: patrols went out, and that's foot on the corpse. Dead bodies stacked around like cordwood."

"How come so few weapons then?"

"General, they had two nights to collect the weapons. They had time to fetch those, but not all the bodies; and, if we found three hundred and twenty-two dead, we probably killed twice that number. As we all know, the Viet Cong can't afford to lose a weapon."

General Ivanhoe paused a moment, got up out of his chair and walked to the briefing map. He sat down and asked, "Why did you extract when you did? Why didn't you reinforce and keep the pressure up? The VC must have had a reason for fighting that hard. Maybe trying to protect something? Could have been a hospital, or a big rice or weapons cache in the area. Did your troopers thoroughly search it out?"

Morgan noticed a subtle change in the Colonel's attitude. The Iceman's intelligent and probing questions were hurting and putting him on the defensive. But still he handled the pressure with cunning aplomb. And Morgan felt a perverse loyalty to his colonel, his leader – right or wrong.

"We searched that whole area very thoroughly, sir, with our long-range patrols, and with battalion patrols as well. I won't say there might not have been some cache hidden in the area. We could search a month and still not necessarily find it in that sort of country. But that isn't why he fought. He wasn't trapped, in my view, sir. It was the success rather of my 'decoy and lure' principle. He thought he saw a soft US target and went all out to swallow it for a psychological victory. But our superior firepower won through, as calculated, and we just tore him apart."

"You took heavy casualties too."

"We did, sir, we did ... but we handed out a whole lot more."

Abruptly the general stopped his questioning; whether because he was satisfied, or because he suddenly realised there were a large number of junior staff officers listening, Morgan couldn't know. The press were then called in for their briefing and the VIP party left.

It was obvious the Colonel was greatly relieved at the general's departure, and he puffed up with fresh confidence at the relatively easy questions of the journalists. He was relaxed and patronising, and this time when asked about casualties, he brazenly replied:

"Of course, three hundred and twenty-two's only the body count, which as you know is a very conservative estimate. My considered guess, from being at the battlefield and personal experience in these combat matters, is he took a whole heap more dead – maybe two or even three times the number of dead VC bodies we counted. As a rough rule of thumb, we always calculate about three wounded to one dead – especially using fragmentation weapons – so my personal conservative guesstimation is around five hundred actual VC dead, and fifteen hundred to two thousand wounded ..."

28

It was Christmas Eve. Throughout Vietnam a truce of sorts was observed: the US bombing of North Vietnam had been suspended for forty-eight hours, and in the South, no US-initiated operations would take place until after the truce. Of course, normal base camp perimeter security patrols would continue, and the Colonel made it very clear that no patrol or sentry should hesitate to return fire. But the H-and-I artillery fire program was suspended. For a pleasant change the camp was noisy only with the sounds of revelry: radios playing hymns and pop songs, and occasional high-spirited yells from unit Christmas parties.

Christmas Eve was also opening night for the brigade headquarters officers' club: a large barn-like building with a concrete floor and a tin roof. Inside, it was gay with colourful and elaborate Christmas decorations: streamers, balloons, silvered paper bells and cottonwool-covered brush. A professional-sounding group of four blacks (drivers from the headquarters company) were hired as the band. Moaning the latest pop songs and gyrating to the latest dances, the singer could easily have made a living on the nightclub circuit in any major city back home.

The Vietnamese bar girls looked tiny and much more feminine than the handful of American nurses there, big and galumphing in their green fatigues and boots and all looking more like somebody's sister than somebody's mistress. Even so, the American girls were feted and got the attention of Hollywood starlets. Their faces shone with the joy of social and sexual success as partner after partner claimed them to rock, twist and shake the night away. With their red faces, stringy hair, and fatigue jackets wet with armpit sweat, they made improbable belles of the ball – but that night, belles they surely were.

"I am intrigued with your process of pacification ..." Junod said to Morgan as they leaned against the bar, drinking instead of competing for a sweat-soaked dance partner. Morgan had invited Junod as a belated peace offering after his premature – and later regretted – walk-out from lunch. Junod was obviously enjoying the party as a welcome change from his usual isolation – after three double bourbons his face glowed and his Gallic hand gestures were increasingly flamboyant. In well-intentioned Christmas spirit, Morgan had vowed just to enjoy Junod's iconoclastic wit and not take it personally.

"I am grateful to you for inviting me tonight, because simply by coming to this party, I am able to understand the Americanisation and pacification program so much better. Take these bar girls, for example. You have five here – and some in each of the other clubs? Perhaps your brigade employs fifty or sixty bar girls alone, and also I am informed you are hiring house-girls, some typists, and of course women labourers to develop your camp. Are you issuing all these girls with the Pill? Or do you have a special fund for the bastard products of American soldiers and Vietnamese female labour? It will be a worthy civil aid program. Perhaps you should consider giving all such bastards, conceived in this camp, US citizenship ..."

One of the bar girls pushed past Junod to give a drink order to the barman, and as she did so, a young cavalry captain cupped his hand and slapped her ass.

"Be nice!" the girl said, turning angrily, but softening when she saw how handsome the captain was.

"See what I mean?" Junod said.

"I guess you get a charge out of needling us," Morgan said. "Payback for us helping you guys win lost wars."

"Any other attitude would be subservient ... but bear-baiting is always fun." Junod smiled merrily. Both he and Morgan were enjoying this mutual mockery – Junod especially. And tonight his new friend Bill Morgan seemed far less prickly than last time.

"Have you ever admitted we aren't the only bad guys in this movie?" Morgan demanded with mock severity. "I seem to remember the VC murdered and mutilated thousands of village officials, and then a lot more thousands of innocent villagers – men, women, and children ... And I haven't even started counting ARVN soldiers at all. We didn't start this war, you know. They did. You Frenchies were in the game for a bit, but cashed in all your chips after Dien Bien Phu. You French guys just couldn't hack the pace – so we inherited your French mess."

"I don't contest our failure," Junod conceded airily. "What I do criticise is the muddled madness of American methods." He stopped to light up a

Gauloise with a brigade Zippo Morgan had given him. "Examine the case of the unfortunate Dong Tuy villagers – and the destruction of their village – a monument to the impulsiveness of your Colonel, and the vindictiveness of the Province Chief." He paused sardonically, and exhaled a blue cloud of Gauloise smoke. "And now, the farcical appeasement of your Colonel's conscience, where he is letting them return to the bomb craters that were their homes."

"Okay. We make mistakes. Dong Tuy was a mistake and you've had my views on that. But you conveniently ignore the other side of the coin, and the bigger picture. If we weren't here, most South Vietnamese don't want to be Communists. Out of thirteen million in the South, I doubt if half a million are hard-core Communists, and no more than a million sympathisers – mostly through fear. In other words, a small and violent minority is trying to force its will on a very unwilling majority."

"But a very apathetic majority – surely?"

"Like hell. There's half a million men serving in the Vietnamese armed forces alone. And they're fighting, and dying, and taking god-awful wounds every day of the week. I don't call that apathy."

"But South Vietnamese soldiers die so lazily, so apathetically. No élan, no spirit – they die like the sheep they are. And almost none are volunteers."

"A lot of our boys aren't volunteers either, but that doesn't mean they don't believe in what they're fighting for."

"Perhaps you are right and all your newspapers are wrong. But these Vietnamese boys? They have no special beliefs, and no choice. Most would far prefer to plough a paddy or tap rubber trees than die in a war of your continuation."

One of the prettiest nurses dancing, a tall athletic brunette, deliberately swung her ass into Junod's hip and said, "You guys talk too much. What's a girl gotta do to do get asked for a dance?"

"Take off all your clothes," Junod laughed. "Then you would have my full attention."

"In your dreams, buster." Then she danced away and pretended to ignore Junod.

"You've won a heart without even trying," Morgan smiled.

"It always works. We made eye contact soon after I arrived and then I ignored her ..."

"Might work for you flashy French guys ..."

"It works universally – providing you make that all important eye contact first. But tonight is hopeless. There is nowhere to go even remotely civilised ..."

"You give up too easily, you modern French. Napoleon would have found a way."

"To bed that nurse?" Junod laughed. "Or win an intractable counter-insurgency?"

29

"Maybe I'm just a compulsive optimist, but I think you're over-selling our role and selling the Vietnamese short." Morgan had returned to their earlier debate. "History shows how well they absorb foreign influence – Chinese and French – and turn it into something new and Vietnamese. And I'm hopeful they'll turn our influence into something new just like the South Koreans."

Now Morgan was on a roll, no doubt booze-inspired, but Junod encouraged him with indulgent affection, like an older brother.

"Take their religions; the Cao Dai sect is a good example. On my last tour, my Special Forces camp was in a Cao Dai province, and I did some homework ... Chieu and Tac didn't have the sect really organised until 1926, so it's still very new. But that's what makes it a model for a possible Vietnamese future. You know much about it?"

"A few trifles," Junod said dryly. "Clearly for a change, I am to be subjected to a Bill Morgan lecture – how can I complain?"

"It's a mixture of Buddhism, Confucianism, Taoism and spiritism, and it's modelled on both the Catholic Church and Western democracies. I'm not suggesting the whole of Vietnam will become Cao Dai – far from it – but culturally, economically, and politically I see the same sort of evolutionary development. Now, of course, our American influence is strongest. But eventually we'll leave, and we'll leave something good behind – enlightenment, progress ..."

"No, Bill. Your biggest legacies will be American voter frustration and fighting the war for the Vietnamese."

The two men were enjoying this verbal jousting – Junod because he was normally so deprived, and Morgan because this was the first time he had put these arguments into something like a coherent whole.

"You're way off base there, Jean Paul. The Popular Forces and Regional Forces – and they're not regulars – often kill more VC and take more casualties than their army. And the PF are mostly rejects from the army. But they protect the bridges and roads, and their own hamlets, and die for it, when it'd be much easier to surrender and be VC."

"I cannot agree," Junod said heatedly. "It is not easier to join the VC when that means risking their lives fighting you – you, with your bombers and jets, your artillery and tanks, and your inexhaustible supply of conscript manpower."

Morgan handed Junod another drink and glanced at the dancing. A black girl with frizzy red-dyed hair was undulating in front of them. A pencil-moustached black lieutenant danced with her, cool and elegant – a snake hypnotising a willing rabbit.

Junod continued, "Think how terrifying your H-and-I program is alone. Americans sitting in their barbwire bases all over the country and each base bristles with artillery pieces – your base camp has so many guns it is like a porcupine. Mighty battleships, belching smog and nuclear fallout, swarm up and down the coastline pouring thousands of tons of naval gunfire into the hinterland. Overhead the sky is blackened with your American Luftwaffe laying their lethal eggs. And where do all these tons of explosives fall? Is there any pattern? Is a poor VC safe anywhere? No. These bombs fall everywhere – apparently without rhyme or reason. At first the VC thought they were too clever for you and began to feed in false intelligence through double agents so you would fire at the wrong targets. But you have tricked them with your bad map reading, pilot error and the inaccuracy of your guns. So that, in fact, a shell or a bomb may surprise them and land anywhere at any time. Alas! The poor Viet Cong. I don't think you kill many of them by this tactic, or interdict many supplies, but I am sure you harass them. They must have a big headache problem. Perhaps that is your plan: give them so many headaches and sleepless nights that their logistic system breaks down trying to keep up the supply of barbiturates, headache powders and earplugs."

"In the middle of all that crap, Junod, you made one good point – the VC logistic system. You conveniently overlook that what keeps this so-called civil war going is the logistic support and seven thousand troops or so per month that North Vietnam sends across the demilitarised zone. This is an outright invasion from the North."

"My dear Bill, you must improve your backhand. You have left yourself wide open. You said 'so-called civil war' as if North and South Vietnam were not parts of the same country. Then you demolished your argument by referring to the demilitarised zone, which you should have remembered was an artificial line agreed to at Geneva in 1954 to split Vietnam in two, after we French had faced up to the facts and admitted we could not afford the cost of such a war any longer. Unfortunately for your American taxpayers, I do not foresee any Dien Bien Phu disasters for your army to shock your Government to its senses and save your taxpayers their billions of dollars and their sons."

Junod shook out another Gauloise, lit it, and through the cloud of smoke scanned the room for his eye-contact nurse. Morgan was so closely in tune with Junod now, he read the look and instantly guessed why.

"What a hypocrite you are, Jean Paul. I saw that shifty look – caught you red handed not-ignoring that nurse. But at least in terms of honesty, you did admit our US Army cannot be defeated."

"Of course I concede that. But I was not looking for that nurse. I was merely scanning the room to see if the Province Chief and his entourage had arrived."

"Sure you were – just like you didn't need our army's help in World War II to get rid of the Nazis."

Junod smiled disarmingly.

"You have a wild imagination for a stoic, Bill Morgan, but getting back to our argument – for the huge American Army, your Colonel's Tombstone City tactics were very sensible and practical. What did the newspapers say? Two hundred dead and wounded Americans compared to an estimated five hundred dead VC. What cheerful statistics. How many Viet Cong and North Vietnamese troops are there? Perhaps a quarter of a million. Okay. What is a conservative US to VC soldier body count ratio in combat? Let us say two-and-a-half to one. That sounds so statistical. Therefore how many predictably dead men must your Pentagon planners feed in to your personnel pipeline for victory? One hundred thousand dead Americans exactly. Or, if the North Vietnamese keep sending more troops in – say ten thousand a month – then you simply have to add another four thousand dead Americans a month, and victory is complete. With your big healthy population of teenagers, you can fight this war indefinitely. But you aren't solving the problem: you are overwhelming it."

30

Later that Christmas party evening, Meredith beckoned Morgan over to the Colonel's table in a corner of the club, where he was sitting with the Province Chief and Lieutenant Colonel Gillespie. There was an extended band break so the Colonel could talk to his guests. The Province Chief was talking volubly about the economic difficulties in the province, where no rubber was being shipped out, and several isolated villages were completely cut off by road and could only be reached by air. This meant there was practically no normal inter-village commercial activity; most villagers were restricted to local subsistence farming – so tax revenue was way down. A worse problem still was the large refugee population subsisting on handouts.

"How can I help you best, Chief?" the Colonel asked. "I think the start we've already made by hiring four hundred locals will help out a lot. That's four hundred jobs and incomes that didn't exist just weeks ago. And we've knocked the stuffing out of the VC Main Force with Tombstone City. They'll be licking their wounds for a long time to come. I wouldn't be surprised if the VC decided to clear right out of this province and leave us well alone."

Old Leather was getting carried away with his own propaganda, Morgan thought sadly. It was painful to hear him talk so boldly and brashly now, but the truth was Old Leather had been very subdued in the weeks since Tombstone City. No bold new operations had been planned since; only safe local patrolling was allowed.

All aggressive operational suggestions made by Meredith, or the three battalion commanders, had been sidestepped in favour of aggressive discussion. As Meredith said, "The Colonel's had his fingers burnt. Those Tombstone City casualties were too heavy; they frightened hell out of him. He nearly lost a whole battalion, and he's scared the Iceman doesn't like him and doesn't believe him. One more big battle turns bad on him, he's scared he'll be sacked. So he's putting up a smokescreen, blowing heaps of smoke that Tombstone City was a brilliant victory. And not just to convince General Ivanhoe, but to convince himself."

Yet Morgan still felt respect for the Colonel, even now, in spite of all his faults – many of which Morgan had been reluctant to recognise – for the Colonel still possessed many admirable qualities.

"I hope you are right," the Province Chief said to the Colonel. "Already this month we have had thirty-two VC ralliers surrender, which is very good. I think we have reached a turning point because of your operations. To consolidate now, and get quick results, I would beg your assistance to open more province roads."

Old Leather's face lit up. Clearly he liked Colonel Phan's latest request, and it seemed to trigger a new wave of confidence in him.

"Certainly see your problem, Chief. Our tactics frightened him away from the villages, you say – and opening the roads would be a big psychological victory for us. What do you think, Frank?"

"I think it's a fine idea, sir. Road convoys are a straightforward military operation. We can lay on all the air and artillery firepower we need, in case Charlie has a go. My only question is, how often do we run the convoys? Properly protected convoys eat up a heap of assets."

"A few times a month is all," the Province Chief said.

"But," Meredith went on, "a few times a month each, to the number of villages and hamlets in this province, adds up to a lot of convoys. Frankly, sir, even though I agree it would be good to open up the roads, I think it means diverting too many troops and assets from our primary mission of destroying VC Main Force."

"Bill, what do you say?" the Colonel asked. "I bet a dollar it's something different."

"For a change, sir, I agree with everybody. I think it's vital we open up the roads – otherwise what are we here for? But I agree it'll tie up a lot of troops and assets."

The Colonel pondered a few seconds then made his Delphic Oracle pronouncement. "I think you're both over-rating our enemy. He can't be every place at once. I think we've started to lick him, and a series of surprise road openings would send a powerful message to the villagers about who's really winning this war.

"It's not enough for the VC and us to know we're winning. The people have to know it too. I think we should do a heap of road-running over the next month. It's mostly open country and I don't think he'll dare touch us – apart from a few mines and sniper rounds. And if he does pick a fight, that's the very fight I want. We'll tear him apart. Yes, sir, we'll tear him apart."

For added emphasis and reassurance, Old Leather gripped the Province Chief's shoulder – Colonel Phan smiled beatifically.

A few minutes before midnight the music and dancing stopped; the officer managing the club asked all the officers to move back to the walls and the women to move around him in a horseshoe in the centre of the room. There was a long roll on the drums; the lights were gradually dimmed and finally blacked out. There were a few nervous shrieks of female laughter when the drum roll stopped, and the room remained dark. Then the lights were snapped on to reveal, in the centre of the horseshoe of girls, a Father Christmas. Roly-poly round in his red Santa Claus suit, with flying boots and cottonwool beard.

Santa Claus began to delve in his huge sack for presents for the girls. The club manager first ushered the embarrassed bar girls up to meet Santa Claus. Each girl got five pairs of stockings and three cans of hairspray. They were obviously delighted by the gifts, and Old Leather led everybody in a round of applause, at which the bar girls bowed shyly and giggled behind cupped hands.

The third American girl had just accepted her gift when the mortar fire began. There was no mistaking the sound: the first rounds seemed close, and then one exploded almost next to the club, showering it with earth and stones and pinging pieces of shrapnel. Nearly everyone threw themselves to the floor in a knee-jerk reaction. There was a moment of stupefied silence, then a confused shouting was just starting when the Colonel's commanding voice cut through it all.

"Everybody steady – and stay where you are. I want no panic just because of a few mortar rounds. Club manager, escort the ladies to the bunker at the rear of the club ..."

You had to pay him, Morgan thought, he was magnificent in this sort of situation. That controlled drawl he'd used when he said, "escort the ladies to the bunker ...". He could have been a Southern plantation owner a hundred years ago, just before the Civil War, organising games for his daughter's coming-out. Steady as a rock, calm in a crisis; he'd have been superb in the Civil War.

The girls were streaming across the open space between the rear of the officers' club and the bunker when a mortar round exploded within five yards. Two Vietnamese and five American girls were killed, and one Vietnamese and nine American girls were wounded.

Since there was nowhere else to put them at the time, the dead girls were laid out behind the bar in the club. Morgan and Junod helped carry them in, disregarding the continuing mortar fire and the crashing of the brigade artillery, now responding with retaliatory fire. He was standing silently above the dead girls, running his torch over them, a feeling of pointlessness about life in general weighing heavily upon him, when Junod spoke:

"War always seems worse when women are killed."

"Yep ... and this was supposed to be a truce." Morgan found there was too much to say. An unreasoning anger began to well up. "So, Junod, who's wrong now? Who's the aggressor, who's illegal, who's immoral, when you start breaking cease-fires and murdering women?"

"I grieve for these girls too ... But please don't forget that far more VC women, and innocent Vietnamese women, are dying from your air and artillery mistakes than these few girls."

"For Christ's sake, Jean Paul – this was deliberate. I don't say we haven't made mistakes, but you can't equate mistakes with deliberate actions."

"No. Mistakes are worse – more frightening. I am sorry for these dead girls. Very sorry. But I ask you to remember to be sorry for the VC women you kill too."

Morgan was to remember Junod's words vividly when he went to the Tactical Operations Centre a few minutes later to find out more about what had happened. He'd left Junod with the remainder of the uninjured girls in the bunker at the rear of the club. As he'd run to the TOC, several VC mortar shells burst nearby, but it was almost impossible to recognise their particular bangs under the deafening roar of the brigade's own artillery.

"What are we firing at? Do we know where the VC mortars are?" Morgan asked the duty officer between his hurried telephone and radio calls.

"Looks like they're firing from Ap Moi hamlet, according to radar reports and other Intell ..."

"We're not firing on Ap Moi are we? There's still around fifty families living there."

"I know, sir. I wasn't ordering nothing because of that, but the Colonel and the Province Chief decided to fire back anyhow. They're all in back of the TOC now."

Morgan hurried to the Colonel's small combat conference room between the duty officer's section and the fire support control centre.

"Sir, do you realise you've ordered artillery fire on a hamlet with fifty families – just old men and women, plus mothers and kids?"

The Colonel, the Province Chief, and Gillespie were looking at grease pencil lines Meredith was marking on the wall planning map. The Colonel turned slowly to face Morgan. Meredith, from behind the Colonel, shook his head and waved his hand to warn Morgan not to go on.

"The Colonel certainly does, Bill," Meredith jumped in before the Colonel could speak. "He and the Province Chief fully appreciate what this means and a joint decision was made."

But Morgan was not to be put off. The whole thing was monstrous; an impulsive and murderous decision that had to be reversed. Morgan could never live with himself if he didn't do his damnedest ...

"But that's murder, sir. Murder as unjustifiable as the VC breaking the truce and killing our girls. Maybe it's worse – because maybe they didn't know we had women in the camp."

"Shut up, Bill, and get yourself under control," Meredith said brutally. "You're talking like some hysterical Sunday school teacher. This is war and now – and a tough decision had to be made."

"Goddam it, Frank Meredith. Don't speak to me like that," Morgan was so upset his head shook with emotion and his forehead was deeply creased.

"You don't know all the facts, Bill – and you're interrupting the Colonel's conference. Ask Intelligence for a run-down. I'll fill in the gaps when I'm done with the Colonel."

Morgan left and walked through the TOC looking for the Intelligence Officer, Major Shane Driscoll, a laconic Texan with a dry and morbid sense of humour. Morgan was so angry he'd almost hit Meredith, and clenched and unclenched his fists like claws. He was about to ask Driscoll for an update on Ap Moi, when Meredith grabbed his arm and led him aside.

"Bill, you're your own worst enemy. When are you going to learn there are times when shooting off your mouth to clear your conscience means cutting your throat?"

"I'm not worried about my throat. I'm worried about fifty Vietnamese families' throats in Ap Moi. And don't ever talk to me like that in front of the Colonel again, or, so help me God, I'll ..."

"Sure. And if I hadn't shocked the shit out of you, you'd have told the Colonel how to fight his brigade in front of the Province Chief and

Gillespie – riding tall in the saddle of your high and mighty conscience – and probably got yourself sacked. I'd rather not have to tell you this, Bill, I hadn't thought it'd get this bad, but Old Leather's been talking of replacing you. Do I have to spell out why?"

"Replacing me?"

"Seems you irritate him, Bill – as a staff officer. He says you're too stubborn and inflexible, and because you disagree too much, he thinks you're too negative."

"But what does he want? Liars and yes-men?"

"You'd call it that. I'd say staff officers with rudimentary tact and common sense."

"And because of your tact and common sense – Ap Moi gets shelled."

"You're so one-eyed when your mind's made up. You ain't the only guy in the US Army with ideas on how to win or lose the war. If you'd stop and think before emoting like a middle-aged preacher-pacifist you might get somewhere."

"What ideas? I'm listening now."

"First: our base camp getting mortared. Our own soldiers, plus American and Vietnamese women, were killed and wounded by that mortar fire, and we're still taking casualties. Second: every peasant hut round here has its own bomb shelter dug in the cellar. So Ap Moi's not taking any more chances than you and me and the rest of the brigade if they get shelled back. Third: if we don't hit back, the VC get the jackpot – the winning formula to hit us without getting hit themselves. Then they'd do the same thing from every village in the province. Fourth: everyone in Ap Moi knew what was going on – they had time to get out of Ap Moi or get in their shelters. Last point: most of Ap Moi are VC relatives or VC sympathisers anyway."

"I can't agree, Frank. You forget what this war's about – why we're here. It's not just to win battles with low casualties. We're not fighting a war in a vacuum or even enemy territory. These Vietnamese people, especially the women and kids, are the main reason we're here – to save them from a worse war and a worse fate. We do things like shell Ap Moi and we're as bad, or worse, than the VC."

"Hell, Bill, be realistic. You don't make an omelette without breaking eggs. Christ, for a combat officer what's come over you? Why this sudden crisis of conscience?"

31

Next evening the Colonel held a planning conference for all unit commanders and senior staff officers in the just-completed briefing hut. It had survived the mortaring virtually undamaged, except for a few jagged shrapnel holes in the walls. Large-scale maps pinned to sliding partitions on a stage showed the province and big areas of the neighbouring provinces. After the customary evening briefing on the events of the past twenty-four hours, the Colonel rose from his chair and walked a few paces to the edge of the stage. He leapt lightly up on stage and turned to face the conference. As he did, he stamped each foot firmly once, which jerked his rucked-up trouser legs back into their correct folds hanging over his boots.

"Somehow Christmas Day seems the wrong day to talk new offensive operations. This is a day when we'd all prefer to think of our loved ones: our wives, or our girlfriends, and our families. This is not a fitting day for war, and for that reason, we sought a truce with the Viet Cong. Deliberately and cold-bloodedly, they chose to violate that truce by mortaring our base camp last night on Christmas Eve, thereby killing two newly hired Vietnamese girls, five American girls, and fourteen of our soldiers.

"Why did the VC do this? I'll tell you why. It's because we've got him on the run. He's learnt he can't stand up to us man to man in close combat. He learnt that at My Trang and Tombstone City. So what's left to him? He's reverting to sneak terrorist tactics: hit-and-run raids, truce breaking, surprise mortar raids and booby traps. As far as I'm concerned, this is fine business. Using those tactics proves he's losing. But I intend to deny him even the satisfaction of his sneak tactics ..."

Morgan looked round the room to check reactions to the Colonel's briefing. There was no getting away from it, he had them hunching forward in their chairs, keenly attentive, faces registering all the right feelings at each emotive signal: *Christmas ... families ... violate ... man to man ... on the*

144

run ... sneak terrorist tactics. It was an uncomfortable discovery for Morgan that he was still as much a prisoner of the Colonel's rhetoric as anyone.

"How can we achieve this and deny the VC all tactical options against our new home – this base camp? The VC can lay mines and booby traps anywhere along our lines of communication. He's free to mortar us any time he chooses if he's in mortar range of this base. And while there's local Vietnamese living within a circle of our base – a circle of, say, five thousand yard radius – he can repeat the same dirty tactic he used last night and set up his mortars inside Vietnamese villages and hope we won't fire back, because if we do, we're shelling local civilians ...

"He gave me a tough decision last night, a real tough decision, by setting up his mortars in Ap Moi. Well, I'm paid to make tough decisions, and the Province Chief agreed with me, and we shelled him right back. I'm pleased to say that one tough decision stopped the mortaring. And it only cost two lives in Ap Moi. And, as you all know, Ap Moi is mostly VC and VC sympathisers.

"There's a lesson here you all should learn very well. Never get soft about tough decisions and pussyfoot around. We're fighting a war, and sometimes in war civilians get hurt. I want that everybody should be very clear on this – when it's a choice between soldiers' lives in this fighting brigade, and the lives of a few civilians, especially VC civilians, my soldiers come first. You can't win a war if you sacrifice your troops instead of saving them to fight ..."

Meredith's parting words of the night before leapt unbidden into Morgan's mind: *"Why this sudden crisis of conscience, Bill?"* After all, Morgan thought, the Colonel's analysis of last night's events spelt out the problem clearly. But Junod's cynicism posed a more fundamental problem: what was the point of this war, or any war, if you destroyed what you meant to save?

The Colonel continued.

"Now, I don't want to give orders to fire on civilians if there's any other way. And for this problem, I believe there is. We resettle all civilians within VC mortar range of our base. That'll do a lot to solve the mortar problem and the booby trap problem at the same time. This whole circle when it's empty of civilians will then become a twenty-four-hour Free Fire Zone – anybody caught in this area will be VC by definition and will get shot. We'll be getting out detailed orders and frag orders to implement that policy very soon.

"Next thing I want to tell you all about is our road-runner program to open up the rural road network in the province and restore normal economic activity. In outline, my concept goes like this ..."

When the Colonel finished his briefing there was a stir of excited conversation about the two new plans.

"One thing about Old Leather, he's a red-hot ideas man," Morgan overheard a battalion commander say.

"Yes, sir. He's got this show on the road and he keeps moving it along. Long-range patrols, decoy and lure battles, resettlement, road-running. He's a go-go commander."

But Morgan was still deeply perturbed, both by the implications of the Colonel's drastic resettlement program, and by his total omission even to discuss this new policy with him – the responsible staff officer. Whether the Colonel had decided not to discuss it with him because he intended to sack him, Morgan didn't care. The thing that hurt most was the omission without explanation: the least the Colonel could have done was summon him and tell him to his face. It would be intolerable to be kept on staff as a man without a function, an awkward piece of padding who was hard to sack because of his combat record. He had to have it out.

Morgan caught the Colonel about to enter his quarters. "I'd like to speak with you in private, sir."

"Urgent, Bill, or can it wait?"

"It's urgent, sir."

"Then come on in. I'll see if my driver can rustle us up some coffee."

Morgan was disarmed by the Colonel's graciousness, and too intent on what he had to say to notice just how studied and controlled this courtesy was.

"Now, what's troubling you, Bill?" the Colonel asked as he sat back in one of the locally produced chairs of cheap metal and garishly coloured basket-weave plastic.

"My status as a principal staff officer on your staff, sir. I understand you've been considering replacing me."

"As a commander, Bill, it's my job to consider many things. Of course considerations, and decisions arising from those considerations, are totally different things. To answer your question now – yes. I have considered replacing you. But I haven't made a decision yet."

"What am I doing wrong, sir?" Morgan asked harshly, both afraid and relieved the subject was out in the open.

"You've got a very fine combat record, Bill. That's one of the reasons I personally selected you for my principal staff. But combat and staff are very different things. Staff work is a function of smooth interpersonal relationships. On my staff I often find you abrasive and too stubborn. For instance, Lieutenant Colonel Gillespie, the Province Chief's adviser, is one of your main contacts, but you always rub him up the wrong way. And your attitude with me, Bill. I'm afraid often I find you negative, too unresponsive to ideas – and unconstructive. A good staff officer must be creative and constructive and realistic in his approach."

"And I'm not, sir?"

"That's another thing. You've got no tact about you, Bill. Still, tact isn't everything, and if you bear these things in mind, Bill, there's no reason why from now on we shouldn't get along fine. You know, I'm glad we've had this little conversation, Bill. At least you had the balls to ask me … and that's one thing I always have admired about you."

"If I'm still a member of your staff, sir, I'd appreciate the chance to express my views on any matters affecting civil affairs before you make your final decisions. Otherwise, sir, you might as well sack me."

"Bill, whenever possible, it's one of my principles to canvass the views of all my staff who can contribute to the solution of a problem. Sometimes, of course, there won't be time to ask opinions or explain orders. As a combat-experienced officer I don't have to tell you that. Things have been pretty hectic since that mortaring last night, and I just didn't have time to discuss with you personally the Province Chief's and my plan to resettle everybody living within the base camp perimeter out to mortar range. I guess that resettlement decision is what's been troubling you most?"

"It is, sir."

Perhaps the Colonel did feel guilty about excluding Morgan from his recent planning sessions, and he appeared sincere when he asked Morgan to give his reactions.

"It's Dong Tuy, sir. I understand the military logic that says we ought to clear our base area out to mortar range – and for all those small hamlets and scattered houses I agree. But I think Dong Tuy should be different. We've destroyed it once already, and made the whole population refugees. Then later we discovered we were dealing mainly with old men, women and children, and as refugees they were virtually starving because the province administration couldn't cope. Those families had no future without land of their own to farm, so you let them go back … That was before Tombstone City. But now we plan to move them yet again. In their case especially, sir – I think your plan is too drastic."

"And what if the VC use Dong Tuy village to mortar us from? What then?"

"I don't think they will, sir. Dong Tuy is too close to this base for them to risk it. But in any case, sir, surely we're fighting this war to help the South Vietnamese people to a better way of life. Not to create a country of homeless refugees."

Morgan stopped, realising he'd probably said too much, but still convinced it had to be said.

The Colonel paused a long moment before replying. "You're a stubborn argumentative sonofabitch, Bill, and you're way out of line. Even when you might be right, you've got a way of putting things that makes them hard to swallow. I've got a brigade of American soldiers to look after, besides those villagers ... but we'll give your idea a try and see how things work out. Meantime, Dong Tuy can stay."

From the way the Colonel said "and see how things work out", Morgan knew this was a last chance for both him and Dong Tuy. The Colonel rose abruptly and, as Morgan saluted to leave, slapped him on the shoulder and said, "Happier now, Bill?"

32

The road-runner operations started next day and, in the main, were remarkably successful. Of course a few jeeps, trucks and armoured personnel carriers were damaged by mines and booby traps, but no ambushes were sprung against the convoys. The Province Chief and the Colonel were delighted, and the Province Chief himself rode at the head of several of the early convoys when they reopened roads to previously cut-off villages. Morale in the province improved noticeably as, for the first time in months, villagers were able to get produce to market at the province capital without fear of VC road blocks and tax collectors.

The Colonel described the Viet Cong reaction as:

"Fear and confusion. We're running him ragged. His Main Force hasn't got over Tombstone City, and his local guerrillas and trail watchers don't know what's hit them. We're doing so much fancy footwork, driving here, then there; artillery firepower ready to wipe out resistance; air-power patrolling the skies just itching to blast off at anything that moves. I'd say he's frantic ..."

Morgan visited hamlets and villages he'd not been able to get to before except by helicopter. He was deeply impressed by the entrepreneurial spirit the formerly cut-off villagers showed in their passion to get produce to market. A bizarre collection of ox-carts, bicycles and motor scooters risked the roads behind the armed road-runner columns. But a sense of foreboding oppressed him; this good luck couldn't last. Finally he spoke to the Colonel and Meredith about it.

"I'm uneasy, sir. This very same tactic of armed road columns was tried by the French and it cost them dear."

But they trivialised Morgan's pessimism. Meredith said, "Good old Bill – our prophet of doom. Sure there's risk involved, but it's illogical to compare us with the French. We've got artillery and tactical air support the French never dreamed of. And what if we do lose a vehicle here and there?

We can afford to. A truck means no more to Uncle Sam than a straw hat to Uncle Ho. And if they hit us? That's exactly what we want – bring them to battle."

"Right on, Frank," the Colonel said. "All this is part of the trap I'm setting for our VC friend. If he doesn't spring it – and I won't be surprised if he doesn't dare – he should have learnt his lesson by now what he's up against. Then we win a major psychological victory."

At the same time as the road-runner operations were criss-crossing the province, the resettlement of the families living within five thousand yards of the base camp was carried out. Draconian though this was, and hateful as it must have been to those affected, Morgan conceded it had to be done. At least he'd had a modest success by saving the Dong Tuy villagers from another uprooting. Now Ap Moi hamlet contained the largest number of families for evacuation, and it was saved till last in the resettlement program. The main reason was to give the provincial administration time, with brigade help, to prepare for so many refugees. Morgan was especially busy as Civil Affairs Officer, coordinating details between the brigade and the Province Chief's staff.

The same day Ap Moi was to be resettled, three members of a Senate Armed Forces sub-committee were scheduled for a briefing and lunch.

At 0830 when Morgan checked in to advise the Colonel that the convoy was ready to leave for Ap Moi to evacuate the villagers, he found the Colonel preoccupied with preparing his briefing notes for the senators.

"If the convoy's ready, get it rolling."

"I was going to suggest, sir, we hold off a bit. Slip it till this low cloud clears – so we have air support."

"Have we got it covered with artillery?"

"We do. But our gunner spotters couldn't do aerial corrections with this cloud."

"So what? It's the convoy commander on the ground who'll call in the fire. Let's not waste time horsing around for a few clouds. Artillery's better in close support anyway. Move it on schedule."

Morgan realised he was getting nowhere and the Colonel was getting irritated, ostentatiously looking at his watch and briefing notes. So he left without further argument and drove to Canh Tri to double-check the refugee reception arrangements.

There was a sports stadium in Canh Tri and this had been barbwired and re-organised as a refugee screening and holding centre. It already held a few hundred recently arrived refugees from the earlier phases of the Colonel's resettlement plan. The playing field was latticed with temporary barbwire cattle fences and chequered with olive-drab canvas marquees and tents to segregate, shelter and interrogate the refugees. Morgan was met by Lieutenant Colonel Gillespie, who briefed him as they walked.

"We've organised the local band to play for the day and lift refugee morale. We've got two Vietnamese psych warfare teams in to give cultural displays and government policy pep talks to distract them while they wait for interrogation. Your MEDCAPS and DENTCAPS are doing a real fine job too, and our USAID man's here with a big bag of goodies to hand out. He's got little plastic bags of rice, a whole mess of pamphlets and kiddies' pre-packaged school kits to hand around."

"Sounds great, Colonel Gillespie. They should have a ball; I reckon those propaganda pamphlets and bags of rice will just make their day."

"If you think that's funny, Morgan, I don't."

"Sorry about that, sir," Morgan said blandly, and they continued in strained silence. As always, the refugees were a pathetic lot. The handful of older boys and young men looked to be simpletons or deformed, which was hardly surprising – they must have been rejected as unfit for service by both the Government and the VC. Morgan noticed one old man in particular, who hobbled to the barbwire and saluted him. Almost bent double, legs gnarled and knobbed like a hawthorn walking stick, the old man croaked, "America, number one." As Morgan responded with the appropriate payment of the remains of a pack of cigarettes, the old man dribbled.

"When do you expect your Ap Moi convoy?" Gillespie asked Morgan. "Any delay on account of the cloud?"

"No. The Colonel decided to stick to schedule. First trucks ought to be here round noon time."

Just before eleven o'clock, when Morgan was having coffee with Gillespie and several other members of his advisory team, Morgan's driver ran up to report.

"Sir – something you ought to know. I've been listening to the command net. Seems like the convoy's found itself a firefight."

Morgan and Gillespie ran back to Morgan's jeep, and after a few minutes listening, they worked out the convoy was ambushed just two miles from the brigade base on the branch road to Ap Moi, where a narrow bridge crossed a deep creek and the jungle grew down to the road. Morgan decided to go back to base immediately in case he was needed.

Reaching base camp, he could still hear shots and sporadic rattles of automatic fire from the ambush.

"What are we up against?" he quietly asked Meredith in the TOC.

"Don't know yet. The bridge was blown and collapsed behind the convoy – around 20 trucks. Then some trees and culverts were blown up within the convoy. At this stage, they're only taking light fire. Just looks like a neat professional job by local guerrillas. We've sent off an engineer detachment to drop another span across the creek. Still, we're not taking any chances, just in case the VC are aiming to bait a bigger trap. So we're sending a company of infantry along in tracks, to guard the engineers."

"How'd the Colonel react?"

"More annoyed than worried about the ambush. Annoyed at the interruption to preparing his briefing for this Senate committee ... The divisional commander and General Westmoreland are coming too, and Old Leather sure wants to impress."

Morgan wasn't really surprised when the relieving column of engineers and infantry in tracked armoured personnel carriers came under heavy fire just before the blown bridge.

"Would happen now," Meredith said laconically. "Guaranteed – when the Colonel's in the middle of briefing all his goddam VIP senators. Hell, we're getting so busy briefing people about the war, there's no time to fight it."

Meredith headed off to interrupt and brief the Colonel.

When he got back, barely ten minutes later, he said sarcastically, "Well, he agreed to sending in the rest of the battalion to reinforce, but Old Leather's so uptight about his briefing and impressing those goddam generals and senators with his past tactical brilliance – and we both know the new gospel according to Saint Leather: *decoy and lure, long-range patrols, Tombstone, road runner, resettlement* – that today's battle just seems an inconvenient interruption. Trouble is, VIPs get more important than fighting the goddam war."

"Thought I was supposed to be the angry young middle-aged man," Morgan laughed.

*

By the time the VIP party left after lunch, it was obvious to Meredith and Morgan that a major battle had developed. A VC force of battalion or even regimental strength seemed to be involved. With the VIPs gone, the

Colonel finally appreciated the gravity of the situation. The whole brigade might be needed to win the battle. Meredith even pressed the Colonel to request heli-borne reserve battalions from Division to insert around the outer edges of the battle zone as blocking forces. But the Colonel adamantly refused to ask for outside help.

Did he refuse, Morgan wondered, because it might be deemed an admission of inadequacy? Or might the Colonel have been guarding against some future investigation? After all, he had been warned by Frank that the situation was getting serious, and he certainly could have excused himself from the VIP briefing. On the other hand, the Divisional Commander and Westmoreland could well consider that was the job of a competent operational staff, to take the reins in a routine emergency ... The Colonel surely had a lot of balls to keep in the air, and Morgan truly felt for him – the icy loneliness of command.

33

Fortunately the cloud cover evaporated before the ambush was sprung and the battle really developed, so Kurt Braemar was able to lay on plentiful air support. In addition, a company of helicopters became available by mid-afternoon, so it was possible to lift a relieving force across the creek to assist the beleaguered remnants of the Ap Moi refugee convoy. As the reports on the battle came in through the afternoon, it appeared that heavy casualties were being taken on both sides. By five o'clock, two and a half of the brigade's three battalions had been committed to the fight; by then the Colonel was becoming increasingly aware he should have followed Frank's earlier advice and called in outside reinforcements.

At this stage the Province Chief and Lieutenant Colonel Gillespie arrived, the Chief being very concerned to pass on to the Colonel an allegedly vital piece of intelligence he had just received from one of his agents – namely that two North Vietnamese regiments had entered the province and planned to attack the brigade base that night, taking advantage of the diversion of so many of the brigade's forces to counter the convoy ambush. Later, when the Province Chief had left, both Meredith and Morgan were sceptical of the agent report, rating it as just another alarmist rumour. They felt confirmed in this judgement when, at last light, the VC broke contact, apparently to end the battle.

Meredith reasoned the VC wanted to use darkness to collect their dead and wounded, plus weapons and unused ammunition, before quitting the battlefield. His view was that once again the VC had launched an attack on what they thought was a soft target, only to find later the tactical advantages reversed. They were then subjected to the full violence of the brigade's artillery and air firepower, and nearly cut off from escape by rapidly deployed heli-borne reinforcements and blocking troops.

Morgan agreed, but credited the Viet Cong with a deeper, more subtle motive: the ambush was brutal and bloody evidence for the Province population that American troops could not protect them – even in armed convoys. The VC then inflicted heavy casualties on Ap Moi refugees, casualties which could later be blamed on the brigade; the ambush could then be touted as a gallant VC effort to rescue Ap Moi refugees from imprisonment in American concentration camps.

By eight o'clock that evening, when battle casualty figures were consolidated, it was clear that Ap Moi refugees had indeed suffered heavy casualties: twenty-three dead, thirty-four wounded, and nineteen missing. Probably, some of the missing had run away, but there was a fair chance even more casualties would be found in the morning.

Brigade casualties were heavy, too. An alarming thirty-two soldiers were missing. Over one hundred were wounded, and it seemed probable that the figure of thirty-nine killed would increase to over sixty, with more deaths from wounds plus finding the bodies of more of those missing in daylight. The Colonel was horrified at the number of missing – all from the convoy escort group, caught in the initial ambush.

So the Colonel demanded a recount of all casualty figures, and insisted on Meredith and his three battalion commanders all getting involved via a field telephone conference. Afterwards, when the casualty figures had been confirmed, Meredith briefed Morgan in a far corner of the TOC, over scalding cups of coffee.

"The Colonel's scared shitless that those thirty-two missing have been captured by the VC. The professional humiliation of Americans from his brigade being prisoners of war is worse for him than having them dead. And now he's taken that phony agent report from the Province Chief far more seriously than we did. He thinks there's a strong chance the base will be attacked later tonight by those phantom North Vietnamese regiments."

"If that's our biggest problem – I'm happy. I'll get back to my hooch and catch up on paperwork. Gillespie brought me a bunch of USAID reports and other stuff this afternoon. I'll check in later when I'm done."

*

One of the worst things about being a soldier is how much of your life is wasted stumbling in the dark to primitive latrines. Finished with that and his paperwork, Morgan walked back to the TOC. He stopped to light a cigarette; how pleasant the temperature was now – almost cool. He stood, enjoying the comparative silence, and waiting for his night vision to recover from the flare of his cigarette lighter. Moments of peace like this were rare; mostly he was butting his head against the brick wall of the demands of the moment.

Looking back, he was surprised to realise how much more time he'd had to himself as a company commander. Of course in those days, on operations with his company, there was no real companionship at nights – he had to remain very much aloof and alone. Whereas now the TOC was invariably a stage for high drama and, sometimes, depending on the Colonel's moods, a theatre of the tragic-absurd. In quiet times, there were endless professional and general discussions with Frank Meredith. Then overriding all was the reason and framework for his life – his professional soldiering career. His new civil affairs job was all-consuming; so much report reading and writing, so many field trips, inevitable ass-kicking ... Then back at base was an apparently never-ending succession of planning conferences to coordinate and supervise his many projects. Finally, and in the Colonel's eyes, most important of all, were the briefings: congressmen, senators, generals from many armies, war correspondents, and even occasional movie stars ...

It was demanding and interesting work, but at times he missed the blood-and-thunder excitement of combat command and of largely being the sole decision-maker. One of the major frustrations of his new job was all the unresolved issues that demanded patient staff work and political craftiness, rather than direct action. The major black cloud on his career-horizon was dealing with the Colonel – sadly, what had once been close to hero-worship had changed to a sullen and stubborn wariness, inadequately concealed as his delusions fell away. Finally, gnawing like cancer cells at the very foundations of his military beliefs, were Junod's cynical critiques on the American way of waging war. If Junod was right, all was folly. The great American war machine was just a blind Cyclops blundering in the dark, wreaking senseless havoc ...

Amongst the pile of reports Gillespie had given him that afternoon, one in particular seemed to confirm many of his more pessimistic views. It was a survey of the attitudes of a sampling of villagers and refugees. The sampling was the work of yet another CIA-inspired innovation – the Census Grievance section of a fifty-nine-man Vietnamese Revolutionary Development Team, just beginning to operate in the province. The translations from the Vietnamese to English were literal and unedited.

... 153 interviews with Province villagers and refugees were carried out by the Census Grievance Team and translations of prevalent or significant attitudes are attached ...

Statement by Ngyen Van Pha, male ageing forty-seven. Americans are much kind with good appearance and help us many things ... give radio, rice, clothes, medicine ... taking disabled daughter to Saigon for replacement of wooden leg with artificial leg of iron. But Americans prohibited us to plough, they destroying our crops and fruit trees, and if they remain here we can do nothing except charity ...

As Morgan read the translated report, he saw it as a very significant document – so significant he should show it to the Colonel and discuss its implications as soon as possible.

To pacify this province, the brigade seemed to be destroying not only American soldiers and the VC in large numbers, but also the province itself; the landscape, the economy, the people, and the old order of Vietnamese society. Morgan now understood more clearly what Junod had meant when he talked of the American way of waging war. Surely there must be a less destructive way.

"Halt!" he heard an officious bark and realised it was one of the MPs assigned to guard the TOC. After a moment's hesitation, while he tried to remember the password, he heard the MP cock his rifle.

"You better have that on safety, sentry," Morgan snarled irritably – trigger-happy sentries were the final straw. "Or I'll ram it down your fucking throat. Here you are pussy-footing around in a soft job, guarding the TOC, surrounded by enough barbwire to go round Vietnam twice, plus three battalions of infantry really taking risks. Shit! MPs like you, skulking in safe jobs, shouldn't be trusted with real bullets."

Immediately he felt better, but guilty for his outburst; especially when he remembered there was only half a battalion of infantry in the base camp. He was about to apologise, when the sentry replied officiously:

"Name, sir? I'm under orders to report all officers not knowing the password."

Morgan was so annoyed he shoved the MP back with a palm to the chest, so the MP lost balance and ended up sitting on the coil of barbwire surrounding the TOC.

34

Inside, he found Meredith and the Colonel staring fixedly at a marked-up map. As Meredith turned, Morgan said, "Pity we don't have real soldiers pulling sentry on the TOC instead of those useless fucking MPs. Guy on now actually asked me for the password – as if he still doesn't know who the hell I am – God help us."

"Calm down, Bill. It's Colonel's orders." Meredith gave a small wink as he spoke, and a slight head shake. "You realise we're thin on the ground tonight."

"I guess you're right, but I still wouldn't mind seeing some of those MPs do a man's job for a change in a line company."

"They do their job, Bill," the Colonel interrupted. "Obey orders and do their job."

Is he inferring I don't? Morgan thought, angry but trying to hide it. Shane Driscoll, the brigade Intelligence Officer, joined them, carrying another map extensively covered in red grease pencil markings.

Before Driscoll could speak, Morgan pulled the Census Grievance Report from his pocket and said to the Colonel, "As soon as you've got time, sir, I've got a critical report here I think you should read."

"What is it, civil affairs?"

"Yes, sir."

"Not now, Bill. We've got a combat situation to deal with."

"Didn't mean now, sir ... When you had time to spare." Morgan was hurt at this second rebuff, but swallowed it. The Colonel ignored him and spoke to Driscoll.

"What's your take, Shane, on the threat to the base?"

"As you know, sir," Driscoll answered, "we've had reports of a North Vietnamese division infiltrating through to this general area – the Duc Binh war base. Those mountains make a great springboard for offensive operations not only into our province, but the surrounding ones too. Then we've got the normal two VC regiments that operate in this area plus, according to my Order of Battle officer's analysis, another five regiments operating within forty-eight hours forced march of our province."

"If we accept that estimate," Meredith interrupted, "we're threatened by seven VC regiments plus an NVA division. I find that very hard to believe. Trouble with Intelligence estimates is they always paint black pictures. That way if they're right they say, 'I told you so'. If they're wrong, it's just good news, and everybody's happy."

"I'd agree with Frank there, sir," Morgan threw in. "The VC has never attacked a major US base camp yet."

The Colonel frowned, stared intently at the map for a long time, then said, "There's always a first time. It's easy for you staff guys to minimise the threat, but you wouldn't bear responsibility for losing the brigade if it all turns to shit. Who's prepared to swear this isn't some major VC trap? A really big play – like Dien Bien Phu against the French? Hell, we've been pacifying this province so fast, he has to try something. If the threat's only a third of what Intelligence paints it, the VC could still attack this base tonight with three regiments."

The Colonel stopped to light a cigar – an animal comfort thing Morgan could well understand. Finally, the Colonel did carry the entire load, and Morgan felt guilty for his petulant behaviour over the asshole MP.

Now the Colonel was on a self-justifying roll.

"Let's examine the feasibility of that proposition. Phase One: VC baited the trap by ambushing the Ap Moi convoy. Phase Two: he drew the bulk of the brigade infantry into that trap, which was really a diversion operation for Phase Three. And Phase Three might have commenced when he broke off contact at last light, having successfully denuded this base of infantry and prepared it for an overwhelming night attack. Now, what's your answer to that?"

"I just can't see it happening that way," Morgan said stubbornly.

"Why not? What proof have you got?"

"I don't have any proof. I just think it's very unlikely."

The Colonel looked at him incredulously. "So you think it's unlikely because you think it's unlikely."

"Sir, even though I think it unlikely, that doesn't mean I don't agree we should take all due precautions ..."

At that point Meredith broke in.

"I agree with Bill about taking all due precautions. Only professional thing to do is take immediate action against that contingency. I made a few notes on an outline plan.

"Step one: immediate stand-to by all troops still in base – only exclusions are essential radio operators and clerks to man the TOC.

"Step two: artillery program continues, but reduced, at commander's discretion, so artillery fox holes are manned.

"Step three: issue Frag Order to one battalion to move immediately back to base to thicken up base defences.

"Step four: instruct other two battalions to move into blocking positions to cut off VC escape routes.

"Step five: ask division to chopper in one battalion for base security till our own battalion gets here."

"Fine professional plan, Frank. All steps agreed, except five. We don't want division sticking their noses in and asking damn-fool questions. We'll handle it all ourselves."

Morgan had to admire Frank's deft touch. It was a masterly performance in how Frank handled the Colonel. Of course, step five was a teaser to find out just how seriously the Colonel took the VC threat, and craftily put at the end of the plan, so the Colonel wouldn't lose face.

"Coffee anyone? I guess that's about all civil affairs can do right now?"

"I'll have a coffee, Bill," the Colonel said, "and while you're up, show me this great report of yours. I'll be up all night anyway, so might as well have something to read."

Morgan sensed the Colonel only wanted the report to pick holes in it; his main focus would be the threat to his brigade, so Morgan's timing could not have been worse for getting the Colonel in a receptive mood for changes in civil affairs policy. Reluctantly, he handed the report over and walked off to arrange the coffee. The Colonel skimmed through the report first, and then read more thoroughly.

Statement by Le Duc Phan, male ageing thirty-eight: American planes and guns destroyed our houses, brought us a big loss. Also they destroy the bridge and bomb my brother and father to death. Now my wife and daughter must be working in American camp because we are refugees. Perhaps my daughter is pregnant, or she must become prostitute to help us homeless, which is much shame ...

Statement by Phan Van Kim, male ageing fifty-three: American forces have a better discipline than Vietnamese soldiers. Our children, ducks or flower they never steal. But they enter our dwellings and take photographs which is bad and their bombs make die our buffalo and oxen. My rice fields cannot be ploughed and the rubber is died too, so there is no work except the American Camp.

Statement by Minh Thi Phuong, female ageing thirty-three: Americans are very cruel and are killing too many Vietnamese included the Viet Cong who are Vietnamese too. The Americans do not mind to die and very brave, but they destroy everything. This war is bad, killing all the men, my husband, my cousins. I think only young mens are American so I must work for them not to starve, but I am frightened, they are such large and red faces too ...

Statement by Tuyen Duc Trang, female ageing thirty-three: American soldiers are very discipline and brave, but are not impartial to distribute gifts, giving gifts to poor families less than rich families because gifts were distributing at the time of poor people out for working, therefore most of distribution gifts reach to rich people's hands. I am a poor widow, but they distribute me nothing ...

Statement by Duong Dinh Viet, male ageing fifty-nine: Americans destroyed Dong Tuy village and we are homeless not to return. Prohibiting us to go to forest to do business. Our women were afraid of the black Americans because we are told they will rape and eat children. This is a lie we know. Americans are kind, even black ones, but they don't know perfectly to work and didn't ask hamlet chief to help them distributing gifts to people, letting children have it by themselves, so we cannot take gifts because we are adults, not to share with children ...

Morgan returned with the coffee and the Colonel looked up and said, "I find this a very interesting and useful report. There's a few valuable extracts we could take from this for our quarterly report to division. But seems to me, Bill, there's a few civic action areas where you've been making mistakes, and should lift your game. Take gift distribution – why not through the Hamlet Chiefs?"

"That was done by the battalions without my ..."

"No excuses, Bill. Everything civic action is you. Just like everything in this brigade is me. I want results, not excuses – I don't give a damn whose fault it is. It's all your baby."

"Sir. But I did want to point out ..."

"I know what you want to say. On balance – apart from the obvious grievances and gripes we've got to accept in this sort of war – our civic action's shaping up okay. Our soldiers are kind, brave, disciplined and friendly. The locals see us as fair and generous. That's all fine business."

"But, sir – I've got say it – my read of that report is the exact opposite. The emphasis in their grievances isn't our virtues, but the destructiveness of our operations. Like us killing livestock, us closing off forest and paddy, us destroying rubber trees and crops, us accidentally maiming and killing peasants, us destroying homes; and above all, us changing their whole way of life and making so many of them into refugees, forced to subsist on our charity."

"Nobody's denying that, Bill, but I think our President put it very realistically when he quoted Jefferson: '*It is the melancholy law of human societies to be compelled sometimes to choose a great evil in order to ward off a greater evil.*' In this war a measure of destructiveness is inevitable. If you've got any bright ideas how we pacify this province different to what we're doing – tell me. But if you're just turning squeamish, with no practical constructive alternatives ... I don't believe I've got room on my staff for weak sisters."

The Colonel had risen to his feet with these final remarks. He turned to Meredith saying, "I've got personal paperwork to do; then I'd like to see you and the Two in half an hour."

When the Colonel left, Meredith said, "You really stuck your neck out that time, Bill Quixote. Your problem is you're such a lousy politician. Can't learn to shut your fucking mouth or compromise. You let personal feelings interfere with your profession. Like Major Bill Morgan is the only guy in step ..."

35

It was thirty seconds after 0100 when the first VC mortar shells exploded in the base. Obviously H hour for the VC had been 0100 and it had taken thirty seconds for orders to be given and the shells to arrive. Morgan was still arguing passionately and tenaciously with Meredith over the Census Grievance report and they were so engrossed that they didn't realise the base was being mortared until the duty officer came in and told Meredith the Colonel wanted to see him immediately.

"Know what he wants?"

"Guess it's the mortaring, sir."

"What mortaring?" Then both Meredith and Morgan recognised with surprise the familiar crump of incoming mortar rounds, probably still a few hundred yards away. The incoming mortars were masked by the roar of their own artillery firing their normal harassment and interdiction program.

Meredith came back ten minutes later. By then the mortaring had intensified, occasional rounds landing near brigade headquarters, but the main impact zone was the perimeter opposite Dong Tuy.

"The Colonel's real pissed about this mortaring," Meredith said. "He's not even saying 'I told you so.' He's convinced it's the prelude to his big VC attack. You've heard the arty Intell assessment of where it's from?"

"I know where it's landing. Not where it's from."

"VC mortar base plates are in Dong Tuy. They're using their Ap Moi tactic again, but this time from Dong Tuy. The Colonel's cussing mad about it. And he says it's all your fault he let those Dong Tuy refugees go back to their houses. He blames you for talking him into it against his better judgment."

"But we're still not going to shell Dong Tuy?"

"We have to. We've got no choice."

"There's got to be another way. Maybe I could lead the ready-reaction company in a clearing attack and capture the fucking mortars."

"No way. Colonel would never buy it. You might be prepared for suicide, but a company taking on maybe two regiments in a frontal assault? Artillery is instant. And if those VC regiments are forming up in Dong Tuy, we'll tear them apart with the guns."

Morgan was horrified, instantly seeing images of Trinh and his family scattered in bloody body parts in the wreckage of their house. And it was his fault – his own compassion had triggered this nightmare. He had nothing to say.

"Colonel's just ordered everything we've got to return fire. His guess is the VC mortars are softening up our perimeter defences opposite Dong Tuy before they attack. The VC probably mean to pull out the same route."

Morgan's next question was drowned in the crashing violence of their first artillery salvo.

"There they go," Meredith shouted in Morgan's ear. "If there really was an attack lining up in Dong Tuy, those VC are bleeding."

More talk was impossible; the artillery fire was one continuous roar. Occasionally most guns fired simultaneously, and the blast was so painful Morgan had to protect his ears with his hands. He was appalled, and still unconvinced a major attack on the base was happening, imminent, or even likely.

Even if there was an attack, he could not accept there was an overriding military need to shell what was left of the luckless village of Dong Tuy. Surely that was taking precautionary measures too far, when it could mean mass murder in the village.

"It's madness," he shouted, "I'm going to tell the Colonel. There's no need for this. It's overreacting."

"It's madness if you tell the Colonel. He's in no mood to argue, Bill. Those North Vietnamese regiments could be there."

But Morgan felt bound to go. He couldn't just stand by compromising, feeling as strongly as he did. If he, as an American officer, lacked the moral courage to protest at a time like this, he was no better than all those Germans in World War II who remained silent and afraid to protest, even though they knew about the death camps ...

The Colonel was alone in the emergency bunker next to his quarters when Morgan found him. A current battle map, telephone and radio remotes kept him just as informed here as in the TOC. He was sitting forward anxiously on the edge of his stool, head cocked, following battle developments on his command net. At first he was unaware of Morgan's entry, for even though the artillery bombardment was muted in the bunker, it was still loud enough to smother footsteps.

"What do you want, Bill?" the Colonel snapped, his look of intense worry changing to annoyance.

"Dong Tuy, sir." Morgan realised he would have to shout. "Dong Tuy, sir. Stop shelling Dong Tuy. We've only just allowed the refugees to return." Accidentally he sprayed a fleck of spittle on the Colonel's cheek as he shouted.

"Bill, I will not have you telling me how to do my job," the Colonel said angrily, pointedly wiping the spittle from his cheek. "If I'd done what I intended to in the first place and resettled Dong Tuy instead of listening to you, we wouldn't have to be shelling the place now. I've had enough of your half-assed advice. Now get the hell out of here. I've got a battle to fight."

"But, sir, we don't know for sure there is an attack. It's only mortaring. We're murdering that village. We don't have to."

"All right, Bill. I warned you. You've had your say. I'm sacking you. Get out. And clear headquarters first thing in the morning."

Morgan swallowed his next "but", saluted, and left. He stumbled into the darkness suddenly aware again of the violence of their artillery barrage. He felt crushed and numbed by the noise; then realised painfully how terrifying it must be for the Dong Tuy villagers on the receiving end. But his protest hadn't helped them. Frank was right; he had failed.

36

Saturday afternoon in Saigon: it meant half a day off from the tedium of Morgan's new job as a staff officer in the Logistics Branch of MACV. He had formed the habit, over these last two months, of taking a walk after Saturday lunch then burying himself in one of the darker bars to drink the rest of the day away.

He had just settled down in a corner of the bar and ordered his first drink when he felt a hand on his left shoulder.

"So this is where you hide from old friends. You are a difficult man to find." It was Junod, smiling warmly and impishly. "I am in Saigon for the weekend before I return to France ... and I wanted very much to catch up before I go."

Morgan's face lit up.

"How'd you track me down?"

"Three hours on the most overloaded telephone system in the world. One of your fellow logisticians told me this is your Saturday womb – or is it tomb?"

Morgan smiled and shrugged to avoid a direct answer.

"Perhaps we could exchange this stygian gloom for sunshine at the Cercle Sportif? We can drink there, and maybe I can introduce you to some femme fatale security risks in bikinis."

Morgan smiled agreement for Junod's sake, but that jibe about "Saturday womb" was all too accurate. Morgan had problems letting go his old job with the brigade and still obsessively rehashed the past and what might have been – especially his final talk with the Colonel. In a vain effort to find solace he was hitting the booze hard – so far mostly just Saturdays, but he had given in to temptation a few times on week nights, too, and drunk himself into angry oblivion. Fortunately, the pain of his hangovers saved him from that hard road after just a few sore-headed trial runs. He flashed back to his last meeting with the Colonel.

*

"Pity things didn't work out, Bill. I had high hopes for you, but I think what I'm doing is for your own good. It was a mistake to put you on staff – my mistake. All we did was hassle."

The Colonel had seemed chastened, almost humble that morning; ironically, Morgan empathised with him. Both had reconsidered the night's events. Morgan had come to a deeper understanding of the loneliness and pressures under which the Colonel made his decisions, right or wrong. It was easy, he admitted, to make suggestions and criticisms when the ultimate responsibility didn't belong to him, but his commander. For the Colonel, the fact that there had been no large-scale VC attack on the base, embarrassed him too. Even so, there seemed to be no question of reversing his decision to replace Morgan.

"High principles are a very fine thing, Bill, and in that department you have my respect. But this stubborn, argumentative streak in you ... And high principles aren't much good if they're so unrealistic you're no longer an effective officer. Main thing you seem to have lost sight of is a combat brigade's primary mission is destroying VC Main Forces. A combat brigade is not only a civil affairs charitable institution ... You got too carried away with your job as Father Christmas to those refugees; you over-identified with them, to the point you forgot we're fighting a real war out here. That's why I think it's in your own best interests to leave the brigade now. Take a rest from field work and get to understand the technical staff functions of the army. You'd got yourself too close to the problem to see the war. I must say I never thought I'd have to remind a Silver Star winner he was a member of the US Army and not the Salvation Army."

The Colonel seemed so fatherly and upset himself as he shook Morgan's hand to say goodbye that Morgan forgot for the moment he was being sacked. Even the Colonel's very last words, as Morgan gave a farewell salute, seemed to show genuine care for his future army career.

"For the record, Bill, and your Efficiency Report, this is a straight reposting – that's all it is ..."

Sometimes, especially at nights, Morgan wished he had been sacked – publicly and on record – because now he was a mere reshuffled staff officer pawn. His protest had lost all point, and he didn't even have the satisfaction of martyrdom. The Colonel had got rid of him so masterfully, there was no embarrassment at all; no enquiry with the Iceman, the Divisional

Commander posing unanswerable questions. It was a perfect crime – no need for murder, just sentence the troublemaker to the Saigon galleys and chain him to a bureaucratic oar.

But often he felt the reverse. He missed the excitement of brigade operations and involvement in the day-to-day tactical developments – whether he agreed or disagreed with the decisions made. And the longer he was away from the brigade, the more he missed it. At least serving with it, he was a legitimate soldier with a purpose and direction. Scuttling around the labyrinth of headquarters and logistics installations in Saigon, burrowing into piles of statistical reports and invoices in his honeycomb office, he felt himself degenerating into a faceless man, a nameless worker, a soulless insect.

*

Junod's intrusion into Morgan's bleak routine was a welcome relief. Morgan had avoided making new friends in his new MACV job and progressively become more taciturn, morose and lonely. He had been keeping so much bottled up for so long, he craved a friendly ear to release some of his pent up anger and resentments.

"We'll take a taxi," Junod said, when they got out to the street. The afternoon sunlight was blinding after the gloomy bar. "You look ghastly," Junod teased. "All white, or rather, grey. I suppose that must be the destiny of the fiercely conscientious Saigon staff officer."

"What have you been up to?" Morgan asked abruptly – an old trick to keep his misery private.

"Watching our estates run down. I had just recovered from my minor irritation at losing fifty square kilometres of rubber through involuntary defoliation because your spray pilots could not read the difference between defoliant and insecticide, when Christmas came. And to teach the VC a lesson for mortaring your base, your Colonel decided to declare another fifty square kilometres of our rubber estates a Free Fire Zone. You remember all that; but since then ..."

They climbed into their taxi, a mini French Citroen designed like a dung beetle. Junod continued, "My estate workers have been rapidly depleted. Some you converted into refugees, and of course those from Ap Moi were nearly all killed in the ambush just before you left. But at last, I thought, after this great battle your brigade has surely killed off or frightened away all VC and there will be peace. But no. Worse was to follow. Next thing your brigade liberated all the villages that were providing my workers, and then it was discovered that those young men who were not VC were mostly deserters, or else were needed as Popular Force troops to guard their newly liberated villages. You laugh. You think I am making jokes. But even worse again: those few workers left, then quit to work in your base camp because the money is so much better. I call it Robin Hood pacification: impoverish the rich plantations, enrich the impoverished plantation workers. Do you think you could find me a job in your PX?"

Morgan was still smiling when they reached the Cercle Sportif.

"Drinks and bird-watching from the swimming pool?" Junod asked as they walked through the main building to the veranda overlooking the long stretch of tennis courts. What an improbable oasis the swimming pool seemed with its turquoise water and amber-skinned girls, wet and sleek in the water, or purring and lazy in the sun. A world within a world within a world, this was a relic of privileged colonial leisure, set amid the teeming refugees and booming bars of the city.

"I presume you were delighted at the news of your Colonel's promotion to one-star general? I read about it in your Armed Forces newspaper, the *Stars and Stripes*. It was neatly put: '*Province pacification earns combat colonel promotion*.'"

Morgan knew what Junod was fishing for, but took wry pleasure in refusing the bait. "No surprise there. He was an outstanding combat commander."

By unspoken agreement, they were playing a new game. Morgan was self-appointed straight man, and French ex-officer Junod was wielding an ironic scalpel to show he knew the hidden truths.

"So it would appear. The VC haven't tried another major attack in the province since they attacked that Ap Moi refugee convoy and then attacked your base from Dong Tuy. They attacked with two North Vietnamese regiments, according to the newspapers?"

"Yes. It was quite a show," Morgan answered evasively.

"I understand you were lucky and there was no in-fighting as such? Your artillery broke up the attack while they were forming in the village."

Morgan nodded calmly at Junod, his face an expressionless blank as he played their new game.

"Poor Dong Tuy," Junod continued. "Anyway, the bulldozers have made a good job of it now. The new model village your brigade is building for the refugees is most impressive. Of course all new villages are depressing at first: red earth and ugly tin roofs. But I have been amazed at how quickly your engineers have thrown it up."

A pretty Eurasian girl walked by, her bikini brief enough to show from behind the cleavage of her ass. Noticing Morgan watching her, Junod said, "And she is a tigress in bed. I know her father: he is one of the few Frenchmen still running a restaurant in town. Of course in another twenty years the Vietnamese people will be a new mixture. With the cream of your conscripts to service the Vietnamese girls, the new half-castes should be a handsome breed. I hope the night-life and the Vietnamese pussy here in Saigon is compensation enough for leaving your brigade."

"It helps some. But tail's expensive now compared to my first tour with Special Forces."

"It must be very hard for somebody so steeped in combat service as you to leave the field for staff work in Saigon. Do you know what a member of the British Embassy joked to me? 'Every American staff officer in Saigon has a sense of shame.' Is it true?"

37

Like a surgeon, Junod was perceptively probing the weak spots and raw nerve ends, yet perversely Morgan enjoyed it. The man was so mercurial and bubbling with nervous energy, he was a stimulating companion. And Morgan sorely felt the need for companionship. Drinking and talking in the late afternoon sun, and occasionally letting his eyes linger on one of the sun-baking girls, he felt himself enveloped by a warm glow of pleasantly developing intoxication.

"Look," Junod said suddenly, "why don't we eat together? I will call on a girl I know, ask her to arrange a friend for you, and ..."

It was almost dark when they left the Cercle Sportif and caught another taxi to where Junod's girl lived in a crowded area midway between Cholon, the Chinese quarter, and Saigon. They had to leave the taxi and walk down a path at the edge of a narrow-gauge railway line, overlooked on one side by tightly packed shanty houses, and falling away on the other to an open sewer. Several times they stumbled on fist-sized pieces of blue metal stone which had spread from between the ties of the railway line onto the path. By the time they reached the girl's house, some two hundred yards down the track from the road, a gaggle of inquisitive children had collected behind them.

"Wait here a moment," Junod said, opening the gate and crossing the tiny front yard with its solitary shade tree. Morgan felt children's fingers plucking at his trousers, and then one bold hand feeling into his pocket.

"Hey, cut that out," he said, slapping the hand away and turning swiftly to catch the culprit. All the children, except one small girl, scattered like a school of fish and formed a watchful circle. He patted the little girl's shoulder absently.

"Cigarette?" she asked.

"No cigarette," Morgan said kindly.

"Cigarette?" The rest of the children took up the cry in staccato shrieks.

"No cigarette," Morgan repeated, shaking his hands and head firmly, and replacing his right hand on the girl's shoulder. "*Cigarettes number twelve,*" he added.

The girl lifted his hand to her face, put his forefinger in her mouth, and bit it sharply and painfully.

"You little bitch," Morgan cried, nursing the bitten finger and grabbing clumsily after her with his left hand as she darted free.

Junod rejoined him, saying, "She's not home. Have you declared war on these children?"

Morgan explained what had happened.

"Friendly little monkeys, aren't they?" Junod laughed, and they began to walk back up the railway line. They had only gone a few steps when Morgan felt a painful jab in his leg and turned to see a boy with a stick dashing away. A few steps later he was hit in the back by a small stone. He ignored it, but soon after he was hit on the shoulder and head by two larger stones in quick succession.

"Hey, cut it out, you kids," he shouted, turning threateningly and picking up a handful of stones as if to throw them back.

There was a chorus of renewed shouting when he began to walk on again.

"They think I am an American, too," Junod said. "They are shouting, 'No bad girls for Yankee dogs. Yankee go home.' This is a tough area."

They heard the patter and scuffling of small feet suddenly rush at them in a wave, and they were hit by a shower of stones, pebbles and sticks.

"I think we must run," Junod said. "It is undignified, but better for the skin."

They began to run, which resulted in a fresh hail of missiles, and the children began to run after them, yelling and yelping in pursuit.

Morgan stumbled a few yards on and fell heavily on his front, painfully barking his elbows and shins on the railway line. The children were on him instantly – kicking, jabbing, throwing and spitting. As Morgan looked up he saw the main street a long way ahead as a thin rectangle of light at the end of a tunnel. He was shocked by the fall, and was suddenly aware of being afraid. He knew it was absurd; they were only children. Then he felt a dog snapping at his leg. He leapt to his feet, furious now, and lunged at the attacking children. But they skipped away and he felt like a clumsy bear.

Another hail of rocks hit him. There was nothing for it but to run, and he ran hard and fast – gradually outstripping the children – the rest of the way to the street where Junod was waiting, smiling, at the taxi.

"Climb in, Monsieur Gulliver. The Lilliputian hordes have withdrawn."

"That was a real nasty experience," Morgan said, as the taxi drove off. He felt awkward and shamefaced, as if somehow it had been his fault.

"Yes, because usually you Americans are so popular with children. Perhaps you can report them to your counter-intelligence branch as a pocket of juvenile subversives."

Junod was obviously delighted with the incident and relishing Morgan's discomfiture to the full.

"You sneaky bastard, I think you took me there deliberately, knowing –"

"Oh, Bill, please. I am not so clever. I wish I was. Obviously it is just that you have a way with children. And, sadly, now we have no girls for tonight."

"That makes us fully paid-up members of the Saigon Losers' Club. These girls have changed compared to my first tour. You've got to hand it to them – they're really professional little businesswomen. Most of them are doing so well fleecing drunken GIs in the bars, they don't have to sleep with them. The story of a soldier's night off in Saigon now is an empty pocket and a promise."

"How well you put it," Junod said. "Like your adventure in the alley: how frustrating the American experience in Vietnam must be. The Viet Cong relatively are as puny and weak as those children. And yet there you were, friendly at first; then wounded and outraged, threshing and bellowing, capable of crushing them to pulp; but you stumbled and they were all over you, and finally you had to turn tail and run. In fact to make the analogy even better, the first stone was my French Dien Bien Phu, and I fled first leaving you to your American glory."

"I suppose that's why I put up with you, Junod. You can laugh at being a loser."

38

They paid off the taxi in the square between the Continental and the Caravelle hotels, then crossed the road to the grass island stacked with parked bicycles, before walking towards Nguyen Hue, the Street of Flowers, where they picked their way past the pavement stalls with their crafty-eyed hawkers. Sunglasses, contraceptives, elephant-hide leatherwork, painted silk postcards, C rations, lacquer-ware, tigers' teeth, *Time* and *Newsweek*, tortoiseshell ... all crowding the stalls in similar displays. A young pimpled American soldier elbowed past them wearing a red Stetson and a black jacket on which was embroidered a green dragon and the words, "I'm a lover, not a fighter."

"You know, our own province capital, Canh Tri, is now a little like this in miniature," Junod said, "although the brothel area is of course shabbier, and more provincial, I suppose. It reminds me of what your frontier towns must have been like in the Wild West. The Canh Tri Honky Tonk, with its own massage parlours, tailors' shops, bars, laundries, leather shops, restaurants, souvenir stalls, barber shops and painted tarts – but rather awkward, graceless little trollops, too fresh from the paddy. And yet I think the Province Chief and your Colonel may have been right. Business in the town – that sort of business – is booming. Yes, I suppose I'm just a colonial sentimentalist, mourning a dead and gracious past."

They ate in the restaurant belonging to the Frenchman who was father to the girl Junod had commented on at the Cercle Sportif. The place was one of the retreats for Saigon's remaining expatriate French, and although the owner greeted Morgan cordially enough when Junod introduced him, later, when a group of American officers came in, they were told firmly that all tables were reserved – even though the restaurant was less than half full.

"You're an arrogant lot, you French. I think you dislike us even more than the British."

"Why act surprised?" said Junod. "Do you expect us to forgive you – ever – for saving us in two world wars, and now trying to recoup our failure here? Your absurdly extravagant standard of living, your size, your wealth, your steamroller power guarantee a natural reaction of jealousy. To ordinary mortals the American giant is both over-powering and more than a little frightening – especially in war."

"Pity the North Vietnamese ain't frightened and think the same way," Morgan joked back. "Then we could escape this crazy dead-end mess." That afternoon he had vowed not to take offence at anything Junod said; since their lunch row, Morgan had painfully come to realise that Junod was right on so many counts.

"They are as proud and stubborn as you. Unless you obliterate them, the more you bomb, the more fanatically tenacious they will become. I wonder how Balzac would have seen this war? Perhaps to him you Americans would seem like the blackmail victims of a neurotic mistress. Your tragic flaw is your do-gooder's sense of honour. As a result of this misplaced sense of honour, you are neglecting your friends, your wives, and your children, all for this absurd alliance with a destructive neurotic."

"All right, Junod. It's easy enough to be clever at our expense; your country's not involved any more. But it's begging the question. I may not like what we're doing, or how we're doing it, but the problem is, we are. How can we do things differently? How do we let go the tiger's tail?"

"I don't think you can. And I still don't think your leaders appreciate how locked-in your situation will become. As your General Westmoreland said, 'This is a war of attrition.' That is your American way of fighting, and is it likely you will change? I think not. And I think this war is only proving what I said when we first met. You Americans are the most powerful oriental nation of all."

"But we are a nation with a conscience. It's crazy to suggest we have imperialist or territorial ambitions. We don't. We're here to help prevent this country from being overrun by Viet Cong terror and military force. Surely you agree our presence here is for a right and proper end? What other nation would have used the restraint and control we have, possessing the destructive means we do? I'm the first to admit that the war is appallingly destructive; we blunder and make mistakes as any military machine must, but we do mean well. It's within our capacity to win eventually, and when we do, we'll withdraw and leave the place in peace."

These words crystallised the position Morgan had tried to convince himself was the right one as he groped for answers since Old Leather had sacked him. Certainly the Colonel had his weaknesses and blind spots, but he had been a professional commander. Within his limitations Old Leather had done what he saw as best – men of action and decision makers had to be ruthless at times. Progressing from there and his deep-seated patriotism, Morgan simply could not accept Junod's cynical appraisal of his country's involvement in Vietnam as merely misguided and futile.

"But is it enough to mean well?" Junod replied. "And is your concept of 'restrained application of power' sufficiently restrained? What are you doing to South Vietnam in the name of saving her? Look at your own province. How were you pacifying that? As I predicted, you were razing it in the name of saving it. You Americans have too much German blood, I think. You only understand total solutions. Eventually you may solve it as you solved your Red Indians. You will convert the country into a gigantic reservation."

"No, Junod. You're wrong. You go too far. Korea and Taiwan are no reservations. Nor is Germany or Japan. No, Junod, we're an honest and outspoken society, conscience guided; and twenty years, when this place is prospering, will prove you wrong."

"A prosperous American colony? Are you trying to convince me or yourself? Perhaps you are right; perhaps it is worth it ... A generation sacrificed to the future: the Communists would agree with you. After all, prosperity is the religious goal of the century."

After dinner Junod insisted on a second bottle of wine. Both men were conscious that this might be their last meeting – and Junod seemed to feel this second bottle gave him licence to probe more deeply and personally.

"So what does the future hold for Bill Morgan, earnest and proven soldier? Will you serve out your penance, or leave?"

"What do you mean, 'leave'? Leave Vietnam, or leave the army?"

"Both, of course."

"I'd be lost without the army – I can't imagine Bill Morgan outside of the army."

"But I can. I could never imagine Jean Paul outside my army, but I left and so could you."

"But you were court martialled and had no choice."

"And weren't you effectively court martialled too?"

"No way –" Morgan began forcefully, but then realised the fallacy behind his protest, and the painful truth in Junod's question. "But what on earth could I do if I left the army?"

"An infinity of things. Go back to university for a start – maybe a Masters in Economics or International Relations? And why not a PhD?"

"No way," Morgan resisted firmly. "The US Army is my life – I'll stay and see what happens next ..."

Junod persisted for a few more minutes, but finally gave up on rearranging Morgan's life when he looked at his watch and saw how late it was. Junod still hadn't packed and his flight left early next morning. He handed Morgan a business card with his parents' contact details neatly printed on the back.

"If ever you come to France ..."

"And if ever you come to the States ..." But both knew another meeting was unlikely and this was probably farewell. But in the manner of professional soldiers, inured to close friendships abruptly ending, they simply shook hands and walked away. Neither looked back.

Morgan had been aware of a painfully developing headache for some time, and was perversely relieved when Junod finally left. He was such an exhausting companion, and Morgan felt talked-out and tired as he walked up the street looking for a taxi. After two blocks, still with no luck, he turned onto Tu Do; on impulse, he decided to have a drink at the nearest bar to try and ward off the headache.

39

"You buy me drink? I talk with you."

"No thanks," Morgan replied curtly to the importuning bar girl. "No drink and I don't want talk." The girl sniffed at him, curling her upper lip, and glided away, leaving him alone at the bar. He closed his eyes and began to massage his temples with his fingertips to try and ease the pain. He heard a newcomer sit next to him, and, simultaneously, the bar girl asking, "You buy me drink? I talk with you."

"Sure. Hey, one beer here, and Saigon Tea for – what's your name?"

"My name Mei Lin."

"Say, that's a pretty name. My name's Clark."

"How old, Clark?"

"I'm twenty, Mei Lin. How old are you?"

"Guess."

"Nineteen."

"No, Clark. Twenty-four. I have been marry. My husband, he die from Viet Cong."

"Gee, I'm real sorry. Did you have any children?"

"Yes. Two baby I must feed. And three young sister and two brother and mother. My father dead too, so I must work bar."

"That's really tough."

"Very hard. You buy me one more drink?"

"Sure. How long you been working here?"

"I just start work bar. You have girlfriend?"

"Back in the States I did, before I came to Vietnam. But not any more. I don't have a girl here."

"Truth? No girl here?"

Morgan still had his eyes shut as he listened to the conversation. He'd heard a hundred similar ones since he'd been in Saigon and had grown cynical. The bar girls invariably said they were widows with a collection of small children and dependent relatives and no current boyfriend. And naturally, any American male bar-crawling at this hour, just before curfew, was on the make.

"I've got no girl, Mei Lin – honestly."

"You work Saigon, Clark?"

"Yes, I work at Tan Son Nhut airbase."

Probably a clerk or a mechanic getting an easy war, Morgan thought sourly. It was always the way; the Saigon warriors getting the girls and taking the cream. He remembered bitterly the number of dead young soldiers from his old company – no girls for them. He shuddered in sorrow and felt unreasoning anger at the boy next to him. He opened his eyes to look at the boy's face.

The girl was saying, "What's this?"

Glancing from the boy's face with its pronounced Adam's apple, emphasised by fair hair and a crew-cut, Morgan looked down and saw the tattoo on his forearm that the girl was pointing at. Inscribed in red lettering, pierced by a dagger, were the words: *Death before dishonour.*

It was too much for Morgan. "Goddam!" he said, standing abruptly and slamming his fist on the bar.

"Do you have the Combat Infantryman's Badge?" he asked the startled youth.

"No, sir."

"Do you have a Purple Heart?"

"No, sir."

"Have you ever killed a Viet Cong?"

"No, sir."

Instantly aware of what Morgan was getting at, the boy covered the tattoo with his other hand. Morgan continued to stare at him for a long moment, then pushed past him disgustedly into the street.

It had been raining and the air smelt fresh. He breathed in deeply. It was absurd, he admitted, to take out his frustrations on a harmless and ridiculous youth. With a flash of insight he knew he felt guilty himself for working in the relative safety of Saigon – insulated from the reality of the shooting war. He was disturbed to realise that, in spite of his concern and compassion for the Vietnamese, suffering because of the war's continuation, his respect as an American officer for the warrior military virtues was so deep-rooted that close personal involvement in fighting the war seemed a moral role in itself. And such an attitude was almost a sanctification of war for its own sake.

The bars were emptying with the approach of curfew, and he joined the throng of bar girls, prostitutes, pimps, and soldiers jostling for taxis and cyclos to go home.

Afterword

Count Your Dead is based on my experiences in Vietnam as an Australian major attached to 173rd US Airborne Brigade and, later, as the senior Intelligence Officer for the Australian Task Force. All characters and incidents are fictional, but based closely on real events and my observations of real people.

I wanted my novel to reveal how different the Vietnam War was compared to the Malayan Emergency, Korea and World War II. The American way of waging war is largely based on superior firepower and a logistics system capable of bringing that firepower to bear.

Only a handful of senior Australian officers in Vietnam had experience in fighting with the Americans in Korea and World War II. But for those of us who were too young for those wars, and had only been involved in the counter-insurgency campaigns of the Malayan Emergency and Indonesian Confrontation in Borneo, the logistical plenty and organisational steam-roller of the American war machine was a fascinating and awe-inspiring revelation.

The widespread use of helicopters and air mobile operations was an intriguing new military dimension – and the thrup of helicopter engines was the signature tune of that war.

When I first thought up the outline of the novel, I certainly did not expect that publishing it would lead to the end of my army career.

The act of writing it gave me my first chance to view the war in a wider perspective. Until then I was simply too busy with the demands of the moment. What I hoped to achieve was to highlight some of the flawed concepts behind our current tactics and strategic thinking. By the time I finished the novel, I had grave doubts about the wisdom of any democracy, no matter how powerful, ever engaging in a counter-insurgency war. The most critical long-term problem is an exit strategy. In Vietnam the exit was a thinly disguised defeat. In Iraq and Afghanistan the US has expended billions of dollars and many young soldiers' lives. And to what end? Messy and politically unstable situations in both countries, which could easily degenerate into civil war.

The senior general in the Australian Army during the Vietnam War was Lieutenant General Sir Thomas Daly; he was also the Chief of the General Staff. Like many other middle ranking officers, I had met him several times. But through a shared passion for skiing, I got to know him particularly well. In 1967, my wife and I went on a skiing holiday to Thredbo with another married couple who were two of our closest friends. General Daly was staying at the Army ski lodge in Thredbo the same week. On the first evening of our holiday, we were having drinks with an Army friend at the Army lodge, and General Daly was there too. After introductions, I mentioned my two friends were booked in for a week of skiing lessons, and General Daly said he would like to join them in the same ski class. Both my wife and I were reasonably competent skiers, so while our two friends and General Daly had lessons in the mornings, we skied separately and rejoined the three of them each afternoon.

Our two friends and General Daly made fairly rapid skiing progress for beginners; then on the Friday afternoon, such heavy snow began to fall that the General and I were the only ones in our group who still wanted to ski. Visibility became so poor it was difficult even to see the ground from the chairlift. As we skied away from the top station, the General began to have problems with both his ski bindings. They began to release prematurely with frustrating regularity. Visibility became so poor it was difficult to see more than a few feet in any direction. Each time one of his skis came off, it was a major time-consuming effort to put it back on, and he was becoming increasingly tired. He was now in his mid-fifties.

Conditions became even worse – a blizzard engulfed us – and we could barely see each other. The next time one of his skis came off, I ignored his protests and replaced it myself, to preserve his strength. By the time we got off the mountain, I had probably refitted his skis over thirty times. Finally we got back to the safety and comfort of the lodge. Though little was said that stressful afternoon, a bond was formed that needed no words.

I made a number of close friends among the American officers with whom I served, and still maintain a strong belief in the importance of the American alliance as Australia faces the Asian century. Though there is much to criticise about the American way of waging a counter-insurgency war, there is also much to commend about the openness of American society and their readiness to adapt and change. As the twenty-first century unfolds against a background of accelerating European decline, American military power remains one of the few constants likely to continue – at least for the next half century. I therefore remain convinced of the bedrock importance of close military ties between the United States and Australia.

I started writing this novel in the Australian hospital at Vung Tau after being diagnosed with infectious hepatitis. The broad concept of the novel came to me in a flash of inspiration in the afternoon of my second day in hospital. It then took many hours to handwrite, in note form, a fuller version of that first visionary moment. Because I was considered highly infectious, I was largely isolated from visitors and so had many hours of forced isolation to develop my thinking about the book. I began the first draft of the novel a couple of days later, writing in longhand in a cheap child's exercise book that one of the nurses gave me.

Because I had served in three other Asian wars before Vietnam, I had accumulated three months of leave and decided to take it when I was released from hospital and spend it with my wife's family in Switzerland. My wife's father, Brian Hill, had been the Australian ambassador in Vietnam in the early 1960s when President Diem was assassinated and the huge American build-up began. He was now the Australian ambassador to Switzerland and my wife had spent the last year with him in Geneva. I flew to London via US military aircraft and then took a commercial flight to Geneva.

When I arrived in Geneva, I was gaunt and emaciated, having lost some twenty kilos, but over the next three months I gradually recovered about half the lost weight. A major part of my convalescence was working on the manuscript of *Count Your Dead*. During the writing I had extensive and probing conversations with Brian Hill about the difficult issues addressed in the novel.

Midway through my convalescence, I received a cable from the Australian High Commission in London asking me to fly over and brief the new Task Force commander, Brigadier Stuart Graham, who was scheduled to take over later in 1967. I already knew Brigadier Graham very well and had great respect for him as a highly intelligent professional soldier. In a previous posting at Army Headquarters, I had worked for him for over two years, having been the desk officer responsible for Indonesian military affairs, and in that time he was the Director of Military Intelligence. But for now, Brigadier Graham was a student again at the renowned British Imperial Defence College.

On returning to Australia, my new job was senior instructor at the School of Military Intelligence in Sydney. In my spare time in the evenings I continued to work on my Vietnam novel.

The single most important reason I became a military intelligence officer was the persuasive influence of Brigadier Fergus Macadie. He had been a legendary military figure since the early 1940s when, at the exceptionally young age of 23, he had been promoted to the rank of lieutenant colonel in command of an independent force to fight the Japanese, and won a DSO. Later he commanded a battalion in the British Occupation Force in Japan, where he commandeered Emperor Hirohito's horse-drawn carriage for his wedding. My first awareness of Fergus Macadie was when he delivered a lecture to an audience of Duntroon cadets, seeking new recruits for the Intelligence Corps. He preceded Stuart Graham as the Director of Military Intelligence, and the two were very close friends. When I returned to Australia from Vietnam, Fergus Macadie was living in Sydney at Victoria Barracks as General Tom Daly's Chief of Staff. Later, he also became the godfather to my older son, Luke. Because I had such a close relationship with Fergus Macadie, I told him I was working on a novel about the Vietnam War, and he volunteered both to read the manuscript and give his comments. Not only did he read the manuscript, but he also gave me valuable insights into my senior American military characters, and the American way of waging war.

When I completed the first draft of the novel in mid-1967, both Brian Hill and Fergus Macadie helped generously with advice and criticism. The editor of the *Bulletin* magazine back then, Donald Horne, had been a diplomatic cadet together with Brian Hill and others during World War II. Brian Hill introduced us, and as a result Donald and I became regular lunchtime companions and formed a lasting friendship. So when the novel was completed, it was Donald Horne who championed the book for publication with Angus and Robertson.

In early 1968, Angus and Robertson finally agreed to publish *Count Your Dead*. In those years it was Australian Army policy, with factual military writing, to seek Army Headquarters approval before publication. However, because I had written a work of fiction, I decided this condition did not apply.

Then, early in 1968, I was advised I was being posted to Washington DC to work with the American Defence Intelligence Agency (DIA) as an exchange officer. It was normal practice in that period for an American exchange intelligence officer to work with the Directorate of Military Intelligence in Canberra as well, as part of a reciprocal agreement. Because my wife Marianne was then pregnant with our first son, Luke, and because there was a prohibition on pregnant women flying within six weeks of their expected delivery date, a family decision was made that my wife would travel to Geneva to give birth, where her family could look after her. So I learned of the birth of my firstborn son as I stepped off the plane in Hawaii en route to Washington. And it was mid-July before my wife and infant son joined me in Washington.

When *Count Your Dead* was finally published in August of 1968, it was a comparatively major media event in Australia. The novel was front-page news in the *Australian* and the Adelaide *Advertiser*, and featured prominently in the *Sydney Morning Herald* and the Brisbane *Courier-Mail*. There was a mini media circus in Washington, too. I was inundated with phone calls from major American newspapers, radio stations and television channels. Amongst the newspapers whose reporters contacted me were the *Washington Post*, the *New York Times*, the *Wall Street Journal* and the *International Herald Tribune*. Because I had not then decided whether to stay on in the Army, I gave them all the same bland answer: "I am not available for interviews – I have spoken through my fiction." The American media soon lost interest. With hindsight I am fully aware that response was a kiss of death in terms of generating ongoing publicity for book sales, but back then I could only follow the dictates of my professional soldier's conscience.

Along with the media telephone calls, I was also contacted by Colonel Bill Henderson, a Defence attaché with the Australian Embassy in Washington. Henderson had been my first battalion commander after graduation, and for my first six months with his battalion, I had been his intelligence officer. One of his staff organised an appointment for me to see him the following day.

Meanwhile, the fact that my novel had been published in Australia and that, in many sections, the characters' dialogue was critical of the American way of fighting a counter-insurgency war, created major concerns within the Defence Intelligence Agency about whether I should continue to work there.

So I was informed that I had an early morning meeting with a US Army general who had recently commanded a division in Vietnam. When I was shown into his office, he already had a copy of my novel flagged with yellow tabs marking controversial statements. During the course of that interview, he made several frank and insightful comments on the current US Army practice of commanders inflating body counts – an important element in the novel, and the reason for the novel's title, *Count Your Dead*. He had clearly speed-read the novel the night before, and said, "Hell – inflated body counts – almost every commander did that – the line starts here ..." and pointed to himself. He then generously said that, providing I would give my word not to write another book critical of the US DIA, I could remain with the Agency. He added as an afterthought that the Agency would very much value the sorts of insights I had shown in my novel being applied to the new intelligence issues confronting the Agency.

Later, around midday, I had my first meeting with Colonel Henderson regarding the book. He began the meeting by showing me a telegram he had received from the Adjutant General of the Australian Army, the officer responsible for administration and discipline throughout the Army. The telegram contained words to the effect that many of the views expressed in the novel were contrary to current Army policy and, in particular, that I was a disloyal officer who had let down my comrades still fighting in Vietnam.

As I read the telegram I compared it with the wisdom and generosity of spirit shown by the American general who had interviewed me earlier that day. After thinking over the allegation that I was a disloyal officer, I told Colonel Henderson I felt honour-bound to resign from the Army forthwith. I could not accept the charge that writing and publishing a novel meant I was disloyal to my comrades still fighting the war. This reaction seemed to disturb Colonel Henderson just as much as the Adjutant General's telegram had disturbed me.

He then tried to persuade me that resignation from the Army was too extreme a reaction. I still felt strongly, however, that the charge of disloyalty to my comrades was so serious that resignation was the only honourable path I could follow. That evening I discussed my resignation at length with my wife, and both of us reluctantly agreed that I should go through with it.

Colonel Henderson called me back into his office twice more, but with the same result. Next, I was summonsed for a meeting with the then Australian ambassador, Sir Keith Waller, who also knew my father-in-law well.

He too applied his considerable intellect and charm to try to persuade me not to resign. One comment of his still echoes down the years: "John, in five years you will probably be proven right in your views. All this current fuss and bother will simply be an amusing anecdote to tell on the cocktail circuit back in Canberra ..."

Being a professional army officer is very much a calling, and it was just as painful for me as for any Catholic priest to leave my vocation. The Australian Army, just like all professional armies, is very much an extended family with all sorts of associations, shared experiences and close friendships. Nevertheless, trying to look into the future of a still-possible army career, I could only foresee a withdrawal from Vietnam in the next few years, by both the American and Australian armies, and then most probably, especially for the Australian Army, an extended period of comparative peace and severe cutbacks in defence. So for me, my army adventure was over.

I was warmed to receive a handwritten letter from General Daly along the following lines:

I was saddened by your decision to resign, but write to reassure you, if you do change your mind, there would be no adverse effects upon your career from recent events...

Because I was still only 32 years old, I felt young enough for the new adventure of a second career. And because the DIA leadership were comfortable about me continuing to work for them, it was decided to leave me in Washington until a replacement officer could be selected. My wife and I then decided that until I had a new job, it was best that she and our baby son return to Geneva, where at least she would have some help with the baby and the care and companionship of her family.

I flew back to Australia in early 1969, via stopovers in both Hawaii and Fiji. In Fiji, a very young ABC reporter, Richard Carleton, boarded the plane to do a preliminary interview with me. At that stage of his career, he was still considered too junior to conduct the interview himself.

My first TV interview was to be on the ABC on a new and highly rated current affairs show called *This Day Tonight*. When I was finally interviewed, I was very aware of a high level of nervous tension in my interviewer. He chain-smoked before and after the interview, and I asked him if he always get so tense before interviews. He brushed the question aside with a joke. But later I learned that the very next day, he had a heart attack and died.

By the end of January 1969, I had completed the round of media interviews and left the army. My next published book was an Australian political thriller called *McCabe PM*. It was published in 1972 by Pan, and was a major bestseller with sales of around 100,000 copies. Since then, I have raised a family and published seven books in all.

Then in 2003 I was contacted by Sydney University Press and asked whether I would consent to *Count Your Dead* being included in their twenty-five book Classic Australian Works series. Of course, I agreed.

But recently, almost ten years later, with the advent of ebooks available to a very wide audience for a very reasonable price, I decided to release *Count Your Dead* in ebook format too. On re-reading the book after forty-four years, I decided it would benefit from a good edit. I have now completed that edit and also engaged a professional editor to finish the job.

Since the Vietnam War finished in the mid 1970s, Australia has joined the USA in two more counter-insurgency wars in Iraq and Afghanistan. Both these new wars were failures in many ways. It is now timely to look back on the Vietnam War and examine thoughtfully some of the lessons we failed to learn back then.